THE BIG

Thomas Kilroy is a lecturer ... University College, Dublin. He is thirty-... years old and is married with three children. He has written two full-length plays for the stage and one prize-winning radio play for the BBC. *The Big Chapel*, his first published novel, has won several literary prizes, including the *Guardian* Fiction Prize 1971, the Royal Irish Academy of Letters: Allied Banks Prize 1971, and the Royal Society for Literature Heinemann Award.

THE BIG CHAPEL

THOMAS KILROY

UNABRIDGED

PAN BOOKS LTD : LONDON

First published 1971 by Faber and Faber Limited
This edition published 1973 by Pan Books Ltd,
33 Tothill Street, London SW1

ISBN 0 330 23551 6

Printed and bound in England by
Hazell Watson & Viney Ltd,
Aylesbury, Bucks

For my friend
Terence Michael Williams

Contents

1 . *The Town*

The town had no very remarkable history before this. This was the time from which its people would measure its age, not with the simple measurement of years, each with its balance of bad luck and prosperity, good harvest and bad winter. Instead they would say: 'Wasn't that the winter of the trouble over the Big Chapel?' Or: 'Didn't his father have a hand in the row over the priest? Isn't he the breed of a chapel burner?' This, although the Big Chapel had not been burned, simply unroofed during the rioting in the town. As the years passed details like this became vague and unsettled. The story turned and twisted with each telling and this is a problem.

Or they might say of a disliked man in the town who had been toppled by misfortune: 'Wasn't that fellow's father baptized by the Red Priest above in the Big Chapel, sure how could his kind have a day's luck?'

It gave a meaning to the place in the beginning, this trouble, it gave meaning to the lives of many families and fathers passed on their allegiance to the priest (or his enemies) to their sons but then, as the years passed, this energy died in the place like a light going out and the town relapsed into timelessness. Time began to pass without much significance one way or another. Mothers began to hide what had happened from their sons, hushing their husbands to silence or whispered half-stories of the terrible events to their daughters. The women wound up the matter between them in secret hoarding. In public the people became furtive about it all before strangers, rock-faced before the questions (Wasn't it here that the priest...?) and it must have been about this time that the place got its bad reputation among travellers in the county.

When the riots were bad the town lost all its business. The paint peeled and chipped on the shops of High Street, that crazy staircase of different shaped buildings up the side of the steep hill; inside in the tunnelling darkness behind the counters the townspeople lurked, with their dusty, half-empty shelves, their boxes, their cats. But when the riots stopped business came back better than ever. That was when they knew they had beaten him, when they saw that circulation of money come back over the counters, like blood, while he withered away in the dilapidated Presbytery. They saw their new prosperity like a sign from the Almighty.

Yet even thirty years after the priest himself had died a farmer was killed by thrown stones in the town and they said it was the old bitterness.

But all that is well into the future. The present is the year 1871 and the years following. Let us say between 1871 and 1883 when the priest died in the home of his sister in Newtown.

It began like this. The parish priest of the place, William Edward Lannigan, defied his bishop, his cardinal, his pope. They suspended him and placed his parish church under interdict. His church was called the Big Chapel. It stood at the top of the high hill of High Street. This street dropped down to the very bank of the river at the other end of the town. This river was crossed by a bridge and here began River Street. On the bank of the river, some several hundred yards to the east of the bridge, stood the Augustinian Friary. Inside the triangle of these three points, Big Chapel and bridge and Friary, was the town, or most of it.

Kirwan, Grace, Delaney, Moore, Nugent, and Bergin. Small shopfronts, small windows, grey, weeping cement walls. No display. No arrogant colours. One or two Huguenot names like Fountain and Dubby seemed to dance in happy comparison over a Grocery and Provisions or General Bakery. But this was an illusion. All the townspeople were solid and modest in ambition, they preserved their secrets from one another and the secrets of the town from the county. That is, until the case of the priest.

In the beginning no one saw the full consequences of it. The people said at first that he was a wilful man given to having his own way, but that it would soon blow over. Then they listened to him. They heard him explain what was at stake (that severe, huge head with its black locks, black brows, the paleness of its

2

anger, the gathering of muscles of its strength). He was transformed for ever and utterly before their eyes, for good or bad, one way or the other. Some of them shrank into silence at what he said and crept away from him and stayed away. Others spat in his path. Others still (but few from the town and this was another thing to be explained, his splitting of town and countryside) went out and became enraged at the injustice done to him and broke themselves across his cause. No one in the place or near it was untouched. Kirwan, Grace, Delaney, Moore, Nugent and Bergin. Each one discovered something new about his neighbour. And almost everyone was to discover something novel and terrible about the familiar places of the town, its four streets, High Street, River Street, New Line and Quarry Road and the Cross that bound them, streets and people, the nexus of all their existence, drawing them to some central point at the butt of the hill like some lode buried deep in the ground. They would say: it was there that such-and-such a thing happened.

It was on the Cross, on a cold November night, 1871, that the Reverend Father Lutterell, curate, read out, not once but several times to a gradually gathering mob, that their parish priest, his parish priest, William Edward Lannigan, had been suspended from his position as parish priest. *Ab omni juristicione spirituali et ab omni officio ecclesiastico.* ('Put it into language, Father,' they shouted from the back. 'He's not your priest,' shouted the thin curate, 'He's of the devil, the devil.') To the suspended priest, who was standing in the darkness of the porch of the Big Chapel all this while on the top of the hill, his few supporters came, running, to say what had happened and that the curate was drunk. He would make no comment on all this, standing there in his long, black cloak but registered this disgraceful fact to add to others in his next letter to the Cardinal.

It is recorded in some old travel books that on this Cross there once stood a market cross, a gibbet of blackened wood with a hanging lantern that gave light to travellers into the town, coming from the four cardinal points of the compass. No one could say when this light and symbol had been removed but it was no longer there in the 1870s.

One or two places in the town had a special significance in the priest's struggle. They ought to be mentioned now. Like the Commons. The Commons was situated a mile and a half below the town, just where the Kilkenny road twisted away towards the north. Here, a warren of British Army cottages built after the Napoleonic Wars and added to since then. There was little disloyalist feeling against the British in the area but some special attitude, between fear and contempt, was reserved for these veterans of the Imperial Army and their breed who lived on the Commons. They were held to be different as their names were different, outlandish names like Stukely or Winkle, common but foreign names like Baker or Thomson or Grainger and the Irish among them, Connors or Reilly having sold themselves away from the town into the licentious marriages of the cottages with women who seemed to come and go, unsettled and unsettling with their English accents standing apart from the men and children even in the same houses.

Before the revolt of Father Lannigan the contacts between the Commons and the town, while sometimes sinister, were at least tolerable. One-armed men appeared and disappeared with the change of seasons. At one time or another every kind of mutilation exhibited itself on the Kilkenny road or River Street or around the timber yards and sawmills near the bridge. The children, lice-ridden and ashen with hunger, walked back and forth to the town to beg in streels of four or five holding hands across the width of the common highway, hardly moving from the feet of fretful horses and the raised whip of the angry driver.

But during the rioting in the town, especially when the Big Chapel was unroofed in November of 1872, the Commons and its brood threatened to engulf the permanent buildings and streets of the town; strange, mercenary and skilful hooligans made themselves available to either side and were hired thoughtlessly before the true consequences of the alliance became clear. It was then the townspeople came to know the cottagers, to know their faces, even their names, in a terrible destructive neighbourliness that brought them more quickly to their common ruin. The Commons would empty itself into the town at the promise of a fight and those same fierce, spirited women with the knowing, hard faces and the unfamiliar voices took to going about in bands. They would enlarge a crowd of fighting men within minutes, taking the blows and cries before them like food.

At the top of High Street, almost opposite the Big Chapel and just before the last straggle of houses at that end of the town, were the schools: a single, plain, two-storeyed building with two solid stone steps up to the large, ugly door and its unnecessary brass knocker. The door was always on the latch, night and morning, until the trouble started when he had a large bolt made to hold the door against the mob. The top step was worn to a hollow that caught the rainwater and made the children skip across the threshold on a wet day. It was for the sake of the schools that he began his doomed quarrel against authority.

They were National Schools, under the Commissioners of National Education in Dublin and he, as parish priest being also manager, was well pleased with the work of the children and their teachers when, with little forewarning, a deputation of the townspeople came before him, some time in the 1860s.

They had come and were shifting about in the cluttered parlour of the Presbytery, six men. One alone showed confidence, a blond, balding man with a hard smile and pale, splintered eyes. This was Hipps, the baker. Paul Hipps. Bun Hipps, the priest reflected mockingly. Gaitered and groomed with his highly polished brogues, the great head razored, laundered, shining silken stock, immaculate frock coat, he had confronted them with massive calm. Hipps and the Doyles, Ger Doyle, Georgie Doyle, China Doyle and Jude Doyle, stonemasons. They were like animals in a nest pushing on top of one another in the confined room, red-faced and clumsy. And Ryan, the farmer. They appeared such puny troublemakers in his sight. That they would be prominent agents in his own destruction, party to his own humiliation before the county, before the world, was inconceivable to him then as he listened sardonically to what they had to say.

'Well?' he queried Hipps, since the others refused to look him straight in the face.

5

'And so we wondered if you could fix up the Brothers in the town,' smiled Hipps as if he were ending a plea instead of beginning one.

'The Brothers?'

'The Christian Brothers, Father,' from one of the Doyles. 'For to start a school, Father.'

'Don't you have your National Schools?' the priest asked with malicious quiet.

'The people wants Catholic schools.'

'What need have you of another school in a town of this size?'

'The National Schools should be closed down altogether.'

'The National Schools is godless schools.'

He turned, at this, towards Ryan, the farmer from Killineck, a barony south of the town towards Tipperary. A thin, scrawny, elderly man with a loose wallet of flesh beneath his chin. The priest had heard of these Ryans, a brother and a sister joined together in a fruitless, fierce union, high-pitched in all their views and living comfortlessly on the largest farm in the parish. He looked sombrely into the burnt, ascetic face of Ryan and saw its animation, like a fever, beneath the skin.

'You forget, Mr Ryan,' he said as levelly as he could although his anger surged in his throat. 'You forget that your own priest is manager of the schools. What have you to say to that? Do you think I would countenance godless schools, as you put it?' As he finished he was almost shouting.

'It isn't me that said it first,' the thorny face was dark and turned aside so that the priest's temples beat in anger at this furtiveness.

'What do you mean?' And then, because no reply came in the hushed room of heavy male breathing, 'Say what you have to say, man. Out with it. I won't tolerate a – a conspiracy in my house, in my parish.'

'The Church's agin the National Schools.'

'They're Governmint schools. Run be the English, heathen schools, to drag away innocent Irish childer. Souper schools!'

'The Cardinal's agin the National Schools. Aye, and the bishop. And most priests.'

'It's only, Father,' this from Hipps, the suave baker, to the

6

priest now speechless with fury, 'it's only that we have our own good Catholic schools now and the good brothers and holy sisters to run them.'

'How dare you. How dare you,' stuttered the priest, 'talk to me – in my own parlour – about what is or is not good for my parish.' It had indeed finally come to his own hearth. Oh, he had heard it said behind his back, that he was a follower of false education, with false ideas, that he mixed with Protestants. And the worst, only the previous June, after ordination in St Kyran's College when in the heat of debate over lunch he said that education was not the preserve of the Roman Catholic Church and more, that education was positive and the pursuit of knowledge and not negative and the limitation of knowledge. All this reported, as he knew it would be, to Bishop's Palace and then that – that sycophant over there to call him over and in his oh so polite voice to say that he didn't approve of this man Mill and his dangerous teaching and how was the parish going? Could he help in any way?

As the priest recalled the robed figure of power behind these six men in his parlour his anger towards them abated. He could say to them: 'You're taking sides in something beyond your comprehension.' What use would it be? What use would it be for him to tell them, ignorant men, that they had become dupes, dupes of ecclesiastical power, that none of it, any of it, had anything to do with God or morality or such but only the policy of Papal consolidation throughout Europe and its direction through the Romanist bishops?

So a second school opened in the town, the school of the Christian Brothers. Mr Fincheon gave over the yard and house behind his shop and contributed a hundred pounds to its decoration. In the very first year the new school took away half the pupils from the National Schools; in the second year Father Lannigan was obliged to let a national teacher go because the numbers were now down to sixty, fifty of them girls. He looked about for means to remedy this situation being determined to keep the National Schools open at all costs and, after much persuasion on his part, managed to establish Master Scully as Headmaster of the National Schools. From that moment onwards, it might be said, these two men, priest and teacher, became enlocked together in a particular tragedy within the larger catastrophe of the place.

The new Headmaster showed little enthusiasm for his post. He moved about the schools and back and forth to his cottage-like house at the Cross with a kind of fated certainty as if he had, in this choice, begun his own contribution to the incident of his own death, three or four years into the future. His family would remark afterwards, when he was dead, of how he began to fail once he took the priest's offer. But for all that the National Schools under Master Scully made a rapid recovery, standards rose; the Master himself, whose reputation in the town before this had been ambiguous, was spoken well of by many parents. The priest personally offered weekly classes in Latin, Greek and French. In the visitation of Major McAllister in 1868 a child addressed a mathematical problem and its solution to the class, first in Latin, then in French and the Major remarked on the fluency with which it was transcribed on to the writing-slates by each of the pupils. Horticulture, Astronomy, Geography and Galvanism were added to the curriculum, and a large globe, five maps and some scientific apparatus arrived from the Head Office of National Education. It was about this time too that the priest had the schools affiliated to the School of Art, Design and Science, South Dulwich, and a notice to that effect appeared in the *Kilkenny Journal*. The following Sunday instead of a sermon he spoke about the schools (they would remember this in their evidence in the four actions which he took for libel). He told his congregation that from now on the schools would be called *The Academy* and this was painted above the great ugly door and its two steps. *The Academy 1868*.

It is difficult to decide between truth and lie in the years immediately following; each side claimed to have acted in extravagant contradiction to what the others represented as the true account. It is known that a people's deputation reported to the bishop through the curate, Father Lutterell, that the parish priest had drawn pupils from the new Christian Brothers schools by provocative and unchristian enticements and persuasions. It was stated at a Government inquiry many years later, by a witness under oath, that Father Lannigan had proclaimed on the public highway, during those months, that he was surrounded by a conspiracy. That it sought to destroy not only him but the lawful state. That it would establish the authority of Rome instead of the law of the land. That the Ultramontanes were gaining power and having formed an unholy alliance with the Liberals were seeking to change the traditional nature of the Irish Church. Episcopacy and dictatorship instead of freedom and local tradition. That the conspiracy had singled him out because here in this town he would tolerate no intolerance, no sectarian evil, he would provide the best schools first and worry about the system afterwards.

There was good reason to believe that Father Lutterell of his own initiative had also reported to the bishop that the parish priest, in turning schoolmaster, was neglecting his parish duties and that, furthermore, he had also turned shopkeeper. Father Lannigan's sister Judy, a Mrs Rowen, owned a small tea and sweet shop on the corner of Quarry Road and Martin's Lane. It was burned out, the first of seven targets fired by the mob in 1872. But before all of this he had persuaded her to leave ('I will go then, William, for you, but if you'd heed me you'd leave this terrible place too') and had given her his blessing, she kneeling in the rain beside the cart that took her and her boxes down the road to Newtown. She would come back the same road again, by Cappagh Eve and Singlebridge, to take him on his own final, funereal journey from the place, more corpse than living man, wrapt and gaunt against the bitter autumn, scarcely noticed by the people, to the County Home. That would be in 1878.

At the Cross in the town was a road-house. Above the door was a sign that said here stopped the Bianconi cars on their way from Clonmel to Kilkenny Station. While travellers might take their rest or refreshment inside the house the horses were watered or changed in the stable yards opposite the Friary down on the New Line. This road-house was operated by a man called McNamara, an outsider to the town who had married into the place. Beside this road-house, and flanked on the other side by the disused Protestant cemetery, was the home of Master Scully.

*   *   *

9

Master Scully and his wife Henrietta. And his sons Marcus Anthony, Nicholas and James Florence Scully, called Florrie. And the girl called Emerine.

When the priest asked him to take over the National Schools he tried hard to avoid it. He had his own little school, hadn't he? Even as the excuse formed on his lips it ridiculed him and his spirit shrank; the five pupils, soon to dwindle to three with the going away of his own son Nicholas to Maynooth and the Hanley boy to England. The truth was that his own school had never been a success, enough to keep his household going, no more.

For over twenty years before the trouble Master Scully had kept his small private school, called the Latin School or Low School, over a disused carriage shed in River Street. The carriage house opened on to a rough field which ran down to the riverbank at a point opposite the Abbey Meadows. Osiers grew there and the field was known as the Weaver's Plot. It was said that baskets were made in the locality before the Famine. The children of the Latin School had the run of this field and for years Master Scully could be seen each morning at the gates, shouting, 'Keep away from the river, keep away from the river, now,' waving his short arms in the long sleeves and nodding his head, the great mane of fair hair forward and catching the sunlight.

From the beginning a section of the townspeople had objected to the Latin School. They said it was 'a wrong kind of school,' they said that Master Scully was 'against the clergy'. For one thing he took Protestants as well as Catholics and it was known that Protestants, like Mr Butler and Mrs Heffernan, gave Scully money to keep the school open. On one occasion following a demonstration of Classical prints from the British Museum it was reported widely that the children were being shown indecent pictures. But the greatest slur that could be put upon the school was that it was different. It was trumpeted on the corners of the Cross, it was whispered in the hatching groups around the Chapel yard after Sunday Mass that those who sent their children to Scully's school had 'airs and graces above their station'.

'I know my enemies' the little Master would say to his family when they were gathered together. He would prance about the kitchen floor trying out his defiant speeches in front of them but he never took his defiance into the street. 'I know my enemies even if I don't know them by name.' And, later, when he had given himself finally, reluctantly, to that doomed alliance with the priest, 'His enemies are my enemies. I don't care who knows it.'

Henrietta from her serving table or from the kitchen hob would say, 'Hush, Master, not in front of the children.' To the day of her death they would never hear her address him as anything else but Master.

She was the daughter of a Protestant clergyman from outside Thurles in County Tipperary. 'My father,' she would sometimes say on a point of self-defence, 'my father was a man of God', and this was her only reference to him. Yet she had become a Catholic on her marriage. When it was all over she died in a home for indigent Christians in Dublin, in 1888 or 1889, it is said, of cholera.

Having fathered four sons, two of whom had died at birth or infancy, Master Scully took out a female child from the local Orphanage in Kilkenny. This was Emerine Scully, familiarly known to the members of her new, elected family as Nina, but of how she got this unusual name there is no explanation. This action of Scully had one curious effect since it seemed to provoke, more than all previous provocation on his part, the antagonism of the townspeople. It was said widely and even to his face that the girl was his illegitimately, but there is nothing to support this, except that while the three boys were fair-skinned and blond, with ragged yellow eyebrows and the prominent frontal bones of the father, she was dark with a gipsy growth of black hair to the waist, while she and they still resembled the Master. That shadowed, guarded look that was hers, constantly, even in smile, was given a curious support, a kind of masking, by the burnt colour of her skin. Later on – and she was older then, of course, and no doubt unkempt in death – the Manchester Police Report of 1879, before the suicide had been identified, described her as of 'Possible Foreign Origin'. It also said she had two moles on her face, one on the right cheek-bone, the other on the neck, like a stone hanging from the left earlobe.

The three Scully boys who survived childhood were Marcus Anthony (who had been so named by a drunken, ecstatic father quoting his Latin into the vacant face of the midwife, old Mam Grant who used to live on River Street), Nicholas and James Florence Scully, this latter younger than Emerine, a boy of six in fact during the worst incidents of the Big Chapel. He would remember little of it all, except the marriage. Strangely he liked to talk of the marriage later on in his life as if it were the single incident of value to be protected from the pitiless years of his childhood. He had been in fact the groomsman, the frail, minute attendant on the couple in the unroofed, polluted church on that startling spring morning in 1874. His memory was this: that the painted shaft of light across the great Assumption canvas behind the high altar was vivified by the real, spilling fall of sunlight through the broken roof away above his head. Angels came through the torn beams, the jagged slates, for the child. When he could take his eyes from this high miracle, transfiguration was everywhere. Even the moving mats of green leaves on the sanctuary floor, blown in through the broken windows, were not a desecration to him, they seemed even more luxurious than the red carpet itself on the altar steps, the warmth of which he knew through his knees as an altar boy. His memory, years later, would only refuse the faces of the others present at the bridal ceremony. He would vaguely remember the figure of the priest like a giant shadow above, beyond his downturned eyes. Of the bridal company, nothing. This was the last ceremony of its kind performed by the excommunicated priest in the condemned, interdicted church, this ceremony of marriage of Marcus Anthony Scully and Emerine Donovan (Scully) because they had discovered another name for her by then.

When they spoke of him with dislike and distrust the people said that Master Scully hobnobbed with the Protestants. They were thinking of Horace Percy Butler who was only one man, however, and could not be called a Protestant at all. He believed in nothing except the scarcely predictable course of his own consciousness. It could hardly be said that they were friends or that they had very much in common, the Master of the town schools and the Master of Whytescourt House. On the first Wednesday of the month the carriage from the big house outside the town would arrive at the Cross and the two men would leave together for Kilkenny to be in time for the meeting of the Archaeological Society at 2 PM. Scully would bring his transcripts of the monuments of the dead from the cemetery behind his house and Butler, with nothing, would question him on the road, in his dry, pendantic manner about the living incidents of the town. It was his one contact with the happenings in the town and later he would transcribe the remarks of Master Scully into his journal, with the same diligence that Scully himself copied the broken words of the dead from the tombs, and this journal of Horace Percy Butler is a major source of information of what happened in the place between 1871 and 1874. After that year the man's mind gave out and the entries become almost unintelligible.

There was one particular view of the town, memorable after a sun shower, from the bottom garden of Whytescourt House. The river ran black and deep here between the sun arbours and lily-ponds on one side and the first brick wall of the town on the other that rose from the very edge of the water, being washed by it in flood. There was such a compactness about the whole town when seen from the lawns of Whytescourt that it even appeared to be walled like an ancient settlement. Windows and doors scarcely showed themselves in this massive display of walls. Instead the town seemed to elevate itself, sleek, glittering roof above roof in a beauty of black and pewter-grey shoulders, with an occasional fleshy side of pink brick, all rising and converging on the steeple of the Big Chapel on the heights. At the very top of the town, with Slievnamon in the distance, was the Workhouse. With its castellated ramparts, its square towers and high turreted chimneys, its long, high outer walls, its arches, the Workhouse completed this image of fortification. Seen from Whytescourt in the steam of warm after-rain, the town looked snug and washed on its hill, massive and crouching like a dark coated thing, with its weakness hidden in the white limbs of its hidden streets.

This was the favourite view of Horace Percy Butler. This was where the people saw him in the evening, taking the air broodingly near the river before walking back to the big, square house behind. He would come here in his shirt sleeves, straight from his study, often shivering in the sudden river breezes, an emaciated figure in light breeches and long stockings. His head was small with a round, punctured nose and sunken, unhappy eyes behind the pince-nez. He was seldom known to smile and still among the people he had a singular reputation for generosity. To some degree this feeling among the people was pity since all knew from the gossip of the labourers and the drovers that he was a failure in the running of the estate and this in some way brought the lonely figure of the man down to within reach of their pity. They knew and knowingly forgave him that for all his forty-odd years he had hardly ever even gone back into the stables and yard and fruit and vegetable gardens that ran back for a quarter of a mile behind the house. The gardens reeked with neglected growth, not just of ordinary fruits, for Mr Butler's father, the old army man who was supposed to be a secret Catholic, had been an avid experimental gardener and from the public highway quite a distance away, with the wind right, one could be smothered in the heavy garden smells of rotting berries, of the quince trees, the Dutch medlars, of the wild pears and plums that were wild without thinning and pruning. The older people said it would turn in his grave the dead old man who had prided husbandry above every other virtue, who in his day had brought back the Duke's Cup from the Dublin Show for his drainage and the Gold Medal of the Royal Agricultural Society for the best labourers' cottages in the province of Leinster, so zealously did he keep his staff and tenants to his own example.

Still for the son they had a curious affection and tolerance which could have nothing to do with familiarity or patronage on his part. His mother, old Mrs Butler, was still alive in 1871, bed-ridden in an upper room and attended constantly by a German lady nurse. The son, too, might as well have been crippled so seldom did he venture out. He spent most of his days cooped up in the monkish room at the top of the house, what everyone else called the study and he the Observatory. If

he ignored the cultivated fruits and flowers of the Whytescourt
gardens Horace Percy Butler had still a passion for the living
produce of the earth but for the wild flowers and not the
attended, demanding shrubs that grew about the house. His
whole being revolted at the constraint, the manipulation of
what was natural, but this might not have anything to do with
his avoidance, his abhorrence even of the cultivated flower-
beds. In his Observatory, with glass and blade, he dissected and
identified the wild specimens that he gathered on his walks and
very occasionally corresponded on his finds with a botanist
clergyman in County Antrim. But more often he simply left his
specimen in broken petals and vegetable skins once his curiosity had been satisfied and went back to his reading or – and
this would explain his name for the room – to looking through
the standing telescope at the window. He was almost stone deaf
and although he persisted in taking a hundredth grain of phos-
phorus daily and a teaspoonful of Fellows' Syrup of the Hypo-
phosphites he knew there could never be a remedy. Everywhere
he went he carried his ornate Conversation Tube with its
shining ivory ear and mouth pieces. In those years of distress
in the town Mr Butler had a dog, an Irish setter called Lincoln.

On an afternoon in August 1871 Horace Percy Butler
walked back from the riverbank to the house, followed by the
dog Lincoln and carrying in his hands, almost reverently, a
long-stemmed white river flower. He moved carefully along
the paths as if the flower were so fragile as to disintegrate at
rough handling. At the edge of the gravel fronting the house
(three storeys, six windows on each upper level, five at the
ground and a splendid door, altogether a square and perfect
structure of white limestone) he stopped a groundsman and
said that he had heard a disturbance in the town and what
could be the meaning of it. The man muttered in reply but
Butler either did not hear or had already forgotten his own
question since he passed the man without stopping. In the
house itself he rapidly, delicately ascended the great oak staircase, his eyes running about the emptiness of the hall with that
alertness of the deaf. At last he reached his room, that narrow
cell, and laid his flower on the cluttered table near the window
with a sigh, a slow exhalation of breath, both satisfied and

satisfying, his whole body partaking of the pleasure from the flower that lay girlishly, ruffled, between his hands. He stood a moment looking at the hollow stem and the white flowers and the passion of the body gave way to a curiosity that moved his mouth without sound. Then he sat down at the same table and, clearing a space, made in the journal the first entry that is of interest to those who would understand the events surrounding the Big Chapel.

He began under an entry that recorded the recent visit to Dublin of the Prince of Wales and some remarks on the Phoenix Park rioting of the week following. He wrote: 'Cowbane (Cicuta Virosa) or Water Parsnip (Sium Latifolium L.) beneath the crossing stones and just opposite Marnell's Wall. Curious so far south.' He considered a moment and then, as was his custom, he continued on without separating the entries. What he wrote was this:

Scully informs me that he will send his son Nicholas into the Roman ministry at Maynooth. Said nothing. He said the boy is clever, will learn something, will have a profession, respect ETCETERA. That he will use his mind. Laughed at this. He said why do you laugh. Said I had read Mr. Ingram's pamphlet and others on the abominable teachings of the college, confessional sexuality ETCETERA. He said no Protestant could hope to understand such [things]. Said nothing to this and he became discomfited. He asked if I knew how the priest Lannigan in the town had been suspended having taken legal action against his Bishop in the common court. Said if Mr. Lannigan put on the Roman collar he had best let himself be led by it. He could not reply to this. There was noise today from the town but it might have been thunder.

The name of the town is Kyle. Tradition has it that the name came from great forests in times past. But in 1871 the land was completely clear of timber and prosperous with a good view of Slievnamon and the Commeraghs to the south and with low, rolling hills to the north and the near city of Kilkenny.

2 . December 1871

Nicholas Scully standing in Kildare Station. Athy, Carlow and Bagnelstown. Just three stops and then Kilkenny. The great locomotive, No 1–48 in high lettering on its side, high chimney, rounded dome and huge, coupled wheels nearly six feet high. Florrie would love the sight of it, thought Nicholas. He had a collection of drawings of Mr McDonnell's locomotives already at home. His father would say that whatever transpired James Florence would leave them all behind yet with his inventions and engines. Tonnage, cylinder and piston sizes. Built at Inchicore. A credit to the country, smiled Nicholas wryly at the thirty tons of labouring and diminishing exertion moving past him to its suspiring stop.

He tried quickly to find an empty carriage (not because, he argued fretfully to himself for the umpteenth time, not because I can't stand to meet them, talk to them, talk to them, say this that and the other to them, small talk: it is the smell) but the best he could manage was one that already contained a woman with a bandaged child and a freckled, ruddy, squat man who turned out to be a cattleman from Waterford.

'The country is on the up and up,' this fellow was saying to the woman but with both his red, glaring eyes on Nicholas all the while. 'Is it the Fenians?' he then asked dramatically and without a change of tone, 'sure the Fenians is rightly dead and buried and the bad cess to them for their mischief making. Risins and revolutions how are ya! Tisn't that'll put mate on a plate and a cup of stirabout in a fist.' Nicholas kept his eyes averted and his heart sank at the prospect of having to address this man. 'Tisn't that'll feed us or the childer, I'm tellin ya that now.' The woman clucked in the corner and the man appeared to take the sound as encouragement, ambiguous though it was. 'God forgive me,' his voice became wheedling and pious in a way that Nicholas found especially upsetting. 'I think the Famine and the emigration has done the country more good than harm, though God mark me if I'm wrong.' This is for my benefit, this is directed towards me, Nicholas fumed: he thinks I am still a cleric: I will say nothing.

At last they jerked off out of the station, convolving pillars of smoke passing the windows and once out from under the station canopy, it seemed, the rain returned, at first pricking the windows with wet hail and then slashing down as the train gathered speed. It was only three o'clock and yet Nicholas could scarcely see into the nearby speeding fields. To make matters worse the man had produced a pipe and began to stoke up foul-smelling tobacco. In the gloom the pipe at his chin reddened and died, reddened and died like an engine. And all the time, without his looking in that direction, Nicholas could feel the raw, inflamed, whisky eyes measuring him up and down. Trying hard to regain his peace of mind Nicholas looked towards the woman and the child and smiled. They looked back at him out of a darkness that had moulded their faces into a mask, the child's being almost completely hidden in great swathes of bandage.

'Excuse me, mister,' said the horrible man, leaning forward and pointing, 'that bag,' and he indicated Nicholas' wooden clothes box on the rack above, 'that bag is a danger.'

Nicholas, standing, swaying, painfully shifted the box on the rack, a great blush pulsing like a tide all over his body. As he looked upwards he believed that even his wrists were crimson with embarrassment. And all the while his contented tormentor sat behind him watching, testing. A meaningless fury shook Nicholas from head to foot. I will sit down and look and stare at this – this vegetable. The man looked back at him, however, quite at ease with himself.

'Excuse me, mister,' he said again. In his effort to glare the man into silence Nicholas saw with a shock that the blotchy face had delicately fair eyebrows but this refinement threw every other feature into high relief. Elsewhere the hair sprouted from the big head in rough, red tufts.

'Yes?'

'Excuse me asking but would you be from the College?' They had left Kildare Station and Maynooth behind but the man caught it all with a twist backwards of his head.

18

'Yes.' His reply was taken with delight by the man who beamed across at the woman as if to say: I told you so. 'Yes,' repeated Nicholas cruelly, watching their faces. 'Yes, but I've left the place for good.' He wanted to say more, to say that he had left everything, all that they in their ignorance and superstition continued to hold and abide by, faith and God. But he could not bring himself to do so before the silent, dark face of the woman, who was listening to what was being said in a great vulnerable swoon of weariness and timidity.

'Well and aren't you still wearing the uniform?' The man mocked him with eyes half covered, his mouth open to laugh. Nicholas had difficulty in keeping his voice level.

'I can't just throw away clothes like that.' His throat began to fill up with pity for himself and his lot. 'If I could change them I would this minute.' (One pair of coarse black corduroy, fifteen shillings. One body coat and vest, thirty shillings. One upper coat of Kersey, a pound. Two pairs of brogues, and they had to sell a table that used to belong to grandmother, and mother's ivory sickness crucifix but she said it was not been sold if it was been given to God. And now.)

'Clothes don't grow on the side of the road, you know.' He hadn't meant to say that at all, to sound so apologetic, so too much like a boy, but that was how it came out. 'Anyway it's my own business, isn't it,' he ended in a fierce whisper across to the man.

'No bones broken,' he even spoke back in a whisper too, in a sympathetic, smiling, paternal way that infuriated Nicholas even more. He resolved not to say another word to the fellow until they got to Kilkenny. 'There are some that are made for it, some that are not.' The thing to do was to avoid looking at him altogether. 'I was just saying to Missus here,' this was in a shout, a burst of raucous goodwill and fellowship, 'I was just saying, wasn't I?' to the woman, 'that it's less clergy and more cows the country needs, hah? Only joking,' he added jovially, 'only joking, ha, ha.'

I will look into the rain for the rest of the journey, Nicholas told the streaming window. The great plain of the Midlands with scarcely a single fence went away from the train into the distant mists. It made him feel even more desolate, this great unfurrowed piece of land without post or stone to break the green blanket of grass. There were sheep out there, sometimes even moving herds of them but they had given up their shape to the grey afternoon, sodden and miserable lumps of dirty white in the rain. It is because I am going home that I am so miserable and why should that be, why should that be, why should that be?

'The worst winter since 'forty-eight,' from across the way. 'Nothing like the floods in England been seen for ages,' this, loudly to the woman in the corner who clucked and moved briefly to life, her shifting about in the seat a response.

What was so shaking, what was leaving him without a particle of hope was this dread of going home. It had all been settled and Dada had written not one letter but two in the last two weeks to say in that meticulous handwriting that everything would be all right. Oh there would be heartache but it would be hidden from him around the table in the kitchen and everyone would say, isn't it grand to have Nicholas home? The idea soured in his mouth but it was not even this (he could live with this because it saved them and him, too, pain) that shook him every time he thought of the where he was going and why.

They were running through cuttings and the high banks on either side shut out what little light was left to the carriage. In this partial darkness they sat and the sound of the breathing seemed as great as the funnelling roar of the engine and the rattle of the wheels on the lines. It seemed to Nicholas in his despair that he was trapped in a box. He had to prevent himself from jumping up and pulling at the grimy window. He gripped his fingers between his knees until he drove the blood from the mounts of the knuckles and his hands looked skeletal.

'I wouldn't take it so hard. Sure there's great prospect nowadays for the young.' The whisky voice. The dull red seat covers. The brown, stained woodwork. The yellowing ceiling fogged by the man's smoking. Nicholas gave a coughing laugh. 'Sure lookit here, young fellow, I mind the time there was the Famine.' To the woman, his dependable, 'I seen times, I'm telling ya. Godalmighty I seen them go outta Waterford on the boats with their bellies stuck to their backs and the smell, the smell mind ya, of the hunger coming off them. Oh they don't know how well off they are these days, the young wans.'

Nicholas gave another swallowed laugh of contempt.

'Oh and they always know better.' He had succeeded in enraging the man who was leaning over towards him, trying to engage him although he was still addressing the woman. 'They can't be told anything. Oh no. Young hop-off-me-thumbs with their heads in the air. Going around with their ideas and notions and — and — fantastications beyond their years.'

This produced its silence that endured for some time while the man muttered to himself, eyes flashing, stomach heaving, a silence that Nicholas enjoyed with a grim satisfaction. It is not, he assured himself, that I want to hurt them, or to show myself, make myself different, apart, safe, or is it? Why bother about it since the fact of my, of my exception is obvious. Famine! It is simply our ignorance is a more exacting master than the English and their landlords and their peelers. If we knew better we would do more. What used Father Lannigan say? God made knowledge, never fear it, fear ignorance.

Rashly, after a while, he said: 'It's our own ignorance that has us the way we are.'

The fellow leaped up alive in his seat. 'Is it now, is it now?' Sarcastically, 'Do ye tell us so? Did ya hear that spake, Missus?' The woman, dumb. 'God bless us all,' breezily, 'they'll be telling us next we've no rights to the air we're breathing. Clerics,' he added savagely, 'clerics, Godalmighty,' and although he clearly wanted to, he could say no more.

'I am not a cleric,' Nicholas shot out angrily.

'Oh, of course, of course, I misremembered that.'

'I have given it up.'

'Oh, of course, of course. Ye've given it up. I seemed to hear you say as much.' Taunting.

'You may,' conceded Nicholas loftily, 'excuse me of anything else. But not that.'

The man laughed, his humour restored. 'Priests is people,' he remarked generously, pulling on his pipe, 'if it weren't for the priest in the dark times the people'd have been without anyone to stand by them. Oh sure I well remember—' and he went on into a long rigmarole about his childhood outside Dungar-

21

van which involved a famous Father Quinn who had died, after years of dedication, in the Poorhouse. He was back to his old humour again and even embraced Nicholas within it with many asides and advices on what was worthwhile in the clergy and what not.

When he had finally finished Nicholas, judging his moment said : 'They are creating a clerical dictatorship in this country, an outpost of the new Roman Empire. They would set up the bishop and his Pope as the true ruler of the land. That's what our clergy is coming to.'

'That's quare talk for a young fellow like you.'

'I'm nineteen,' Nicholas asserted hotly.

'Oh, God bless us, God bless us,' wheezed the man, his eyes streaming with laughter. 'Will you listen to that?' he appealed once more to the woman, 'will you listen to who's talking?'

'Are you a Gallican or an Ultramontane,' Nicholas furiously demanded, 'or do you even know what that means? You don't even know what's going on around you. Do you know what it means to be an Ultramontane?'

'Begob I don't,' the other conceded but with lively humour in his eyes, ready to break out again into laughter at it all. 'Is it politics ye're talking about?'

'I'm talking about religion,' Nicholas, coldly. Was there any use in talking about anything?

'Them are big words.' The man was watching him shrewdly as he would judge a young animal in the fair yard. 'Are they your own?'

Nicholas was speechless with mortification and helplessness. It was obvious to him that he was being mocked. How would Father Lannigan deal with the fellow? He was the one who'd explain what was at stake in the great struggle. 'They may not be,' he said slowly, 'my own words. But if they're not itself I know what they mean.' The figure of the priest stood beside him, he could feel the great square bulk as a living presence, could hear the florid voice expounding, could catch the spirited spring of attack in the voice. He himself wouldn't be able to do justice to the great debate and even if he could these ignorant figures in the dark compartment wouldn't be able to follow what he was saying. And the pity of it, the pity of it was that these were the very ones who had to be told, who had to be taught, more than any others. It was their gospel, the gospel to be preached to the poor and the ignorant, the gospel of freedom, freedom from authoritarianism, freedom from superstition. If it wasn't their gospel then it didn't have any meaning at all. The shadow of the priest with soutane and cape in a black flow, seemed to cross the compartment between him and the others and Nicholas felt bowed down by the burden that it brought.

'Never mind,' he said quickly to the man, at length, who had his mouth open, half laughing, before him. 'It doesn't matter. Nothing matters.'

'Oh it doesn't, hah? But lookit, come here now. Aren't ya going to spell the big words for us? I mean aren't ya – Missus and meself. Lookit, Missus and meself and the young lad there – sure we're all mad to know what you're talking about. What did ya say it 'twas – ulster – something or other, hah?'

'It doesn't matter.'

'Oh begod it does matter.' He was enjoying himself. 'Oh begod it does. Doesn't it matter, Missus?'

'You're making a mockery of me.'

'Ah now, young lad, who says that?'

'You're just jeering.'

'Ah now, no wan's jeering, no wan's jeering at all.'

'You don't know how serious it all is. But you'll know, one day.' He had quietened the fellow but couldn't go any further. He tried to recall that sermon of Father Lannigan in the Big Chapel in September, the Sunday before he left the town. Word had got out about the law case against the curates and how the bishop was supposed to be going to suspend the priest. The church had been half empty because they were afraid. They had gone to the Friary instead, the Londregans and the Healys, Mr and Mrs Moore, and even Mr O'Brien, the apothecary who was such a stalwart in the church collections. Even Timmy Reilly, the sacristan. And others.

'Would I be right,' asked the man in the compartment, pulling on his pipe and putting on a serious face, 'would I be right in suggestin' that you're in a bit of trouble over the religion, young lad? Sure, lookit here,' looking about the compartment as if he were surrounded by hundreds of people, 'don't we all go through a bit of a lame season, so to speak, now and again? None of us is perfect. Well I knew Dr Cronin from Waterford that became the assistant to the Pope himself after living in the biggest—'

During the Mass he had turned again and again from the altar to run the deep-set eyes from person to person in the pews, counting maybe or checking if others had come late, the flow of the Mass, so triumphant normally in his voice, now a broken and sporadic sound. The wine and water had not been put out, the Sunday announcement book was misplaced, he was savagely impatient with the altar boys. When he finally turned to give out the name of the Sunday feast, the prayers for the dead and the other weekly information, he was unable to proceed. He had looked about his church with a deep, grieving expression the like of which Nicholas had never seen before. They had held themselves together, the few families, the few individuals in the seats and none of them doubted now that their gesture in attending on that Sunday had singled them out from the community of the town as clearly as the mark of disease or disfigurement and it was with this discomfort that they, at first, received his words. Nicholas could feel this shiver of recognition from his father who sat to his right, as was his custom, at the end of the pew occupied by the whole family.

'An attempt is being made to destroy your freedom. Not my freedom, mark you. But yours. I'm not fighting my cause alone, my people, but yours and never forget it. An attempt is being made to introduce a discipline into the Irish Catholic Church which would make the laity the slaves of the clergy. I have an acquaintance of more than thirty-five years' standing with the Canon Law and Theology of the Cisalpine Schools of Divinity. My knowledge of that law and that theology teaches me loyalty to my Queen as well as to the Head of my Church. It teaches me to give to God the things that are His but still to give Caesar his due. This Canon Law and this Theology, my dear people, will ignore the pretensions of a Pius IX as it would of a Pius V or an Adrian IV when such pretensions are inconsistent with the civil rights of the Sovereign or the Sovereign's subjects. Our Lordship the bishop,' the people exhaled here,

24

slowly, with his sharp pause, 'our Lordship the bishop has been educated in a school of Theology which would allow Rome and its representative to flout the law of the land. This school of Theology we call Ultramontane. It is new and it is powerful but its basis is power and not Christ. It will say that no Catholic can defend himself in the public courts against his ill-treatment by priest or bishop. It will say that the cleric is above the law of the land and unimpeachable. It would make the wearer of this collar,' in his frenzy Father Lannigan appeared to struggle at his throat, hands rifling the cloth to get at the white band beneath, 'no matter what his vice, above the law of the land. It will make you the slave of the priest, the priest the slave of the bishop, the bishop——'

'After that,' the man was saying, 'he never looked back. Went from strength to strength. Oh sure I knew the father and the brother well, grand people them Cronins if a bit fond of the drop. But I'll say this much,' tapping the knee of Nicholas who rocked, stupefied, in the seat opposite, 'wance he took a hoult of himself never touched a drop thereafter. There's a man for you, Doctor Cronin,' he shouted over to the woman, informatively as if for the first time, 'Doctor Cronin outta Waterford below, now a big noise beside the Pope himself.'

'The wretched man,' Nicholas murmured ambiguously, his mind still on that scene in the church. 'I mean someone else,' he explained to the dragon eyes that burned at him from across the way. 'I was – thinking of another priest. But then,' smiling thinly, 'aren't they all wretched?'

'Priests is people like ourselves,' challengingly the man watched.

'That is the beginning of the truth.'

'Lookit, young lad, I've a notion what's up with ya.'

'What?'

'Oh never mind now but I've got you measured rightly. I know what's biting you, I'm telling you.'

'What's up with me? What's biting me?'

The man squinted intensely. 'It's that College.'

'Maynooth?'

'Aye.'

25

'You mean Maynooth—' Nicholas had to laugh. Without breathing.

'Aye, all jokes aside now. Two weeks at home with a bit of flesh on you and you'll be right as rain again. It's them perfessors up there. Sure it's common knowledge some of them isn't Christian much less Catholics.'

Again laugh, shortly, choked off.

'You mean they've – ruined me?' And again laughter, like vomit in his dry throat so that the man looked gravely into his face. 'It is. I mean it's—' Nicholas stumbled, 'it's a strange. I mean – for an Irishman to say.'

'But isn't it true now, young fellow. Own up to it. Isn't it true there does be every sort of an idea given out be the perfessors up there? To be testing the students like. Sort of lettin' off air. Luther notions and the divil knows what else. The whole country knows that. Sure is it any wonder young fellows do break down under it before they're even in gallup. A saint a' God'd break under that carry-on.' Sucking his pipe furiously at this outrage. 'I'll tell you wan thing, young lad,' he confided thickly, his body heaving, 'the people of this country is getting wise to carry-on like that. I'm telling you that now, boy.'

Nicholas mocking: 'I believed you were a great supporter of the Church.'

'Oh I am, I am. Don't get me wrong now.' His look of slight fear had taken in the woman, his one ally. Nicholas looked at her too but she wasn't paying any attention to them. Rocking the child in her arms to the movement of the train, both apparently asleep and yet not at rest, not recovering themselves like normal sleepers. There was something guarded about their bodies, something wakeful as if it had been a long time since they had slept in a normal way.

'But come here a minute, come here a minute and tell us something,' the man grasped this chance to speak his mind to Nicholas. 'Aren't there some queer hawks of priests above in that place?'

'Do you mean – independent men?' Civilly, coldly.

'Aye, aye. You know what I mean. Trying to stir up divilment and the like. That class of thing.'

'If you mean men who will not be cowed, yes. But most of

26

them belong to the bishops.' Should he tell about Dr Kenny? Not that he knew a whole lot about him himself as the Juniors didn't study Moral. Except an unhappy, grey face under a biretta on the walks. And his denunciation of the Index and the censorship of ideas. Nicholas had memorized the sentences that had been transmitted from the Senior House after the row with Bishop Healy. 'If we are obliged to avoid everything that is dangerous to faith and morals we should leave the world altogether. Why did God make flesh?' They said he was against Infallibility too and that he spoke out in favour of mixed marriages with Protestants. 'Those that say what they believe, suffer. Was it ever any other way in the history of the Church?' He looked away from the man, hoping he would leave it at that.

'But come here, young lad. Come here now. What about that row out in Rome last year when John McHale stood up to the Italians and the rest of them.'

'Do you mean the Vatican Council?'

'Aye. Aye. That's right, that's right.'

Nicholas couldn't resist it. 'There was an effort,' he said from a great height of knowledge, 'to control the Pope and his bishops. But they had their way and now we have the Infallibility of the Pope.'

'When he speaks outta his chair,' the fellow's eyes were blazing with excitement, 'isn't that it? When he speaks outta his chair he can speak no wrong.'

'As you say,' Nicholas agreed, drily, 'when he speaks outta his chair.'

'Oh I was only explaining it the other day.' The great root of a face was comical in its earnestness. 'When he speaks outta his chair he can do no wrong. That's what the Latin means, as I was saying.' And he repeated, over and over again, his explanation, his words.

'There are men in the Church who see its power for what it is,' Nicholas began quietly but suddenly he had a burst of energy. 'They speak out against it. Against Rome and its silken tyrants. And they suffer for it. They are the true martyrs of your Church,' he asserted accusingly to the man. 'Martyrs of silence. Not like these others. Lunatics with their self-tortures

27

and their fasts and their – their love of blood.' He was breathing with difficulty, could feel his own blood, beyond his control, race and spill through his body, a hot wash of repulsion that was also, in a strange way, not disagreeable.

'When he speaks outta his chair he can do no wrong.' The man was still muttering this, mesmerized, head bobbing. 'Isn't that a quare thing now for you?' He had clearly not been listening at all. Nicholas could plainly see that much. They will listen only to what they are willing to hear. His face tightened with contempt for the lot of all preachers. Tied to their flocks. Sheep-dogs. 'Does it mean,' asked the man in slow, unhappy bewilderment, 'that he can't even tell lies like the rest of us? Begod God is generous. That's all I say.'

Nicholas gave a sharp, derisive laugh into the wet window at his elbow.

'Oh you can laugh all you want to, young fellow. You don't know the half of it.'

'I don't, ha?'

'Begor, you don't.'

'That's what you think.'

But he was strangely moved by the man or by the intimacy that seemed to come out of their contradiction and he could not rid himself of the thought of his father. They went onwards in the heaving, creaking compartment and for the second time Nicholas had the illusion of being imprisoned on this narrow, spittled floor beneath their feet with its filthy little rivulets of rainwater but this time not terrifyingly, simply a fact, evidence of their common lot, he, the man and the wombed figures of the mother and the child in the dark corner.

'And it was at the same meeting that they condemned the Fenians? Isn't it so?'

'At the Vatican Council?'

'Aye.'

'Well,' Nicholas began, 'there was a decree' – but the man snapped at him in a way that shocked him into attention.

'Arse-lickers with the British Queen. Oh they'll go on about Faith and Fatherland. But bejasus they'll make sure they're on the side of the Government and the money bags.'

Nicholas wanted to say something taunting about this change

28

in direction again but the grieving, bent face opposite stopped him.

'Between ourselves. I don't want this to go beyond the two of us, now.' The hoarse, choking voice. The big hand like a lumpy, comical potato holding his knee at which he stared not daring to look into the face. 'The brother took the oath. Me own brother. Below in Dungarvan.' Again, inescapably, the blood-shot eyes, remembering, two mourning, flickering coals in the wrinkled face. There was the quick glance to make sure the woman wasn't listening. 'He was read off the altar below in Dungarvan with six others. Had to take the boat to the States the next morning.' He took out a filthy rag and wiped his eyes and Nicholas tried to withdraw himself. He put a finger to the window and smeared a flat circle in the fogged glass. Then he erased it with the butt of his hand and the icy cold shot through his wrist. I will not, he vowed, allow myself to be – to suffer for someone that I don't even know. And they didn't speak to one another in the compartment again until the girl got on outside Athy.

The train had lurched and stopped at a level crossing and this big girl, the daughter of the gate-keeper, was pushed up into their carriage by several hands. She brought the fierce biting winds with her off the low fields together with numerous baskets that threatened everyone with their size.

'I'm always in dread of the train,' she began right away, chortling and rustling her many skirts and shawls. She wore a fringed cotton cap tight about her head and it seemed to squeeze out her fat, shining face and black ringlets. 'Every other day of the week there's them fierce crashes beyond in England. God forgive me,' she added with a bleat of laughter, 'I thought ye's were going to go through the shut gates yerselves this very evening.'

The cattleman stirred to life again with the company. 'It's like this, Missus, don't you see,' he explained as they moved off again, 'the more trains, the more lines, the more lines the more men to watch them. Something's bound to give in the end.'

'What're ye calling me Missus for, sure I'm not married at all,' giggled the girl with the baskets, kicking Nicholas on the legs with the side of her foot. Her many skirts made a wind across the floor. He tried to smile at her to placate her great, uninhibited femaleness that crushed him up against the carriage wall. He was anxious to please but still didn't want to have anything to do with her. She was coarse and he thought of Emerine and this arrow of memory hurt: a woman too she, Emerine, like this perspiring, odorous baggage on the seat beside him but the arrangement of the parts, breasts, arms and limbs or hair so different. Nicholas shivered with a great spinal wrench from the root of his body. 'Anyways,' went on the girl, subsiding at last, 'trains or no trains I'm melted with the weight of this stuff. I'm bound for Crowleys in Athy, d'you know. Sez I to me father, wouldn't you wait till the morning mail and the rain might have lifted. Sez he is it chickens instead a' eggs ya want to be bringing them.' And she gurgled again at this exchange. And went on in a rush to talk of the price of produce and how it would be nearly worth their while to bring it all as far as Dublin for what she was told was that the prices there were beyond belief. But the father wouldn't have it. 'Sez he d'ya want to end up being taken be a sailor off the boats, sez he.' And this prospect clearly delighted her for she revelled in it before each occupant of the carriage in turn.

'God girl,' said the cattleman, somewhat offended, 'don't make a mockery of that. I'm telling you now there's more truth than you'd imagine in that remark. Isn't that right, young fellow?' he appealed to Nicholas in his earnest way.

'Arrah go on outta that with you,' said she derisively.

'Oh no, now, it's the gospel truth, sure I've heard meself of the young country girl who – well now I don't want to go into it but 'twould make your blood cold, the story, so it would.'

'She got what she wanted or she didn't know how to avoid it. Much the same either way. Isn't that right, young fellow?' She bore down on Nicholas with her huge ham of a thigh and in his consternation he felt he'd smother as under a great plumed bird, falling, drenched and plump out of a wet sky. Then she swayed away from him again on the seat and he smiled coldly and muttered some useless contribution, exactly what he wasn't sure. The man clicked his tongue in disapproval and they were all glad to get rid of her in Athy. She got off

30

with more great shoves and pulls and shouts and the four of them were left together again, comfortlessly, in the carriage.

While the train was still standing in Athy Station the man raised himself half out the window and surveyed the wet, dripping platform. His great rear stuck back into the compartment like a cow's in a byre and Nicholas sniffed in distaste. He hoped he would move soon but instead the fellow crossed his brogues behind and appeared to be settled for a while. He would shout now and then at people on the platform, apparently knowing them all by name.

'What did you have for the Leger, John?'

'I had a shilling on Pretender but the whore faded away.'

'What was she at?'

'Six to five on, I gather.'

'Divil the bit it matters now.'

'Oh Divil the bit is right.'

'How's the Missus?'

'Oh thriving, thriving.'

To distract himself from the great haunches in the breeches almost level with his nose and, too, to take this chance of speaking to her with the fellow's back turned, Nicholas bent towards the woman. As pleasantly as he could. Of the new bookstalls that they had now in all the stations. And, quickly, to the no answer, how nice the waiting-rooms were, so clean and with turf fires. Was she ever in the one in Kilkenny? She shook her head, guardedly. That he himself was from Kilkenny, the county that is, and was on his way home (can she not speak? can she not say anything?) but still and all he liked the travelling. Trains especially. So fast now and great service to the people. Did she see how the Great Southern was offering Kilkenny to London now in only twenty-three hours for only twenty-two and seven pence—

The man broke this desperate ramble of words by backing back into the compartment, shaking himself of raindrops and closing the window, grunting, fastening the long leather thong on its catch.

In this uncertain interval Nicholas asked her if they had been to Dublin and said quietly that the little lad was so good and so quiet on the long journey.

31

'They've been to the hospital,' interrupted the cattleman brusquely, not looking up, excluding any more questions.

'They took one eye out of him,' the woman sang out unexpectedly and in an unexpectedly high voice, shrill and monotonous. At this the train began to move, began its enclosing, imprisoning rhythm again and Nicholas felt that now, finally, it was insupportable to be with them. The child had not even stirred. It had been standing like that, sallow and fearful against her knees for a long time. Its thin, barefoot legs were like sticks. Now, with a cold horror that sank within him like a stone, Nicholas perceived that indeed the bandage was down over one eye but for all the animation that it showed, the other, dark and unblinking, might have been equally sightless.

The rain lifted a bit after Carlow and a wet sun came to the windows of the train.

'Thanks be to God,' said the man, 'the clouds is scattering.' He had been making occasional remarks like that for miles without anyone attending. Nicholas was watching the dark green light of the day outside, mucus light out of the full, clotted throats of the ditches. Thinking of the creatures of this light. Formed by sodden fields. Slime. Himself too.

'Home soon,' pronounced the man, spitting on the floor and squinting out the window. 'You'll be home soon, young fellow.'

No answer. Don't answer. He is, conceded Nicholas, what is called a friendly. One wet, green thing in the ditch crawling towards another. Outside, the naked branches of the December trees sped past and he began to construct his first, arriving words. To Dada that he had, that he was or something like that. Maybe had prayed and that God guided. The face of his father under the bush of hair knowing more than was said knowing that what was said was untrue. Or Emerine? The memory of the great devouring silences that had grown between them in the months before he had left for the seminary. One day she had said to him, the darkness of her body in the words, that she would be offering up her morning prayers for his intentions. His lips curled in a smile and in the window at his side he was vaguely mirrored, green and wasted and unhappy.

In the other corner the woman was feeding the child, furtively and with many bird-like lifts of her head towards the men, from a coarse canvas pouch between her knees. It was yellow meal that she had dampened with sugared water and this she kneaded with her fingers into small pellets. The child opened its mouth docilely and scarcely chewed at all. When she had finished the woman hid the bag and what was left somewhere on her person and all this too, secretive and searching, was accompanied by the quick, raised, apprehensive looks across the carriage.

'Ye'll be glad to be home?' the man asked after much sighing and blowing. 'It's always a good thing to come home after the while away.' He didn't seem to want an answer. ''Course when the ould people die—' He didn't finish this. 'Is yer father still alive?'

Nicholas nodded.

The man nodded back. Understanding. 'Where's home when the light is out?' He was trying to resume his old, original humour of the beginning of their journey together but his grin was forced. 'That is if you don't mind me asking.'

Nicholas told him in one word and as he began, 'Did you ever hear tell of—' he was already shocked by the effect of his information not only on the man who had suddenly sat up, sucking in his breath but on the woman from whom there was a strange gurgling sound at the mention of the name of the town. He was a little frightened at this. And immediately thought that something else had happened at home of which he wasn't aware, maybe the murder of Father Lannigan or of his father who, as Master, was still up to his eyes in it, and all of this ran into the one word that he was able to breathe to them, 'Why?' Neither the man nor the woman answered him but they looked at him with a new kind of pity. In her last letter his mother had said the people were roaming the streets of the town every night in bands and that no one knew how the business would be settled between the bishop and the priest.

Suddenly the cattleman bent across in his direction, no longer mocking, nor arguing, a deep, worried look on his face. Nicholas observed the mass of pockets in his clothes, two extra-large ones in his old frock coat, pockets in his waistcoats, pockets in his pants, they all gaped with pathetic, open-mouthed appeal in his direction. Between the man's crotch, he noticed the abdomen sunken in the bulky sack of age. Despite himself Nicholas was moved to pity for the man in front of him and it was some moments until he could bring himself to hear what he was saying.

'... I met a man the other day,' the cattleman was whispering, pleading, fearful, 'who said that blood was flowing like water every other day in that place.' The great dog-face implored Nicholas. 'If I were you, young fellow, I'd avoid the place entirely.'

'But it's my home,' Nicholas tried to smile all this away. He even turned to the woman uneasily. 'It's my home place, don't you know,' he tried desperately to reach out to the corner of silence in the swaying carriage. And at once his head pounded with images of home, threatened it would seem by this incomprehension around him, an incomprehension dangerous and vital that stretched out beyond the carriage and into the misty day of the fields, or not threatened but already obliterated, by something far beyond his control because he knew now as each thought struck him that home would never again be like this and he was not going back to it: images of home, images of the kitchen and of his father trimming his moustache before the old mirror with the print of the shoe on it, of his mother stitching linen on a cold night, the knuckles of her small hand raw and worrying the thread, of the damp in the hallway where wet boots were left to dry in pools behind the door, of Emerine. Of young Florrie. Of Marcus Anthony. Of Emerine. Of Emerine crying. Of Emerine laughing. Of Emerine crying when the cat died in Cody's Yard. Of – 'I have to go home, haven't I?' he gulped. But the man only glared back at him, mouth open, chin dribbling.

They had travelled in silence for several miles and Nicholas had begun to think that his escape from the closed carriage was near at hand as Kilkenny couldn't be very far away. He had started to plan how he would leave Kilkenny on his arrival there, how he would go down to Rose Inn Street, crossing the bridge and on up to the Parade. There he would surely find a car going out the Clonmel road or maybe even the Workhouse wagon driven by Jimmy Durney and his two comical tinker horses. Jimmy would stop for him and there was the advantage that he wouldn't have to say anything on the ten-mile journey to the idiot driver. Witlessness is an easy companion and he had had enough talk for one day. And how he'd carry his wooden clothes box. It secretly shamed him to have such a battered clothes box and would like to have left it in Maynooth but that it belonged to his mother ('Look at the nice lining in it, Nicholas. Sure it will keep your linen away from the damp.'). He would carry it under one arm and not by the straps so that people would think it was just any old box. He was even considering having a boy carry it across the city for him, when the man spoke.

'They say,' clearing his throat, his voice almost gone in uncertainty, 'they say that priest was wronged.'

Nicholas nodded, warily.

'I heard that said for a truth.' Nicholas tried to look at the floor in indifference, dreading anything more. The man wheezed like a bellows. 'I heard it said, I heard it said that his own people have riz agin him.'

'They are – divided,' Nicholas, with studied factuality.

'Aye.'

'Those that are for him,' Nicholas went on with that impulsiveness which he hated in himself as a humiliation, 'are called Reds. And those against him are called Schismatics.'

'Aye,' repeated the man heavily to himself and in his own thoughts, 'when the man is down kick him, kick him.'

The train hummed on the rails and Nicholas, wiping the window, looked out, hoping to see St Canice's in the distance. He was a little less fearful of talk with the man now. Chat was safe but deep within him he knew was some level at which the trouble in the town stormed in a madness, waiting to be let loose, with what effects he didn't know. He even began to feel a certain obligation to explain a little to the man in the carriage, moved perhaps by his sympathy.

'The townspeople,' he explained, 'would destroy him. Don't you know how it is? Isn't it always the same in a town? Aren't

35

townies the same everywhere? I mean the viciousness. But the country people, the people from out the country—' He didn't finish. It didn't seem necessary. The man understood. He knew what it was like.

'Aye,' repeated the man again, sucking on his dead pipe.

The cosiness between them lulled Nicholas. He began to think of what else he might say.

'They were saying below in Waterford that the church is closed on him and no one let in or out. Is that true now?'

'Well,' said Nicholas, 'not exactly. He's still saying Mass and everything but the Church has suspended him.' He smiled sardonically into the window beside him. 'In other words his Masses and his prayers don't belong to the Holy Roman Catholic and Apostolic Church.'

'Go way,' breathed the man. 'Is that a fact?' He was looking at Nicholas in awe as at a foreigner in strange clothes. 'Do you mean to say that if I went into him to Confession maybe that I'd be still the same as I went in after coming out?'

Nicholas nodded. 'Or to get married. Or to get baptized.' He was rather enjoying himself and gave a high laugh at the man's expression who in turn tried to smile but was still too much in awe at it all to manage any kind of expression on his open face. 'Of course,' Nicholas added, carefully, 'of course there are many who don't believe. I mean all this business of cutting him off. My father, for instance.' This he threw in because he didn't seem to be getting anywhere with what he wanted to say. 'My father is Master in the schools,' he added senselessly, irrelevantly, crimson in colour.

They had both forgotten the woman and child all this while but she must have been listening to what was said. Suddenly out of the corner, to disturb their familiarity came that high-pitched monotone like an arrow.

'The priest is cursed, cursed be God like the father does curse his own flesh and blood. And anywan that touches his hand is touched with it.'

She continued to mouth at them without saying any more and they both looked at her, shocked, as she gathered the child into the protection of her skirts her eyes scattering about them like icy raindrops.

36

'I am going home,' said Nicholas to the man, ignoring her in his anger, 'to give myself to a cause.'

But there was no answer from the man and he felt confirmed within himself. No more was said about the priest after that but the man seemed to have grown towards him after their exchanges. He began, after a while, to give a long, rambling account of his own life to Nicholas, some of which he had already mentioned before. Nicholas would nod into the big, bulbous face but in truth he hardly heard much of what was said. A story of land lost and shillings earned at fairs in Cahir, Cappoquin and Carrick. How he broke a man's arm in a public-house with a blackthorn when life was young and everything depended on his name and the name of his father. Of a drover he knew by the name of Powers who would walk twenty heifers up to Meath and be back in Waterford for his breakfast. But them were the days. The people nowadays didn't know the meaning of honest work. Nothing now but jobbing and idling and robbing under the name of dealing. On and on it went and Nicholas was left with the cold feeling of many dawns on frosty roads and the smell of dung and hard bargaining of red-faced men, stinking of beer.

At last, Kilkenny Station. Nicholas was already on his feet lifting down the wooden box from the rack as the train passed the signal box. He tried to get out of the carriage without attention but the man insisted on getting to his feet, unnecessarily helping with the door and with a final, embarrassing gesture, saluting Nicholas with a hand to his head as if he were raising a hat to a priest.

On the platform all was flowing life again and Nicholas tasted the heavy fog of coal smoke from the engine with a kind of grateful pleasure. Crowds were embracing all around him and ladies passed, lifting their skirts off the platform or moving daintily aside from the porters. It was like a return to the community of the living again and Nicholas found himself standing there in something like a daze, his unwanted clothes box at his feet, being buffeted by the flow of people. In the very centre of it all stood the resplendent station-master, braided and polished, his moustache surveying everyone and everything with unmoving sternness.

37

It was then that Nicholas noticed the man leaving the carriage that he himself had just left, climbing down with cramped legs and a slow weariness. He was bent almost double and Nicholas was moved to watch him cross the platform against the throng where he went behind to urinate. There was such a kinship now between him and the man that Nicholas felt obliged to wait and to watch and when agitation began around him to send the train off again on its way to Waterford he even felt apprehensive that the man would miss it. He looked over heads in the direction of the urinal and wondered if he ought to go and alert him. Whistles blew and flags waved and Nicholas tried to attract a porter's attention above the din, pointing over his shoulder but he wasn't understood. He looked again and still no sign of the man and now the last doors were being banged shut and great gasps of blue smoke began to fill the station as the engine panted at the front of the train.

When he had decided to leave his box on the platform and go and search for him the man finally appeared, blinking and fumbling into the light. Nicholas watched him with a perceptible pain as he made his crab-like way through the press of people and angry porters. They shouted about his great, hanging head but he seemed indifferent and finally at the very last moment he was pushed and goaded back into the carriage, just like one of his own animals, or so it seemed to Nicholas, and the door was shut upon him. Nicholas felt a great surge of pity for the man which left him stupefied so that it was several minutes before he could leave.

He picked up his box and walked out into the station yard and began to go down the hill into the rain-darkened city. He had forgotten all about the appearance of his clothes box and carried it carelessly by the leather straps. The streets were black with the wet and from the heavy skies there was little promise of a change.

3 . *Christmas Eve 1871*

In reviewing the events of the old year we would be avoiding our duty to the public if we did not appeal for the restoration of law and order in our misfortunate neighbour island. Our concern is directed chiefly towards the small town of Kyle, a name quite unknown to most readers a few months ago but which has come to rival the Red River Settlement, Tasmania and Calcutta in the conversations with which we settle the matters of the Empire. It is not too great an exaggeration to say that in recent months this small town has witnessed scenes scarcely paralleled by the worst excesses of the Paris Commune. This is not the occasion to enter into the cause of the misfortunate clergyman Mr. Lannigan. We would simply offer to all those concerned in the treatment of civil and religious strife in Ireland the principle, well-founded, well-tried and acceptable to all men of goodwill, of 'a stout constable, an honest justice, a clear highway and a free chapel!'

The Times. January 1872

According to a telegram which reached town last evening Kyle was again (on Christmas Eve of all evenings!) the scene of a lamentable and very unseemly 'affair!' In the course of the customary and annual festivities in the town, held as usual on the town Cross, the Reverend Mr. Lutterell, curate to the suspended P.P. the Reverend Mr. Lannigan, was grossly assaulted by supporters of the latter making a mockery of all that is Christian and respectable in this land of ours. Despite the very painful attentions of the mob, the same Reverend Mr. Lutterell asserted the ruling of his authorities on the recent distressful happenings in the town. Whereupon, it appears, a riot ensued. Aid was quickly invoked and shortly thereafter this intrepid clergyman, being nothing daunted by his rough handling, returned to the scene of his initial encounter, reinforced by a police sergeant and two constables but by now the mob was out of control. How the 'affair' ended we do not know but we apprehend the public will hear more of it.

A Dublin Paper, December 1871

By nightfall the streets were filled with carts from the country-side, pulled by asses and gennets and horses, heavy with the farmers and their wives and staring children in for the last of the Christmas shopping or just to look. Mostly just to look because there was little enough to spend that Christmas. There was such a confusion of wagons at the Cross coming from north, south, east and west at once that the constables were sent for and the big countrymen yelled at one another, their sticks in the air while the wives and children cowered in the carts behind them, covering themselves with old greatcoats and sacks. Down the hill past the Big Chapel came a great cavalcade of the Mullaghnagreen fellows with their dirty ponies and still dirtier women, the youngsters of the town running alongside yelling and throwing mudcakes at them. The people in the shops nodded and chuckled as they watched and the shop-keepers, one and all, said they could do without that kind of trash without a halfpenny between the lot of them. Half drunk already weren't they on their wild mountain poteen. On swept the big dark men and their fierce women, all shouting and talking in their Tipperary accents, sweeping down into the mêlée at the Cross.

Grace's Boot and Shoe Establishment. Nugent's American Flour Stores with its one door and half a window. Dubby's Depository for Medicated Produce. Bergin's Bread Shop and Tea Hall. Mr Fincheon's well-known Grocery and Provisions. 'There ought to be a law to keep them outta the town.' 'Aye.' Yellow grain pouring golden and dry as sand into sacks. Pigs' heads grinning, thick ears flapping, on a row on a shelf. Canisters marked Tea and American Sugar by the wall. 'Isn't it the likes of them that has the town stirred up?' Great slicks of brown porter on the floor straw of Jude Hennessy's pub, the old man rolling barrels out of the kitchen with his witless giant of a son standing back at the roars of complaint of the father.

'Priest-lickers!' Down on the Quarry Road beside the Skin and Bone Shop (BEST PRICE FOR ALL BONES) the Jew Sullivan was selling off yards of calico colours to the poor out of the cottages, held back by the cute Corkman until this very evening and stored in an old loft down by the river. He had bought it cheap straight off a Liverpool boat on the quays of Waterford. 'Is there fightin' on the Cross?' The foreign lilt of the Corkman. 'Asha it's only the crowd in outta the country.' 'There'll be quare support for his riverence above on the hill so if trouble starts.' 'His riverence is right! Bad cess to him and his mischief.' 'We'd be better off without priest or chapel.' 'We would so.' 'Isn't it them that talk religion that cause the most trouble.' ''Tis so!'

After a while the wagons and carts were lined up on either side of High Street and down on River Street near the bridge where the road was wide and the countrymen went off into the pubs in shouldering, clumsy banter, backslapping and pushing. The women and children were left in the carts to sit and stare or gossip among themselves from cart to cart but they were guarded when townspeople passed by. There was much to see when the candles and lanterns were lit in the shops and the night was dry even if the wind was bitter at times on the streets. A fiddler and two whistle players had started up at the Cross and when the big bonfire was lit in front of Myler's stone wall the dancing started and stopped and started again as couples came and went out of the crowd, four-handed reels and sets and a solo hornpipe by Mrs Eily McKey, the wonder dancer from Crossbeg.

At about eight o'clock the excitement on the streets became intense. A dozen carriages or so, harness jingling, fine geldings between the shafts, tall-hatted coachmen fore and aft came through the packed streets, pale faces in the dark interiors. Major Wymnes and his party from the city. Mrs Johnstone and her two daughters from Hibbel Hall. Somewhere in the line the Honourable Horace Percy Butler and his guest from Dublin, Mr Watters the lawyer. All on their way to the annual Christmas Punch Party at Killgrange House. The severe, apprehensive faces at the windows, the hint of fur, the curled whiskers, the white of lace. 'God bless you, sir!' Shouts and cheers. 'God and Mary give you long life, m'am.' 'It's the gintry, it's the gintry,' was the cry on all sides and everyone tried to identify the figures in the carriages or the coachmen on the horses. On the crest of the hill of High Street the whips cracked in the frosty air and the horses leaped forward, the coaches lurching on the rough street and everyone bade them godspeed. Wasn't it a fine lot of horses and men, God bless them, and didn't everyone know that Killgrange House was the best estate from here to Clonmel? The carriages finally went into the night past the dark bulk of the Big Chapel and the shuttered schools, a few dogs still barking at the wheels and the road was open before them under the stars. A solitary ragged man spat after them in the dust and cursed the breed of all landlords and their military.

It was known as the Walk. Starting at the top of the hill of High Street at the schools, all the way down to the Inn at the Cross and the house of the Master. On down into River Street past Grainger's, Martin Donovan's stables, the bakery of Bun Hipps, over the bridge and by the timber yards and sawmills. Out the Kilkenny road and there where the fields began again it was time to turn back and maybe do the Walk once more, the towney girls in their bonnets and shawls, laughing and giggling and pushing among themselves, in linked groups of fours and fives. Mary and Katie and Rose, they would do the Walk maybe five or six times on a dry Saturday evening giving the glad-eye to all the fellows standing outside the pubs, teasing the country lads with their towney smartness. 'Go home and take the mud offa yer britches!' 'Oh lookit yer man with the fancy French coat on him!' 'Stoppit, Judy or I'll bust laughing.' There was always great entertainment on the Walk. And on Christmas Eve there was a special gaiety to it. All the maids in service got off early and flocked like speckled birds, black, yellow, red and green, eyes excited, on the space in front of the schools at the top of the town before beginning the Walk.

One of the two deaths recorded in the violence of Christmas Eve, 1871, was that of one Missy Lynch, a plump parlourmaid in Mr Proctor's, one of the brightly coloured birds of the Walk, found on the river path below the bridge in a disarrangement of skirts and petticoats, her head beaten in and the solid bloodied drover's ash plant still beside her. A man was charged in the January Assizes along with the fifty-two other cases of assault and riotous assembly of the same night but he seems to have been acquitted. When the two brothers, Nicholas and Marcus Scully, were returning through the throng on their way home, still shocked by their own part in the action of the night, they saw this too. A space had been cleared on the bridge and between the swaying legs they saw her lying across a cart, a great argument in progress as to where she was to be taken. Nicholas caught the puffed, purplish face, the look of surprise and then he could not look at the corpse any longer but dragged away his crouching brother with his hand and they staggered off home.

Earlier in the night Mr Fincheon, the careful grocer, had hung two red lamps at his shop door on the Cross and stood beside them for a while, the great white sheet of an apron high on his round stomach, so high it seemed to begin shortly below his armpits. His rolling black moustache and shining ringleted hair, for all his fifty-odd years, explained the name Foreigner Fincheon which they called him but never to his face. He could say he was held in high respect by all the townspeople. When he stood by his shop door, as on this evening, his bulk would reassure all those who passed by of the virtue of the good and honest trade. Everyone knew you could get a fair measure in his shop and he was known to give charity to the poor.

It was he who, nearly ten years before, had given over the house and yard behind his shop with its opening on to Quarry Road, to the new Christian Brothers Schools which had caused all the trouble between the priest and town in the first place. And he had donated over one hundred pounds towards its decoration. For this they said he was a Schismatic and a bishop's man but Mr Fincheon liked to think that he was beyond the row between priest and town, between priest and churchmen, that he had only acted then, as any man of good-will would have done, for the sake of the whole town. And besides, in the beginning didn't Father Lannigan himself agree to

43

having the Christian Brothers Schools? He, Fincheon, certainly didn't see himself as one of the roughs who were making their hatred of the priest an occasion of violence, like the Doyles and the Kirwans and Hipps the baker. He was a peaceable man was Mr Fincheon and attended to his own duties first. He did, it was true, go to Mass in the Friary and not to the Big Chapel, thereby separating himself from the cause of the priest, but this was because the Church told him to do so, through the bishop and the Cardinal of Dublin and not because of a personal feeling about Father Lannigan who, Mr Fincheon would allow, was a fine man in his own way.

The two thin Christian Brothers were still holding school in the house behind the shop in the trying atmosphere of late 1871 but Mr Fincheon had nothing to do with them except to wish them Godbless whenever he met them as he would to any Christian.

Behind Mr Fincheon in the shop as he stood at the door were the Christmas hams and fowls, chickens, ducks, geese, grouse and woodcock, a single cock pheasant. There were piles of black blood sausages on the counters with pigs' heads and pigs' feet and great round loaves of oatmeal bread fresh up from Hipps' Bakery on River Street.

He would need to be attentive this night. He eyed gravely the growing bonfire near his door cheered by the crowd and looked unmoved at the dancing and the musicians. He had already urged Police Sergeant Jennings to close the town to the wilder elements from the country, especially from Mullaghnagreen and Cualaliss, pointing out the loss of business which this might mean but indicating that no responsible person in the place would put profit before riot and disturbance. He had not been heeded. It was rumoured abroad the Father Lannigan's supporters were gathering from the four corners of the parish. Even on a normal Christmas Eve it was necessary to be careful and now there was this added danger. Everyone, with business or not, liked to crowd into Fincheon's, and tonight with the smells so good in the place every tom tinker would come to gawk.

But Mr Fincheon as he turned indoors felt well pleased with his own arrangements. In station at the dark end of the shop

44

was his wife Julia, a tall spare woman who was disfigured by goitre; around her neck she always wore a disguising coil of scarves which seemed to push her head up from her shoulders. She seemed never to take her eyes from her husband but in fact there was little that she missed either in the shop or out on the street.

Old Roddy Higgins, with Mr Fincheon now for years, and the two hired boys did the selling and packing but Mr Fincheon himself came forward for the special customer like Mrs Bradshawe the housekeeper from Whytescourt or Mrs Bulmer from Killgrange or old Mrs Hartley-Greene who liked to do her own shopping and was watchful, too, of the weights and scales.

By special consent, it being Christmas Eve, Mr Fincheon's one child, Statia, a daughter of seventeen, was let stand in the shop. She was bumpy and backward for her age and was seldom allowed out of the house because of a certain delicacy of the lungs which made her a prey of the damp. She stood now, moonishly in a corner sucking sugar cane with the young ragamuffins from the town lanes gaping in at her as she licked and licked.

In the house almost directly opposite Mr Fincheon's at the bottom of the High Street on the Cross (not quite opposite since there was also the town Inn on the corner, with its heavy sign suspended creaking in the wind) Master Scully listened to the growing tumult on the streets as the night went on. He had told Henrietta and Emerine to remain in the kitchen, which they did, and the boy James Florence was dispatched to bed. The Master swore and stamped in the hallway when the other two boys failed to return home and as matters worsened on the other side of his barred door.

'Wouldn't you think Nicholas, at least, would have the wit to come in out of the streets on a night like this?' he cried to the women, but they didn't lift their heads from their sewing.

When the hammering began on the front door he feared the worst. At first, so great was his panic, he could scarcely recognize the group out on the street, Mr Proctor, yes, and Mr O'Brien the apothecary with his flashing spectacles but the others were lost to him because of his view of the mob on the Cross. Everyone on the street appeared to be yelling at once and he could see the figure of the curate Father Lutterell standing on a box or a barrel in front of Fincheon's shop but he couldn't hear what was being said.

'What's that? What's that?' he called to Mr Proctor who tried to shout again what apparently he had been shouting already before this, most of which was lost again in the din except something of how he, Scully, was needed to help, to restrain the people.

'I have no command over them, Mr Proctor. Do you really think – do you really think they'd pay any heed to what I'd say?'

Proctor may not have heard what the Master said above the roaring because he seemed to stand back to consult someone behind him. The Master tried to close his door but Mr O'Brien had edged forward.

'There's going to be bloodshed, Master. Some of us must join together and stop it before it's too late.'

'Well and what good can I do, Mr O'Brien?'

'What?'

'I said –' the scene before him had become a nightmare; he could see that scoundrel Lutterell working himself into a fury on his makeshift platform – 'what can I do? What am I...?'

'I said the town is in riot, Master.'

'I heard you say as much, Mr O'Brien. I heard you, man.'

'Well sir,' cried the mild apothecary, his lips shaking, 'something must be done.'

'Where's the constables? Where's the constables?'

'The constables,' someone in the group echoed.

'Is it three men?'

'They'd be murdered anyway.'

'They haven't a chance.'

'Send out to Colonel Fitzgibbon then and have him send in for the militia.'

They seemed to consider this, much to the annoyance of the Master who simply wished to get rid of the lot of them. Mr Proctor, the retired clerk of the Board of Works whose opinion was widely respected, came forward once more but few heard

46

what he said because at this moment a great roar went up from the mob, and it began to move out in four great waves into the four streets of the town like water in a pool when a rock is dropped. In so moving the faces turned towards the awed on-lookers at the doorway, faces mad with some lust or torment the like of which the Master had never seen before. At this he panicked and pushed his door shut. He felt someone pushing on the other side and despite all his effort Mr O'Brien with an amazing force shoved himself almost into the hallway.

'But Master – Master, they're all out at Killgrange!'

'Send for them so. Let go of my door if you please, Mr O'Brien.' The apothecary gave way, stepping back with a grieving look and it was to the finally closed door that the Master cried: 'Let those that started it stop it. It's no concern of mine.'

He wrestled with the chain of the door several times before he succeeded in making it secure. It was then he realized that the two boys were still outside somewhere on the streets. He rushed into the kitchen where Emerine and Henrietta were now standing by the fire, frightened, listening to the roaring out in the town and called out: 'Where are they? God Almighty, on a night like this! Where could they have got to?' And then in a rush of fury and self-doubt, 'Well they may stay out in it, so. I'm not going hunting them. They may see what their fine champion has brought down on us all.'

Six miles from the town, one mile of that a long beech-shad-owed avenue in from the highroad, was Killgrange House. It was a Butler house, one of the chain of mansions or small castles across the landscapes of Kilkenny and South Tipperary which proclaimed the provincial majesty of the House of Ormonde, Kilkenny Castle, Whytescourt, Killgrange, Kilcash. With their curious progeny of erratic and brilliant Butlers, Lords Deputy, county marshals, amateur scientists and philo-sophers, bishops both Protestant and Catholic, and always soldiers. Great mats of green paddock, profusion of oak and beech, land for the horse and horsemen, cover for healthy game.

Horace Percy Butler stood on the terrace of Killgrange

47

House with its three-tiered stone staircase to the lawns below and its gigantic stone lions brooding on the balustrades. He had fled the throng indoors, the interminable conversation about arterial drainage and the uses of Peruvian guano, and he stood apart, too, from the laughing couples outdoors strolling in the darkness. He played with his Conversation Tube which hung about his neck by a black ribbon and considered the prospect across the lawns and into the trees. It was cold but the wind had dropped and Butler watched the tenantry of the estate crowding down on the avenue below him.

While Killgrange was a sister house of Whytescourt, its present occupant was but a distant cousin, a Miss Freemantle. It was her brother John whom Butler could now see between the trees in the distance, on horseback, with two grooms at his side, distributing traditional Christmas gifts to the peasantry. He could easily make out large numbers of men and women and even children all the way down to the main gateway, because most of them carried torches. Sheets of flannel, he had been told, tobacco for the old, loaves of bread and raisin cake for the women and children, a modest portion of ale to the men. It was a custom of the house and Butler had witnessed this same scene on many eves of Christmas (once in a fierce snowstorm) and always with a sense of gloom at the weight of history on his own name.

He mused on the passage of property from hand to hand, from name to name. Gain to one, loss to another. Up one, down the other. All the truth of the Universe is uncertain but the profit and the loss of it. Mr Carlyle, the common-minded Scotsman with an uncommon sentiment. It was the principle of what is described as life, how much passes from hand to hand and for how much. It was intensely depressing; no end to the flow of merchandise, of traffic in coin and loot, no end but the grave. Did they, down there, those ragged wretches from the edges of Killgrange Estate, from their hovels and cabins, did they really believe that they were being given, presented with something for nothing? Or for that matter did they in there, his neighbours and cousins in the drawing-room (in a bluster as he left them over the latest outrage in Mayo where a distant kinsman had been dragged from his brougham in some bog the week before and had been stabbed to death by a scarecrow band of Ribbonsmen), did they conceive of their position as anything but an accumulation of doubtful profit? The essential for sanity was to avoid traffic: in some easeful, minimal investment of attention to preserve life in the flesh; it would all end one day in a little breathlessness, a quietus of the least expenditure. They would talk to him of their lineage and the splendour of their stock. He might have told them then if his sense of history were sufficiently intact, and Butler smiled grimly in the darkness both at his own inadequacy and the relish of horror on their faces, he might have said that in thirteen something or other it had all passed to them through a spattered Norman speculator, all of it stretching before him in the darkness towards Kilkenny and the Tipperary hills. All loot.

'I say, Butler, what are they giving the peasantry?' A voice, a hand on his arm.

'Yes, yes,' replied Butler, without his speaking instrument to his ear.

'Food, isn't it? That's all the beggars appreciate, I can tell you.'

Other voices and he was surrounded by a group which had strolled out on the terrace: old Lord Carrick, old Dunquin, Wymnes and some officers from Clonmel. And with them that dreadful fellow whom he had tried to avoid all evening (Jackson? Jenkins?) who had recently bought the Hubert home. He listened, reluctantly. The fellow was in spate on some anecdote or other.

'There's only one way of dealing with them, sir. Brain, sir, brain.' A protuberant head drinking from a glass. 'I had a hundred men on the job cleaning the bottoms, paying eight-pence to a shilling a day. A fair wage, you say, well. Well, sir. The weekly expense amounted to about twenty-five pounds. A good sum, you say. Very well. Three or four months went by and we were on the uplands, clearing the land, draining.'

'I don't approve, sir, of removing moisture from the land,' said old Carrick.

'Very well, sir, be that as it may be.'

'The land needs water,' appealed the old gentleman to the group. He had served in India and all in the company knew he was ready to launch forth on his pet topic of irrigation in Northern India.

'Well, sir, the point is this. They arrived up to the house. Right on to the front lawn. I don't have to tell you the spot, gentlemen. You know the house. Priscilla saw them from the window and had to be given salts. I sent Reilly out to them and told him not to bargain until they stood well off from the lawn. The finest rose-buds in the county, sir! But I don't need to tell any of you gentlemen that! Well, sir. You'll like this. Just listen to this! The demand was for one shilling and t'opence a day. One shilling and t'opence, I said. Reilly, I said, go out and tell them as follows. The master will not give one shilling and t'opence but three shillings a day if the men be worth it. But with prices rising he can only pay twelve pounds ten shillings altogether in the one week. You see! Twelve pounds ten shillings. Out went Reilly. I could see them lean their heads to where he stood beside the fishpond. A good man, Reilly! "Now boys," this is what he said, you see, "now boys, let me pick my men according to the new arrangement." So he began by picking out the best. "And how much is that you want," he asked. "Oh," says the first fellow, "we'll take the top price of three shillings a day, if you please." "Very well," was Reilly's answer, "eighteen shillings a week for twelve comes to ten pounds and sixteen shillings altogether. And that leaves one pound and fourteen shillings remaining. With that I can only have two more of you. Fourteen of you stay and eighty-six of you can go." Well, sir, they soon gathered in knots fighting among themselves and need I tell you that there was no trouble from that day out. Brain,' he chuckled loudly, 'brain, sir. That's how to handle them.'

There was an ambiguous murmur of response from the group of men and all was silence again as they looked down over the lawns of Killgrange. A wind touched the treetops and the peasantry with their torches down on the driveway seemed to move with the leaves in the breeze.

'You see, sir,' the fellow was explaining again to Lord Carrick who had imperfectly understood his story, 'twelve pounds and ten shillings was all that I was prepared to pay! Ha! Ha! Half of what I paid before, you see.'

There was a curious stillness in the air above the woods and but for the crackle of glassware and the rise and fall of talk from the house they on the terrace might have been within the silence of trees. Someone said it might in fact snow but another pointed to the stars and clear patches in the sky. Butler felt the urge to move; he was cramped with the cold, he saw nothing before him to retain his interest but still he remained listening to their odd, listless talk. The officers appeared to be thoroughly bored whispering privately among themselves and were relieved when some of the younger women called to them from the french windows: they were wanted, it seemed, to supervise the festive firing of guns and crackers among the apple trees in the orchard. In a surprising short while, it seemed to Butler (they could scarcely have apprehended their weapons or whatever) he heard the reports and cheering from the side of the house and for a while the lawns resounded with the cheers since the peasantry on the driveway joined in with a will, tossing their hats in the air and jumping up and down.

'The young people enjoy these things,' old Dunquin's voice cranked and wound itself up again like a clock. 'A splendid old custom of Wassail.'

'The young have all before them, Reginald,' joined in Lord Carrick clapping his old friend on the shoulder.

'Well, sir, may they live as long as we and live as well.'

'Amen, to that, sir.'

'I drink to that!'

'To the young!'

'To the young!'

Butler did not have a glass but he bowed slightly from the hips while his companions drank. He was thinking that they included him too with the aged, the venerable, a curious thought which had never occurred to him before. He felt, it is true, that he had always lived in some unmoving state of tired maturity, at least as far back as he could remember without exertion and beyond that, apparently, his memory did not consider it worthwhile to go.

There was, presently, a commotion on the terrace and many people came out including the women, all white and pink and shivering with the cold.

'What in damnation is going on, over there?'

'No idea. Some kind of scuffle.'

It turned out to be a messenger from the town, one of the Thomson youths, who stood within a ring of the men petrified by their questions and shining lace cravats, the ribbons, the silk, the heavy odour of drink. Watters came over towards Butler and yelled that the town was rioting and had they not better get back before the streets were blocked but Butler paid him little heed. The women were hurried indoors and a conference was held on the terrace. Major Wymnes dispatched some of the young officers somewhere and there was a great coming and going for some minutes, many people were shouting orders at once and in the middle stood the pale youth still, quite lost. Butler remarked that he had not been consulted in any of this and knowing the boy and feeling sorry for him he beckoned him over with a finger.

'Who sent you, boy?'

'Mr Proctor, Mr Butler, sir.'

'Speak up, boy.'

'Mr Proctor, sir.'

'What about Mr Proctor, boy?'

'He sent me, sir.'

He could see the young fellow's unwillingness to speak into his hearing tube. They would prefer to be unheard. He believed it was a matter of education of the youth and the native distrust of scientific objects.

'You must speak into the instrument, boy.'

'Yes, sir.'

'Now you must tell me what is the matter.'

'Yes, sir. The Reds, sir, are burning the town in the name of the priest, sir, and Mr Proctor said, sir, that the militia will have to come. And the bishop's men are burning the houses of the priest's men and there's a riot.'

'Did Mr Proctor say that anyone had been killed?'

'No, sir.'

'Have they touched Master Scully's house, boy?'

'No, sir.'

'Have they touched Father Lannigan's person or his Chapel?'

'Not as I can say so, sir.'

52

'Very well. You may return now to the other gentlemen.'

'Yes, sir. Thank you, sir.'

Butler turned his back on the hurried consultations nearby and considered again the prospect of the lawns and trees. The tenants were still out there and did he imagine it or was there a tense attention in the way in which they looked towards the house. It would be advisable to disperse them but no one seemed concerned with this now. Everyone was running about shouting. He continued to look towards the distant people, lined up along the paling of the low paddock, apparently returning his gaze, mute, like animals waiting to be fed. He had the uneasy feeling that he alone from the house was aware of them, that he had become an intercessor in some silent appeal from the distant fence. This in itself was an irrational fantasy: the fact was that there was merely this distance in space and a silence.

Suddenly, from beneath where he stood, a girl in a white gown and long white shawl ran laughing out on to the lawn like an actress assuming her place on a lighted stage and quite oblivious of the movement above her on the terrace. There was something odd about her dress and then he understood: she was one of the mummers. Her hair shone with some kind of glistening material as did her gown while she wore a mask of a similar substance which covered all but her mouth. The young had organized a Mumming Play earlier in the lower drawing-room and this, evidently, was a participant, a now fugitive princess. He was a trifle elated by her appearance at such a curious juncture (which was a surprise since he had been thoroughly bored by the performance earlier) and had begun to reflect on this when, teasing and pirouetting in the darkness, she was chased by two others in costume, a waddling Baron of Beef and a tall, ungainly Saint George with lopsided plumes. They ran away off towards the woods, the long white arms, a flash of orange, a trail of colour, down towards the trees, down towards the darkness, the echo of a laugh and sounds of twigs cracking and no more.

It had all happened so quickly that he thought perhaps he had imagined it. Certainly no one else saw, all wrapped up in their discussions whether the Resident Magistrate should be called, how many men could be brought from Fethard, who should return to the town. The voice of his own guest Watters boomed with opinion. Really the man was impossible. He was in the district for two days; it could scarcely be his affair. Butler looked off into the darkness after his weaving, dancing figures. They had gone in that perfect single moment of distraction, of colour. Something far less tangible than a rioting town. A momentary stimulation. He tried to bring himself back, with little success, to the discussion about him. If he were convinced, at least, that something would or even could be done quickly enough to relieve the unfortunate people in the town. Everyone about him was talking about duty and action. He could not believe that some formula would unravel the intricate suffering of these people but if he were to say this would he not and justly be condemned as a useless individual? Let them send their few soldiers and their respected representatives! When the burden appeared to be so great as to be beyond the scope of any one time or place it was better to make a beginning with a gesture, a word into the wind.

Just three young people running on the lawn! He looked down again into the empty darkness and thought that perhaps after all he might organize the return of the coach party if the town were clear. He noticed with a shock of interruption that the long line of peasants was still in position on the driveway, still looking in his direction, the same stance. He wondered if they too had witnessed his silver princess and her pursuit by her two freakish admirers. Or again if this alone had been reserved to him.

Then, in the town, two strange figures joined the mob as it turned out of River Lane surging on towards the Cross. They were strangers to the crowd. 'Are yis for the bishop or for that shit up in the Chapel?' someone yelled but the marching feet made talk impossible.

The smaller of the two wore a faded sailor's uniform and a battered tri-quarter hat, the kind that was common enough thirty or forty years before. He was carrying, this dumpy little man, a short baton and a wind of rope around his wrist. The other and taller wore a long coat to his ankles with big cuffs on the sleeves and a high chimney-pot hat on his head. His face (what they could see of it) was long and dark-whiskered and savaged by the pox. This one carried a beautifully polished walking-stick with silver graining on the side. As the night hurtled to its climax it was to be revealed as a swordstick. It was said that this was the fellow who stabbed the Purcell woman in the neck when she tried to stop the looting down on the New Line.

'Who's them two?' the Gaum Coady yelled in a loud voice when they reached River Street, and someone laughed. The Gaum was always making a fool of himself with questions. Someone else whispered that they were from the Commons cottages but the crowd just swept on through the dark street, rippling with excitement and no one again questioned the two strangers. Some people questioned afterwards because these two were never to be seen about the town again.

'. . . and let there be no trouble. We don't want trouble, now.' Father Lutterell, standing on a barrel, was shouting above the din on the Cross. 'It's them in out of the country'd give the town a bad name. Let them go back to where they came from and there'll be no trouble. We all know why they're here and who told them to come! We all know your man up there in the Chapel is behind it all!' There was a great roar at this and wild talk of going up to the Big Chapel and pulling it down on top of him.

'We're all dacent Christian people in this town now, men. We've the right on our sides. Isn't the Cardinal himself for us? Let there be no blackguardism now, men. It'd go against us.' He was watching with anxiety as each of the four streets of the town seemed to empty its quota of shouting, jostling men into the arena of the Cross which was lit, fitfully, by the bonfire. He began to perspire copiously. At the start he had been fortified by a lot of drink, now he was terrifyingly sober wondering if what had been started could be stopped.

'Begod we're all with ya, Father! And with His Holiness the bishop, too,' a voice yelled from the back and the crowd rumbled and swayed with assent.

'Now, men, I know ye're good men. Let there be no damage.'
'Burn them out!'

55

'Aye! Burn the feckers out, all the arse-licking lot of them.'
'Down with the Reds! Up the Popesmen!'

Word was brought to the kitchen of Kirwan's pub beside the
Friary that a crowd of fellows were on their way in from
Cualaliss to fight for the priest. The Kirwan family were great
haters of Father Lannigan and the place was a centre of support
for the friars and the bishop. Mr Kirwan and his two sons
collected the offerings every Sunday in the Friary. It was said
that the enmity with Father Lannigan went back a generation
and to a wrong done to old Mrs Kirwan by one of Father
Lannigan's kinsmen. But Mr Kirwan had made himself con-
versant, too, with all the facts of the present case; he had read
out to a large number of men in this same kitchen the procla-
mation placing the Big Chapel under interdict. There had been
many meetings in the same kitchen, trying to find ways to rid
the town of this renegade priest and those who stood up for
him. It was like having an infected person in the place, carrying
a foul disease about, so great was the hatred which swelled in
Kirwan's kitchen. Sometimes they brought Father Lutterell
along to explain points of Church law to them although no one
really liked the curate: no priest worth his coat was ever a
drunkard.

There was a racket then when news of the Cualaliss boys was
brought in. They were known to be Fenians, every man-jack of
them out there in Cualaliss. Didn't they obstruct the Head
Constable himself when he went out to read the Riot Act to
them, a few winters before? It was the most troublesome town-
land in the parish and everyone knew they'd take up with the
priest if only to do more damage.

They had hardly taken in the news when someone else
shouted in the door that a crowd of known Molly Maguires
were seen coming over from Tipperary the night before to join
the Cualaliss boys. The thronged kitchen took all this in with
great mutterings and threats, porter sploshing, eyes red with
the wet turf smoke.

'Bejasus, if they set foot across the bridge below they'll see a
sorry end. I'm telling ye that now.' He was a big fat man who
sat over in a corner, his face red with constant temper.

'What'll ya do to them, Gunner?'

'Aye, Gunner, what'll ya do to them?'

'Are ya going to make bris of them?'

'I'd do fukin' more'n you'd do anyways, any fukin' day of the fukin' week.'

There was great roars of laughter and toppling of jugs of porter at this and everyone said that Gunner was a great man for the talk and they continued to shout over to him with drunken repetition: 'What'll ya do to them, Gunner, ah?' 'Aye, what're ya going to do, boy?' and Gunner's face got darker and darker but everyone knew he wouldn't take offence. He was a good poor soul was Gunner, if a little hasty.

While the pubs of the town filled and spread their selling into the crowded frosty streets, while the town worked itself up into this half carnival, half fury, for and against the priest of the Big Chapel, there were occasional scuffles. But the Cualaliss boys had the first strike. Crossing the bridge a marching twenty of them in groups of fours and fives, they came upon little Jimmy Freely crouching in his doorway, the son of the tailor Freely, a great supporter of the bishop and they beat the youth for the name of his father. Breaking both his arms below the elbows before they quite knew it.

Then running, the bishop's men came to Poll Dwyer's little shop just below the stonemason's shop on Quarry Road. She was next on their list as a Red (she was known to have gone to devotions in the Big Chapel the previous Friday) and was a friend, too, of the priest's sister, Mrs Rowen. Behind them already six places ransacked and knocked about, Mrs Rowen's own place included (she herself must have been with him in the Presbytery above for safety). Six places to show they weren't going to stand for bishop-baiting in the town and, still running, they reached her door. Four or five men out in front like a line of chosen champions, faces wet with sweat, the older ones like old man Ryan grey with the pace, the younger ones red and boiling.

They seemed to falter outside the shop or maybe waiting for the dozen or so lads coming to catch up, standing, their hands on hips or knees, heaving, panting. Someone shouted: 'Where's the torches and we'll burn the cunt outta there.' 'No burning,' someone else shouted, 'remember that. No burning.'

She was waiting for them in the darkness behind the closed door, her long white hair hanging down over her shawl. As the mob straggled up behind the ringleaders, the Doyles and old Ryan from Killineck, some of the Kirwan gang and a few more towneys she couldn't recognize, but what matter she knew the breed of all of them. And knew their bitter cowardice, too, the way they shouted to one another to keep their spirits up.

'The auld hoor is adin there!'

'Break down the door one of yis!'

'Go on home outta that,' cried the old woman fearlessly, 'go home outta that ye crowd of pedlars. Off with ye!'

They might have remained there on the road, bubbling towards coldness and fear but for her voice. But then suddenly, so suddenly that it surprised themselves, they were all in there, in the cramped little shop, pushing her hands and thin fighting body aside. After that a darkness and one or two moments of pause or muttering and then a mad babble and scramble. Old man Ryan standing stupefied for a moment before the few shelves of sweet jars, liquorices and sugar-sticks, a few snuff-boxes and wads of tobacco, dazed by its littleness perhaps, until one of the Doyles swept past him ('Arrah for Jasus' sake') and swept all in a litter to the floor, plunder for the young towneys out of the lanes who were running up in hordes now from the Cross at the prospect of another break-in.

Ger Doyle pushed her out into the street out of the way and she hung on his arms like a lover, moaning, and he dark-faced with embarrassment and fear and anger tried to shove her off but she clung to his hands. Bun Hipps shouted over mistakenly, 'Ah, lave her alone, Ger,' and at this Doyle became what he had only appeared to be until then, savage and mindless and slapped her across the head with his palm, yelling, frothing, 'Get off, ya cunt, get off ya – ya Red. Begod or I'll—' and she collapsed away to the side from his blows crying with the voice of a young girl.

Father Lutterell was still standing on the Cross with a few people still around him when the carriages came back through

the town from Killgrange. He was saying: 'I tried to stop
them. I did all I could. It's that – that man above there in the
Chapel whose reckoning it is before the Almighty.' The Cross
was almost deserted but there were still yells and cries from
different parts of the town. Every time some newcomer would
approach the curate began again to explain, his eyes darting
above their heads, his hands trying to keep the greatcoat closed
against the cold. When the fire began to die down everyone felt
the ice in the air. 'I tried to put a stop to them. But God knows
they were provoked long enough by that – that – above on the
hill there.' It was this more than anything else that appeared to
unsettle him, his hidden antagonist, because the parish priest
had not shown himself in all the uproar of the night. Although
many people had gone up to gape, the Big Chapel had remained dark and shuttered and the Presbytery behind it might
have been abandoned.

Down the hill of High Street came the carriages with twelve
mounted soldiers and Colonel Fitzgibbon as escort. The townspeople on the streets and from their windows watched in silence
half afraid that this was to be the final terrible visitation of the
night. But the soldiers looked ahead content to clear the way
through the rabble. They appeared to halt at the Cross but
were soon off again down towards the bridge in River Street
not even a face shown at the carriage windows, curtains drawn.

As the procession passed him the curate, with his caged and
cornered eyes on the coaches, cried out again with a renewal of
spirit, 'Look, am I a man to want trouble? Can any of ye say
I want trouble and factions? But can ya stop the flood when its
on top of ya? No man wants peace in this town more than me.'
And then as the last outriders disappeared into River Street, a
last cry, 'Wasn't I the one who saved his life? Didn't I stop the
bloodshed the day above on the Fair Green when the people
were intent on tearing the clothes offa his back?'

With the first touch of daylight, Christmas Day 1871, the town
showed itself like a place that had experienced war. But there
was still one or two candles to be seen in windows over High
Street. It was an attempt to make the season return when it
seemed to have passed the place by. To display the spirit of

peace against the destruction which was everywhere.

Shivering groups of townspeople were standing in the shelter of doorways and young fellows were poking the embers of the great fire by Myler's wall. Once or twice carts went up or down the street with country people finally trying to make their way home. There was whispering in the doorways which broke off with the sporadic yelling that still came from parts of the town. There was great talk of the young one out of Proctor's who had been beaten to death at the bridge. Out on the Carrick road, one man said (and they all pushed closer to hear him), they were still fighting, terrible bloodshed. There was little to be happy about this Christmas, a woman cried, and several others clucked in agreement.

The light of dawn when it came was barely strong enough to light the shadows of the houses and for a while the town was drenched in this greyness, neither sunlight nor dark. Shuffling and complaining with the cold the few people on the streets could scarcely have known for what they were waiting.

Then came the Friary bell of the Angelus, the first of the day: it began tremblingly as if uncertain of its reception in the wasted town. It was almost at once overpowered by the second bell which leaped out in sound over the rooftops, great single beats rising higher and higher. For some moments they didn't appear to recognize the Big Chapel bell but then several at once told the others in excitement. They began to drift out into the streets apprehensively to stare up the hill at his church. He hadn't shown himself all night. They had found it hard to understand why. But here he was now unmistakable as if he stood in bulk on the hilltop belabouring them with his words. Each one felt his presence. They knew he was up there in the Big Chapel although they couldn't see him, he was up behind the tall columns on the porch, pulling the heavy bell chain, his body in the long black cloak lifting with each beat, right foot in the rung, pulling on God's signal, Gloria in the rising, drifting darkness.

The Journal of Horace Percy Butler, Christmas 1871

In the beginning of the entry he had written: 'It was an untrue report that there had been burning.' But this statement apparently dissatisfied him in some way because he had partly obliterated it, one of the few such erasures in the complete manuscript. He had skipped several lines to the entry proper.

Returning from the punch party at Killgrange House. Contrary to my advice Fitzgibbon had insisted upon an escort. We were consequently stoned at several points on the road. Mrs. Johnstone and her two daughters in the front carriage, four other carriages behind. All stopped at the Cross. Indescribable scenes of disorder. Watters was insistent that we wait for the R.M. The crowd was ugly and for the safety of the women in the party we moved on. A full horse cart together with what appeared to be furniture, ablaze outside the Inn. Fincheon's shop and several others appeared to be totally ransacked.

In Lower River Street saw Scully's two boys and others carrying a child. Stopped the carriage although Colonel Fitzgibbon said it might be a stratagem. Replied that I knew the people. They asked if we had anyone who might make splints since the child's arms had been broken by the priest's supporters.

I directed them to Mr. O'Brien but they said he was elsewhere engaged. The child in their arms appeared to be lifeless. I questioned the Scully boy who had been a Roman student and is not unintelligent. He informed us of two deaths in the town and the possibility of more from the injured. One of the dead was from a seizure but no doubt due to the violence. We left.

Watters took up his chant again that the Revolution was upon us. That once the masses were given any freedom there would be no restraint. Etcetera.

For myself I remarked that the primary matter was to induce moral and social habits in the population. Something which the churches had failed to do. I did not express this latter view in the presence of the ladies but I believe my point was taken.

I do not feel disposed to record anything further of this Christmas.

4 . Christmas Day 1871

After the big dinner there was a Christmas present for each of them put out by Henrietta and Emerine on the leaf-table in the front room. And each of them laughed or cried out, 'Look what I've got!' or, 'Is this for me?' although in fact the gifts had been settled on after long discussions months before. All throughout the long, darkening Christmas afternoon they remained there on the table, the no-surprise presents (a small Real Russian Leather Purse for Emerine herself, bought in Baldwin's of Henry Street six weeks before by Mr Cuffe the landagent out at Beecham's, on Henrietta's instructions, while he was up in Dublin to negotiate the purchase of drainage pipes for Beecham's Bog; a wicker work-basket for Henrietta herself with bright new needles and inlaid with pink satin: TO OUR ONLY MOTHER, with tiny red hearts embossed on the lid; the New Almanac and Diurnal Indicator for the Master; an erasing knife for Nicholas and a carpenter's measure for Marcus while the boy Florrie put back his Coloured Novelty Ball to complete the display having had tantrums early in the morning until they gave it to him to keep him quiet) and the family gathered before the small grate with the annual visitor who came without fail each year to spend Christmas afternoon with them, Mrs Biddie Dawson the genteel widow from High Street. It was a Christian charity, Henrietta always said, to have her because she had now no one of her own.

All, except Nicholas. He sat alone in the kitchen. He couldn't bring himself to be with them.

('Oh, Nicholas has to be different!' His putative sister, taunting. Her tremolo. Her virginal attack. He tried to frighten her with the violence of his glare but ruined everything by flushing himself, grinding his fingers in humiliation at his own clumsy weakness.

'I will sit here in the kitchen all day if I want to . . .'

'Sulk!'

'Nina, now you leave Nicholas alone. If he wants to stay...'

'Sulk, anyway!' And she swished out with the others.)

There was this much to be said about this house, at any rate, you could always count on someone to respect your need to do as you wanted to do! It reminded him of the credo of the Master. Ye must do as ye think fit! How often they had heard it since they were small boys, he and Marcus! Only that very morning on their walk of conciliation the Master had said the same thing. There would be no compulsion in his house, he said, as long as he drew breath.

Earlier there had been the quarrel between the father and the sons and Henrietta said they should take a walk together before their Christmas dinner could be blessed with prayer. And they went. It had all started because Marcus said he wouldn't go to Christmas Mass with the rest of them to the Friary when he'd been going to Mass every Sunday of the year to the Big Chapel. With Father Lannigan. Very well, conceded the Master, pale and calm but then Nicholas said he too would go with Marcus...

Ye must do as ye think fit, he said to them more than once as they went down River Street. He hadn't demanded that they go to the Friary this morning with Mama and he, Nina and Florrie, had he? No! If they thought to side with Father Lannigan he wouldn't stop them. He knew they were wrong but he wouldn't stop them. Oh, better than most people in this town he knew there was much to be said for the man...

'Not enough people are saying it then.'

'No, Marcus, son—'

'It's true, Dada!'

'Marcus, don't you know there's nothing that's simply right or wrong. Don't you know that, son?'

'He's in the right!'

'He was in the right, you mean.'

'He is now.'

'Maybe in the beginning. Only maybe – but he won't humble himself. Will he put himself second to the people of the town? Will he? Oh no! Not Father Lannigan!'

'He's in the right! He's in the right!'

'He's only a man like the rest of us. Not a saint of God and what have you to be laughing at?'

Nicholas said he wasn't laughing. Only remembering something.

'What something?'

He said he was only remembering a man he had met. On the train from Maynooth.

'What man?'

'Only a man. That's all.'

'Well what about him that makes you snigger?'

'Nothing. Nothing. He only said the same thing. Priests are people. That was how he put it.'

'That's nothing to grin about.'

No reply. There was no reply. And they walked back together through the marked streets of the town, burnt timbers like bones rising out of the ash where the fire had been at Myler's wall the night before. The daylight was going out like a flickering candle in the kitchen and Nicholas felt that anything could happen, even the end of the world. Yesterday, it seemed, but it was much further back, they had been father, mother, brothers, sister and now there was this small, white-haired frightened little man. There was this lump of a person called Marcus. There was this creature of perverse, flaunting innocence, this living irritant, this non-sister, half-sister, this female whose whole existence now seemed intended to draw out some poison in his own flesh, some sickness. Sick Nick. Two things were more difficult to understand than anything else: how growing made men different and the same at once, and then why they continued to call it love when it had passed into pain and anguish.

He was still crouched in a stupor in the corner of the kitchen when the boy Florrie passed through out to the yard. He shook himself then and tried to bring himself to get up and join the family in the front room. When they had got back from the morning's walk he had found himself alone in the same front room with his father and he had tried (oh, he had tried!). They had gone through the Master's manuscript book once again, transcriptions of gravestones of the town, papers for the Kilkenny Archaeological Society, genealogies and the beginnings of that history, never completed beyond the first few para-graphs ('No one knows for certain when our fair town was first settled, or by whom . . .'). You have been working hard at your manuscript, Dada.

'Every time I open it, I know peace.' Finger tracing beautiful copywork, chiselled stone in the cemetery. '*Hic pacet Johannes Nangle sub marmore duro.* That's my favourite. The Nangles. Nangle. It's not a local name, you know. Mr Butler thinks they may have been tallow-makers.'

You have been working hard at your manuscript, Dada. Not looking at the book but at a newspaper cutting marking a page Holloway's Cure-for-All Ointment. Bad legs, bad breasts, Abscess and sores of all kinds. The Mother's Friend. Dropsical swellings. Sore nipples. Piles. Sold at Professor Holloway's Establishment, 533 Oxford Street, London. Also by nearly every respectable vendor of medicines. All that money he spends to keep upright, skull whitening, rounded, shrinking shoulders.

'I will take the past any time in preference to the present. It's all ended there. Dead and buried. Oh, it isn't that I'm turning a deaf ear to all that's happening around me. The town rifled by factions and riots. And all in the name of God Almighty. No, I won't be party to it.'

You have been working hard at your—

'The way they've taken the Poorhouse off him! They're stripping him of all he ever had. Could you credit it? Wouldn't you think now they'd stop and leave him be. He took a great pride in being chaplain to the paupers. I was above one day in the yard of the Poorhouse when he came out after giving out the rosary in the Eating Hall. And the way they all crowded around him, men and women, before they were sent back to their separate quarters, God help them. I saw him lift up his hands like a bishop and they all knelt down on the cauld flags to be blessed. Poor creatures in from God-knows-where. In out of the ditches and off the roads. He stood in the middle of them letting them hold his cloak with their sticks of hands. What's the meaning of it all, Nicholas? What, I ask you? Rain or shine, day or night he'd be up there in the Union giving the creatures comfort. Wasn't he good to them? Isn't it enough to be good to them? Who cares about the law of the land!'

The Master had been half bent across the table as in pain. Don't, Dada. Don't.

'Oh, I had sympathy for him at the start. He was wronged then. That hoe-boy Lutterell and Hipps and that gang down the road. But it's one thing to defend your own name and another thing entirely to rise the people to hate, just because you can talk to them off the height of an altar!'

Nicholas tried to stand up in the kitchen and almost fell over with cramp. It was time to make an appearance before the family and Mrs Dawson. He had tried. He had tried to reach his father with words, the touch of a hand now being beyond him. 'Oh, it's going to kill me, it's going to kill me,' the Master had kept repeating with a fierce aquiline conviction that even now, hours afterwards, still set the eardrums beating in Nicholas' head as if (and the crazy connexion persisted in his mind) he had dived deep into the weir below the bridge, a summer-day dive, deep down among the sodden green weeds and bog-brown corners near the bank, away from the sun. All that he had, love or at least pity, had flooded his being for the bowed figure in front of him. For a few minutes he thought he was part of a miracle. But then it was all over. They ended as they began, bickering.

'To be wrong is to be wrong is to be wrong.'

'Which is the greater wrong – to wrong an institution or your own person?'

'Don't give me your seminary smartness!'

'It's not seminary smartness. Father Lannigan has been accused, tried and condemned all in his absence. Is this natural justice?'

'Don't you shout at me, boy.'

'I'm not shouting.'

'He's been suspended by his lawful superiors for dragging his fellow priests and even bishop into the common court. He's now threatening the Cardinal himself.'

'And why not?'

'What—'

'Why not? Why can't you prosecute a priest in a civil court? Why? Why? If there's no crime, what's to be afraid of?'

'Pilate's Court! Pilate's Court!'

Nicholas picked his way through the gloom, stumbling, determined to try at least to put a face on it. After all it was Christmas Day. And they had a visitor. He felt very righteous with himself as he opened the door.

In the front room the Master half dozed before the smoky fire, a small bucket of punch at his feet which he warmed from time to time with a poker. It upset Henrietta to see him so silent when he should be happy with his family in the Grace of God. She knew now that he'd droop like that all day, probably drinking more than was good for him and going more and more into himself. As she sat still and silent opposite him, looking into the fire, she worried about having invited Mrs Dawson with all this trouble in the air. She had warned everyone beforehand that there was to be no talk of Father Lannigan. Mrs Dawson was a Protestant and scandal was scandal. The children seemed to be happy enough, thank God! Emerine was sitting curled under her skirt on the floor leaning up against Marcus' legs with a worn copy of *A Christmas Card Annual* on her lap from which she read them Christmas stories from time to time, *A Fashionable Dairy-maid's Disaster* and *The Folkestone Express* or *How the Guard Saved the Christmas Travellers*. Nicholas was out somewhere in the kitchen and Florrie was playing with boxes behind the chair of Mrs Dawson.

'Child,' said Mrs Biddie Dawson to Henrietta shortly after she had spread herself in the chair beside the Master. She referred to all the Scullys but the Master as child. 'Child, ye must pay more attention to your hair. I remark that so many ladies today do not have the required combs to keep the hair in place. Bone is preferable to the novelties one sees nowadays. Only the other day I had occasion to say to Mrs Bulmer (she's the new housekeeper, don't you know out at Killgrange). Mrs Bulmer, I said to her . . .'

Henrietta merely smiled into the fire. She was used to Mrs Dawson's outbursts which from anyone else would be hurtful. But Mrs Dawson was always telling people about their slovenliness, to stitch up their skirts and tidy their hair. And it was easy to understand: she was such a neat presentable creature herself. She was still smiling into the fire while Mrs Dawson went on at length with her gossip from the downstairs of Killgrange. She liked to show her familiarity with the gentry, Mrs Dawson, even if it was only by way of the servants' quarters.

'I must tell you,' said Mrs Dawson nodding to no one in particular, 'that everyone in the county was at Killgrange last night for the festivities. The Reverend Hillsop came over from London with his wife (she's the first cousin of Mrs Carpenter, that was, of Clonmel, one of the Island Carpenters, don't you know). They say he has a prospect of being a canon of Westminster.'

'They were firing off crackers and guns in the orchard. Marcus heard them. Didn't you Marcus?'

'I didn't.'

'You said you did anyway.' Emerine pouted.

'An ancient custom,' observed Mrs Dawson. 'We have many ancient customs of Christmastide that are not derived from the Teutonic races. It is a disgrace the way people have begun to forget the old ways. Not to speak of the disgrace of the town last night. May the Lord forgive them! I won't say more. I'm not one to speak of others. I mind my own affairs! I'm not one to condemn the Roman Church and its ministers.' Her face was shaking below the tight bun of hair but no one dared look in her direction.

'Father Lannigan,' growled Marcus from where he lay stretched on the floor. 'Father Lannigan,' he began again.

'Don't, Marcus,' whispered Emerine.

'We've had enough of that,' said Henrietta sharply, 'for one day.'

'He hath prepared for him the instruments of death,' chanted Mrs Dawson, more loudly than ever. 'He ordaineth his arrows against the persecutors.'

'Agh,' Marcus swept his hand in disgust before his face and Emerine caught it in flight and held it, pleading silently with him.

'If you don't mind, Mrs Dawson,' ventured Henrietta trying to catch the woman's attention, but Mrs Dawson all puffed-up had closed her eyes and leant her head back revealing the rolling folds of her throat.

'He hath graven and digged up a pit,' she cried loudly, 'and is fallen himself into the destruction that he made for others.'

At this there was silence. The Master had said nothing all this while but was stirring his punch before taking another cup. Florrie crept around the chairs to his mother and she held him by the waist. 'Look at the fire,' she whispered, 'the way it's smoking!' And indeed it had begun to cloud the small room with gusts of pale, drifting smoke. 'Run out,' she whispered again to Florrie, 'and get us a bit of dry turf in the shed. There's a good gosoon!' And Florrie went because he didn't want to stay. 'It's always the same,' Henrietta poked a stick in the grate. 'Whenever there's a north wind we have no chimney.'

'What about games?' asked Emerine brightly. 'What about *The Old Soldier* or *How, When and Where*? Where's Nicholas? I can pick out some out of the book. Dada, will we play word games?'

'Games,' said the Master, 'yes.'

'Nicholas!' Emerine called. 'Oh where has he gone to?'

'Never mind him, Nina.'

'But we need him for numbers.'

'Sir,' said Mrs Dawson to the Master in her most composed manner, 'if Mr Gladstone wasn't so anxious to give way this way and that way to the Fenians there'd be little to trouble us.'

'Yes,' nodded the Master, 'yes, yes.'

'There's a game here,' Emerine tried to interest all of them in her book, 'called *So Says the King of France*. Look! One of us has to be the King of France and no matter what he says or does everyone has to copy him and then if you don't you have to pay a forfeit. That's the way to play it, you see.' She flushed at this point and put her head down over the book.

'I don't like that game, Nina. Pick another.'

'Oh, Marcus you're always the same. You never want to do anything I say. No matter what I pick no one wants to play.' Tearfully.

'Child,' announced Mrs Dawson, 'Prince Albert Victor will be eight years of age this January, bless him. Such darling children! And such a mother! What a shame she lost the baby

69

in April! I must tell you that Miss Lucy in the Lodge told me that she, the Princess Alexandra, I mean, perceived a man one day on the common road stealing apples. Such a creature! She simply ascertained the unfortunate man's improvidence and at once provided for his invalid daughter who was speedily removed to hospital.'

'What was she doing out on the road?'

'Who, child?'

'Princess Alexandra.'

'Child, the Princess has no airs and graces. She is well known for her contacts with the common people. And the Prince of Wales, too, but in a different manner. Ahem! Well anyway it seems this fellow was not where he was supposed to be and with all those apples.'

'I can't believe,' persisted Emerine, 'that a Princess would be abroad on the road just like that, so I can't.' She was angry almost to tears that no one wished to play her games and that no one had asked her to continue reading from the stories.

'Nor me, neither,' affirmed Marcus behind her.

'Well I think it's a nice story,' said Henrietta, wishing the children wouldn't annoy Mrs Dawson like that.

'Let us pray,' intoned Mrs Dawson joining both hands and they all looked at her in shock thinking she was going to pray there and then. But this wasn't so. 'Let us pray daily for the speedy recovery of the Prince stricken by the fever. Let me tell you the Archbishop of Canterbury has sent out a beautiful prayer for the occasion of the Prince's illness. I dare say it may even be read in some of the Roman churches.'

'No, I don't think so, Mrs Dawson,' said Henrietta warily.

'Well that,' replied the widow, 'leaves me in some surprise since the whole Empire, Christian and infidel, are praying for his recovery. Jew and Mahometan across the deserts and the mountains, and even, as I understand, the Parsee fire-worshippers.'

There was a suitable silence at this.

Henrietta managed to distract Mrs Dawson with talk about the Prince's visit to Dublin the previous August and of the awful Fenian riots in the Park during the visit. The two women

70

agreed together that nothing could be done properly in the
country without some wretches to upset everything. Mrs Dawson went on to further account of the Royalty so that even
Henrietta was a trifle bored. The woman had such an appetite
for these things. People even said she resembled the Queen herself but this might have been a matter of conscious imitation.
They had heard her so often on this same topic, even describing
the interior details of Buckingham Palace, the Ballroom with
its throne dais, the golden canopy brought back all the way
from India, the ornate ceiling of the Blue Drawing-Room. All
of this, Mrs Dawson was fond of telling the Scully children in
her odd pouting way, was evidence of God's appointment.

To withdraw her from the subject of the Court Henrietta inquired about Mrs Dawson's spinster sister who was a district
nurse in Liverpool; going around 'the dens' as Mrs Dawson
put it, with her little bag of lint, ointment, bits of linen and
guttapercha. From this it was but a short passage to matters of
health, death and the nourishment of good food. Mrs Dawson
gave out a list of her own prescriptions for the sick, extracts of
beef, Valentine's Meat Juice, gruel and arrowroot and her own
special recipe for linseed tea. She talked about food and death
as if they were two facets of the same fact, rolling her voice
with the same fullness when she talked about beef-tea and the
striking down of the poor in their tenements. Earlier when they
had offered her a little piece of hackin pie or Emerine's tipsy
cake she had demurred, belching slightly, saying that 'sweet
things contradicted my digestion'. But she had taken a little of
the roast apple left over after the dinner, 'since it's a blessed
feast', chewing the spongy, hot fruit off her spoon between one
opinion and the other.

When she had finished about the social work of her sister,
Marcus grumbled in a low voice that the poor of Ireland had
less attention than the poor in England and the Master who
surprisingly had heard him said there was no poverty now like
when he was a boy, when he walked for fifteen miles to Thurles
with his piece of turf for payment to have his lessons from the
blind schoolmaster. How many a youngster would put himself
out nowadays to walk five, never talk about fifteen, miles to
have his schooling? Was there any love left at all now for learn-

ing, he asked, his eyes blinking with the drink and the smoke from the fire.

'Hush, Master,' said Henrietta, 'and don't be annoying yourself.'

'Well, is there?' he cried.

'Sir,' clucked Mrs Dawson. 'Far be it from me to speak slightingly of your Church. But isn't it the Roman clergy that—'

'Well, is there?' cried the Master more loudly looking about wildly from one to the other. 'Can any of you answer me that?'

But no one did because they all knew the mood he was in and he soon lapsed back into his corner nodding that it was all clear to himself if to no one else.

Henrietta gave her husband a few sharp glances to show her feelings. The Master paid her no heed, however, and went on to fill up a particularly full cup of punch for Mrs Dawson.

She took a large draught, paused and cried out in a suddenly loud voice that Mr Dawson, God grant his eternal soul peace, was a learned man who knew much more than those who claimed to be his superiors.

'He was a fine man, God rest him,' said Henrietta.

Marcus poked Emerine in the back and she barely contained a giggle. She knew what he was thinking of, how they had often together imitated Mrs Dawson's frequent and lengthy laments for her dead husband.

'How did the poor man die, Mrs Dawson?' asked Marcus innocently.

'Marcus!' cried his mother, quite angry now and Emerine bent her head into the book on her lap. 'Children!' said the mother again, her face whitening and darkening by turns.

'Child,' answered Mrs Dawson in a trumpet call, 'he died of the Decline!' not appearing to notice the mirth or the anger in front of her, not noticing that she had given out this epitaph so often in the Scully home that it had become an old joke among the children. What angered Henrietta more than anything else was that Mr Dawson (whom she had never known herself) had given his life, as she saw it, unselfishly for others. But children were so heedless, heedless! How often she had explained that Mr Dawson had been a fine public servant, respected by the people and gentry alike, and who had finally taken the Famine fever in '46 while serving with the Board of Works on the Road Relief Scheme down on the New Line. ('How many more of the poor are buried with him, Mama?' Marcus had replied to this with his sharp temper. 'Poor people who should never have been asked to lift a shovel, rotten with hunger.') Marcus was becoming such a hothead! Well, Mr Dawson's monument was the still-unfinished road on the New Line which suddenly became a rough track once you passed the gate of Townsend's orchard. You could see where the poor creatures had stopped the paving and how the grass had grown into the stone. When the Famine passed the works stopped everywhere.

'I weep,' shouted Mrs Dawson suddenly to Henrietta's consternation. 'I weep,' she roared again but without a trace of a tear, 'for a man worth weeping for and not some penny-boy with his eye on advancement.'

'He was a fine man, Mrs Dawson,' answered Emerine, a little frightened by this vehemence.

'A good man!'

'You've no need to say that in this house, Mrs Dawson. Don't you know what we think of Mr Dawson. You have no need to say such a thing.'

'If I do not say it, who will?' she bellowed unabated, her jaws working, her face turned away. 'He is gone into the Light,' she said more quietly, 'blessed are the dead who die in the Lord.'

They all murmured some agreement or other and there was a silence. Henrietta wondered wretchedly what time it was but did not want to offend Mrs Dawson again by sending one of the children into the kitchen to look at the clock. She would surely take it as a hint to go, which was true in its way but it was better to be patient. It had got so dark outside on the street that she might soon mistake the time and go of her own accord.

'Why don't you read, dear?' she turned to Emerine. 'I'm sure Mrs Dawson would like to hear you read.'

'We are counselled to read from suitable literature on holy days,' said the widow primly. She sat up at this, in her great wide ruffled black skirts, her bonnet on her lap with that smell of must from her clothes which the Scully children knew so well. 'Holy Scripture is preferable to the books of the world but a little entertainment is not out of place.' She coughed at this and set her head erect, the straight black hair combed away from the wide, white face and her large marble eyes touching upon each of them in turn.

'Well, I was thinking—' Emerine stopped.

'Go on, dear,' said Henrietta, 'everyone would like to hear you read.'

'She reads,' confided the Master heavily to the widow, 'she reads beautiful. Beautifully.'

'Not enough attention is paid nowadays to proper speech. I remember Mr Dawson, God give him peace, read the Psalms every night of his life before retiring.' She touched one eyelid delicately with a pudgy finger. 'Aloud, of course.'

'But what'll I read? I've read them all already.'

'Go on, Nina.'

'Read that nice piece about Christmas.'

'Is it out of *Between Two Hearts*?'

'Is it?'

'I'll see.'

'Go on, Nina.'

Pause.

'Oh, I don't know.' Skimming paper. 'It's such a long piece.'

'Christmas!' intoned the Master, with his eyes closed, 'Christmas was close at hand, in all his bluff and hearty honesty. The season of – of hospitality, merriment and – ah, open-heartedness. Mr Dickens,' he explained to Mrs Dawson, nodding his head.

'Oh, Dada!'

'Never mind, dear. Just read from your book.'

'The old year – um-hum!' persisted the Master, 'like an – an ancient philosopher. I love that part. Like an ancient philosopher, calling his friends about him. Or something like that.'

'Dada!' shrieked Emerine and the Master relapsed into his seat.

'Well. Are you going to read or not?' Marcus, pushing.

'I will if only I'm let.'

'Oh, go on!'

She looked about her, tossing her long hair, to ensure that

74

everyone was attentive. Her mother leant over the hearth, elbows on knees, smiling towards the fire, but her father and Mrs Dawson looked in her direction. Clearing her throat she began in a high, nervous voice: '"Who does not hail Christmas? Who, as it approaches, is not sensible of a happy feeling begotten of an influence which pervades humanity, a feeling of good-will towards mankind and of love towards friends? Who is there so dull that is not imbued with this spirit of peace and joy? Who is it that does not respond in the fullness of heart to a happy sense of rest and enjoyment; rest born of consciousness of a holy serenity which fills the hearts of all good men and imbues the air with an exhilarating breath and an enjoyment produced by this rest, an enjoyment rendered more complete by the bonds of love, friendship and uprighteousness?"'

Nicholas appeared in the low doorway, another shadow in the room.

'Oh,' she gasped, once, 'there's Nicholas!' and she slapped her book shut between her palms, blushing.

They appeared to him like a collection of dead birds in the great hallway of Whytescourt. Sitting around in the half-dark. Except her. He saw her blush, the difference of his arrival and for him, then, it was a sign, her knowledge and his knowledge meeting somewhere across the room as if the others weren't present.

'Where's Florrie?' Henrietta asked after the pause.

'Isn't he here?'

'I sent him out to get turf.'

'Oh, yes. He's out in the yard.'

'Where's that child gone to?'

'I'll go get him.'

'Ah don't bother, Nicholas. Come on in.'

Emerine still red, lip and cheek, was roughening the pages of her book like loose papers. 'Look, Nicholas, we wanted you for to play games. *Question and Answer*. Here it is.' Rapidly, nervously. 'Why is the letter K like a pig's tail?' She looked up at Nicholas, oval, the rich black hair framing the eyes, appealing for a way out of her embarrassment.

'Ah, Nina, stoppit.'

'No, Marcus, you keep quiet. What is it, Nicholas?'

'I dunno.' Smile at her. Smile. Smile. Sm.

'Well the answer is because it's at the end of pork. The word, you see. P-O-R-K.'

'I'd never have guessed.'

'Oh you're too smart altogether.'

A pause while the Master filled himself another cup, spilling the drink all over the place, and then another one for Mrs Dawson who grabbed the cup as it toppled. Nicholas tried to laugh but it came out as a rattle in his throat.

'Will I go look for Florrie?'

'Oh don't bother, Nicholas.'

'Sit down, Nicholas.'

'No. I'll go look for him.'

'Here's another one,' cried his sister (oh my God, sister). '"If ladies",' she read carefully in her best voice, '"could be sent to Parliament, why could no unmarried ones go?" That's one for Marcus.'

'Arrah stoppit, Nina. That's child's games.'

'Go on, Marcus. It's your turn.' Her voice tearful again.

'Well I give up anyway.'

From the doorway he saw how she leant up against him, her, their brother, how she almost across his legs, lay, how her arm fondled. How they. Touched.

'What's the right answer, dear?' Henrietta, polite.

'Oh no one wants to do anything in this house.'

'No, Nina, no. What is it?'

'Because it would be miss-representation.' Sulkily. Her head bent beneath the book again. 'That's the right answer anyway.'

'Oh I think that's clever.'

'I'm not going to bother with any more of them.'

'Child,' boomed Mrs Dawson who had been listening to all of this in some puzzlement, 'what is that volume you are reading from?'

'It's only *Christmas Card Annual*,' whispered Emerine, quite overcome.

'I'll go and look for Florrie,' Nicholas called to his mother, decisively, and came out without waiting for a reply into the hallway. It was all painful and for her he had felt the most pain, trying to rouse them out of a book. He staggered through the

76

darkening kitchen hardly knowing where he was. Her flushed face burning there in the room behind him. He couldn't go on much longer like this, with this boil ready to burst. Wasn't it the truth (if he'd only face up to it) that what he wanted wasn't some ordinary, say love, but some kind of horned destruction which he'd bring down upon her? Jesus God, he cried, I'm truly mad. Again the tossed parlourmaid on the cart at the bridge, the sticky mess beneath the hair but in a horror game in his head it was she, Emerine, on the cart. Opened.

After some time he saw the boy, Florrie, from the kitchen window, standing out in the frozen backyard, over by the turf-box, white-faced, his thumb stuck in his mouth, eyes lost to somewhere else. He'd leave him there. Wasn't he outside because he didn't want to be inside? A small frail Nobody standing outside there in the yard. 'My family,' whispered Nicholas, 'blood, born, breed, begotten, brother.' If they were all to go up in a flame would it make the slightest difference? Curious. He really believed that there was not one single person alive who mattered to him. He was enveloped in a cold, peaceful calm as if an engine had been shut down inside him. Curious, very curious.

The next moment it seemed, but without any intervening movement on his part (he must have lifted the latch on the door carefully, the click carried throughout the house) he was in Emerine's small bedroom under the stairs. Narrow bed, patchwork quilt, intimacy of cloth, stifle of old odours of shoes and clothes and the remains of a scent, or so it seemed to him, of her. He observed this Other, this maker of outrage, this calm, even, if he heard aright, chuckling, would-be violator, observed Him with amazement as He went through her closet, neatly arranged calico and flannel combinations, alpaca petticoats, shaking fingers. Nicholas' head suddenly spun with the smell of cambric and muslin and he sank down on the hanging forms of her dresses (turned inside out to keep them clean) the stiff material marking him, so raw was the skin of his face and down on his knees, he wept. He thought to himself: this is the end. If some of them walked in now they'd say he was a lunatic. Maybe he was. But the mad didn't know they were mad. Wasn't that the truth? Emerine. She was only the figure of it all, whatever it was that made things go the way they were going.

Half-priest, he jeered. Half-man. I've been crippled by the Cross of Christ – not even the whole cross, only the shadow . . .

When he reached the kitchen again, still filled with the smell of goose, he could hear the voices from the front room. His body shook with the cold and he fretted whether he should go back to her room to make sure everything . . .

Suddenly, Mrs Dawson's throaty voice rose up from the front room, flowing through the whole house –

> *'While Shepherds watch'd their flocks by night*
> *All seated on the ground,*
> *The Angel of the Lord—'*

Old Biddie Protestant, smiled Nicholas, smiling at the forced politeness of the others which he couldn't see. He listened. The great lunged sound filled the darkness of the evening. Emerine listening. All listening.

> *'To you, in David's town, this day*
> *Is born of David's line*
> *The Saviour—'*

It was so simple. Simple words: Protestantism. It said a lot about the nature of men that such pain, such fear, such hatred could be made out of so simple a start as that, shepherds and stars. A child's picture. He thought sadly of his mother and how hard it must have been for her. To change her Faith to marry the Master. From the cold indifference of the time before he was now drenched with feeling for all of them. They were in there in the room beyond, pitiably real and alive. Christmas, God save us! Christ hear us! Amen. His mother, he remembered now, as Mrs Dawson's voice rolled through the air, his mother still had her Book of Common Prayer. In that drawer in her room. With the bits and pieces that she called her treasure.

He felt it was time he was out there again with the family. When he reached the front room all was in confusion. Henrietta was trying to get Mrs Dawson to her feet and it was clear that the older woman was very drunk. The Master was no help at all, sunken into his chair by the fire, not even looking up. Someone had lit the Christmas candle on the window-sill and even it was in danger as Emerine and Henrietta tried to raise Mrs Dawson out of her chair.

'Christmas!' she was bellowing loudly, 'God sends his own son in the likeness of sinful flesh and for sin condemns the sin in the flesh!'

'Now, Mrs Dawson, we're just there!'

'If you move back the chair a bit, Mama——'

'Hold on——'

'They shall perish, but Thou remainest.' Nicholas believed she directed this at him in the doorway, her look baleful and perspiring, trying to adjust her bonnet and shawl at once. 'They shall wax old as doth a garment. As a vesture thou fold them up.'

Henrietta looked in helpless anger at the Master, and Nicholas moved himself back into shadow. There was little he could do to help anyway.

'Marcus will walk up the way with you, Mrs Dawson. Won't you, Marcus?'

'Mama, I can go.'

'No, Nina. It's after dark. Marcus, you go. It won't take you a minute.'

Mrs Dawson who had appeared to be on her way stopped when she heard this. 'Child!' she proclaimed, 'I will not be intimidated.' She gave great attention to her words, gripping the two women fiercely. 'They will not cow down Biddie Dawson with their sticks. Chapel-burners! Fenians! Communists!' She shook her head. 'My mother stood up to them. Stood up to the Molly Maguires on the street of Carrick when they'd have murdered the bailiff, poor Mr Thornton. Yes! Give ear, thou Judge of all the earth and listen when I pray.' At this, to the consternation of Henrietta she began to hum and to hum, rocking back and forth on her heels, eyes closed, wordlessly.

'Now, Mrs Dawson,' shouted Henrietta in a high voice, 'it'll be all right! Move back a bit, Nina. Now, Mrs Dawson, the boy will walk up the way with you. Move back that chair,

Marcus. God Almighty, what has come over her! Can't you do something?' she cried to Marcus who was standing all the time with his hands in his pockets.

'What'll I do?'

'Lift the candle for one thing and give us light.'

And in this way they all contrived to squeeze through the doorway and beyond that the narrow hallway with Nicholas standing in the shadow. The front door brought them all to their senses, even Mrs Dawson, with a flood of icy air when it opened. The candlelight ran around the walls in fright and Henrietta protected the flame with her bib.

She got Mrs Dawson out on to the empty street and Nicholas saw one or two candles alight in windows opposite.

'Marcus, you're not to get into talk with anyone.'

'Who'd I talk to?'

'It's no night to be out.'

'Agh, Mama, I can take care of meself.'

'Marcus!'

'Agh, all right.'

He took Mrs Dawson on his arm and she hadn't a word to their cries of, 'Goodnight, Mrs Dawson.' 'Safe home now!'

They closed the door and with a briskness which they knew as anger Henrietta began to lead the way, with the candle, back into the kitchen.

'What about Dada?' asked Nicholas. He could see the slouching figure beside the fire alone in the front room.

'Never mind him,' shouted Henrietta from the kitchen. 'Let him stay there.'

So Nicholas closed the door quietly on his father who might have been sleeping, head to one side and the punch bowl at his feet. The Christmas presents, he saw, were still there in the darkness on the side-table. Then he followed his mother and Emerine.

5 . Spring and Early Summer 1872

Being extracts from the Butler Journal on the Lannigan affair, the Keogh trial and other matters of the day, together with an account of what happened between the boy and the girl on the riverbank.

April 3rd: Travelled [with] Scully to hear Professor Eyre's lecture [in] Kilkenny on *Aerostatics and Urban Travel*. While waiting (for him) was persuaded to enter his house. Mean interior. But clean. Met the Maynooth boy. They say he has become a kind of secretary of the priest. Moody youth. Needs to be sent away. Dreadful lecture about railways on wires over streets. All present said it was enlightening. I said we have a sufficiency of noise.

April 4th: Sent messages to Scully because of our quarrel last night. Said I did not intend disrespect. We are drowning in an old argument. He had said, with very earnest attention to the pronoun – You being an Unbeliever can hardly speak about religious duty. I said the subject was Duty not Religion until now. He became very apologetic and cried that Christ was being reviled again as at Golgotha but in this very town. To taunt him further I recited the Poet's Parody, Our Father Augustus Caesar, who art in these Thy Substantial Astronomical Telescopic Heavens. Give us day by day our real taxed substantial Money bought Bread. Could not remember the finish of it but said we should address our devotion to Man first and our Moral Purpose to the betterment of this life and not to fancy about another, hereafter.

April [undated]: They have asked that I support the priest in the Defence Fund established under Lord Desart. That Everyone is to contribute. I marvel how this fellow Everyone is become our Master in All Things. They say the priest is out of pocket 700L. in his two actions against the bishop, two actions against the curates and one action against another clergyman. They say the priest is deprived of 60L. per a. in his loss of the Workhouse Chaplaincy Etcetera. That his case will be fought up to the Lords. I say the priest speaks too much of money his great charge Etcetera. They say that in supporting him we may uphold our liberties. I say who are We what is Ours? They talk to me of our class. Said to Mr. Langrishe the other day that as a class we were doomed. That we had been separated and had separated ourselves from Moral Action. He laughed. His throat full of port. Now Lannigan is encouraged to sue the cardinal of Dublin because by this suspension he, Lannigan, has been deprived of Workhouse, Schools, Etcetera . . .

. . . If he is a model of anything it is not of any class or faction but of the rights of Solitary Man. To burden him with Defence Funds, Petitions, Assemblies and Concourses is to corrupt his fate . . .

April 7th [?]: Great public excitement in the trial before Judge Keogh of the petition to unseat Captain Nolan candidate of the late Galway election. Undue priestly interference at the polls.

April 10th: Mr. Gladstone meant well when he entered into Irish legislation in the particulars of Irish land, Religion Etcetera. But in so doing he has put himself into the hands of the Romanist priests and their creatures in the Commons. They will bleed him until he faints.

April 11th: Met the Waterford Doctor on the stairs who has come to see Mother. Complained of noises in my ears sometimes like great tides beating other times like cracking of minute particles such as glass or other frangible substance. The fool said it was the atmosphere. I said am I to be a sounding cavern for every passing cloud of electricity? Mother will insist on doctors whose names she sees in newspapers . . .

April (Undated): Trial arising from Galway elections goes on. Evidence of clerical interference, Catholic perjury, denunciation from altars, bullying in confessions and so on. Mother isn't well again today. She talks of death now. Father's death. His grave. I will go over to his grave.

April 30th: On Thursday night at 9.8 pm. London office recd. message sent from India on Friday morning 12.43 pm. Message recd. in London day before sent from India ... Keogh trial continues. Judge Keogh is a Catholic. The Law is a convenience. There are other conveniences such as stone walls and iron gates. The Law struggles with imperfections to correct imperfections ...
Mem: Say to Scully that elsewhere too Roman Priests claim to be immune from Civil Law. Witness Bismark's speech against priests.

May [Undated]: Reports that Lannigan has taken the Scully boy to Dublin to consult his Lawyers. I at once sent word to Scully that he must send the boy away out of this. Proctor conducted to Whytescourt the Scotsman Doctor MacIntosh. He is making an Itinerary of the country. Choleric little man. Given to impatient questioning on sanitation, Poor Law, politics, roads, Hibernian agriculture and Dr. Hancock's Judicial Statistics. We are become the object of the Kingdom where every inquirer must make an Itinerary of our countryside and write about it in books. Said he had come to find the remarkable Mr. Lannigan for himself but that Lannigan had gone to Dublin to see his lawyers. Proctor introduced me as a Scientific Gentleman, Landlord and Master of Whytescourt. In the beginning it was a diversion but the fellow's questions began to upset me and I had to lie down in the afternoon with a compress and I believe an emission from the right ear.

May 12th: Lannigan returned from Dublin last evening to great acclamation on the roads from his supporters. Egress from the Kilkenny Road impossible. Buckley told me. He was coming home with medicines for Mother. The curate

Lutterell although removed by his superiors to another parish was in the town again last night inciting faction. It is said that the Keogh Trial will up-end the Dublin cardinal and his Italianate priests so that Lannigan will have no one to contest . . .

May 13th: The Scots Doctor all morning. I've met your remarkable priest, he cried. You mean Lannigan, I said. Sir, he said, It surprises me that with such a celebrity in the town you haven't taken pains to meet him, he said. Why, *The Times* is full of his case! I wager, he said, that Mr. Lannigan will unmask the Ultramontanes. So, I said, you met him. Yes, sir, he said. I shook the man by the hand . . . We're not of the same persuasion, I told him but . . . I'm for an open Bible but I applaud your fight against tyranny. I said to MacIntosh that he put me in mind of Mr. Stanley and Doctor Livingstone. You are a wit sir, Mr. Butler, he said. He is to come back tomorrow.

May 14th: Spent the morning over Mr. de Moleynes' *Irish Landowners' and Agents' Practical Guide*. I said in view of the unsettled locality we ought not act against delinquent tenants. Mother adamant. Mentioned Father. Doctor MacIntosh didn't come.

May 15th: MacIntosh didn't come. Sent a message to the Inn. MacNamara replied MacIntosh gone out all day with Lannigan. The late Land Act while it has gone some way towards meeting injustice has made for much calculation Etcetera. If Mr. Mill had been listened to we would be at peace on Irish land. Mother said today I was a communist. I said Yes and she was hysterical.

May 20th: Day of great heat. Doctor MacIntosh and I walked and talked in the Oak Arbour before lunch. And also after. He has been all over the country making notes on railways Etcetera. He has visited Mr. Bianconi. He jumped up and down often on the footpath so that I had difficulty following him. The country is not at war, he said, and still one-fifth of our army is quartered here. Can you explain that, sir? Popery, sir, he said. That's the cause of all your troubles here, he said, economic and otherwise. From de Tocqueville to Mr. Dickens the best minds have condemned Popery as a shackle on self-improvement. Oh there are some good priests, he said. But I wish every priest had a wife as St. Peter had and so double his happiness and usefulness. I laughed at this and said he ought to live amongst us a while longer. I write all this as he said. Afterwards he told me that Lannigan had shown him all the correspondence on his own case which the Doctor copied out. Afterwards we went into the farmyard where Doctor MacIntosh addressed the men and made many observations that I made Hawe note down.

May 21st: Took Doctor MacIntosh out by Mockler, Carrig, Singlebridge and back. Avoided the town by coming round by Chapel Lane. He remarked on the industry of the fields and the neatness of the dwellings. He spoke much of godliness and cleanliness so that I began to tire of him. He went on so about the evangelism of the Irish; church union and Archbishop Usher, the Irish Church Missions and Colportage Society. He was of the opinion that Popery was finished and instanced the decline of France and Prussian treatment of priests. He said the Irish would be free of Romism if there were more Lannigans. I said if christ is christ why do Christians differ, but he scarcely heard.

May 22nd: MacIntosh came today but I sent down the girl to say I was indisposed. He insisted upon coming up and we sat in the Observatory while he recommended specifics to mend my complaint. I do not like his constant advice. I said if you are so unhappy with Romish practices why are you not in Judge Keogh's court. He said he would be there for the delivery [of] judgement since the case would last a week more. He went on again about catechising the natives quoting Berkeley to effect. How the Romanists feared mixed education and the passage of ideas. He said it is all the policy of this Dublin bishop sent especially from Rome to

Romanize the Irish. How only thirty years ago these bishops were happy to live with Protestants and share their desks and books of scripture. But this cardinal wouldn't rest until he had his catholic everything school and university. I said it is all the one evil Catholic and Protestant which greatly scandalized him. God is atom, I said. Before he left I said to him: Consider our fields, our hedges how we have proliferated everywhere with escaped cultivation. Petasites Fragrans, Mimulus Guttatus, Acorus Calamus were all at one time cultivated plants and even the common poppy, the corn-salad too, all imported colonists into the countryside through human indulgence. What is your moral, sir, he said, your moral? My moral, sir, I said, is that man is the great despoiler and not the beast that he hunts. He will choke off the life of nature if he is given head ...

We do ourselves little good, I said then, to see ourselves singled out like divinities from our fellow animals. Religion I said is an old comfort that we might be able to meet the beast in ourselves. Religion, I said, was made in the universal darkness of the beginning when there was no other light and man crouched down in the leaves because of his terror. But we are not afraid now, I said. Religion misguides the purpose of correction because it would separate us from the body of the world in which we must work our end. Our evolution is only just begun, I said. I won't listen to Darwinism, he said and left. Then I was able to lie down for a long time.

May 24th: Spent two days in the bed but the heat being so great I was obliged to get up and apply cold towels to my body. Applied to the ear a new poltice which O'Brien sent out but it remedied little.

May 25th: Today I thought I might destroy this journal. Surely the only, the one question is not Does Truth exist? because it does but instead How to find it? *Que Sais-je?* I will recommend Montaigne's essay on the Savages of Brasil to Doctor MacIntosh.

86

May 26th: Went out for a little while today and then came back.

May 27th: Continuance of great heat. Walked as far as North Gate and back. The dog is sick with the worms.

May 30th: Judge Keogh's judgement a sensation. Am in better spirit. Priests guilt in intimidation at polls proven. Captain Nolan's election declared void. Cousin Amelia may now go visit the Trenches if Galway is safe.

May 31st: Decided today to go out. Sent word to Scully and we went to measure the Monolith at Cuffesgrange but neglecting to bring a measuring instrument; we had to content ourselves with perambulations about the fields. I was for a speedy return home, the dew coming down but Scully was all for possible discoveries, Marked Stones, Etcetera.
Observed a cow in a paddock, its head covered. Scully said the people called the covering a BLIND and signified the cow was a thief. I was for relieving the unfortunate animal but he said the people might assault us. I said where, pray, do you see people. I imperfectly heard his warning while negotiating passage of a stream in the dusk and my stockings became wet. Dreadful adventure.
On way home he asked if I was entertained by the Keogh Trial. Such evidence of my worst beliefs of the Romanist Ministry, politics Etcetera. I said, the judge seems honest. He said, you mean he is a catholic. I said, mean what you will. He then asked what ought he do now that Lannigan had been removed as school manager. I said, could you not work as well under a new manager. Said he was troubled. That he had given his loyalty in the first place to the suspended priest. I said, Mr. Lannigan would have no case and Judge Keogh no trial if catholics did not let themselves be led by the bishops, like hounds. He said he wondered that I supported Lannigan. I said I did not support him. I said Lannigan condemned himself when he put on the black suit. Where do you stand then, Mr Butler, he said. I am using myself, I said, as an experiment to keep Tribalism, Faction

and Tyranny of the Majority at bay. Someone has to do it, I said. For the sake of the species, I said. Breeders do less for horses. He laughed and said I was antic. I said, yes.

June 1st: Scully left in high dudgeon last eve because I insinuated that I had more confirmed purpose than he. I am becoming ... When I asked that he send his eldest son to see me that I might engage his prospects he said he saw little of him. He said the boy only frequents his home like an inn, that he has become the subjunctive of the priest. If I drive away visitors soon no one will come. Today I invited Proctor but he made excuses. I suspect his reasons.

June 2nd: A meeting at Gabbot's but I would not attend. Our community Etcetera. Ideal habitation, cellular with sufficient apertures and interconnecting passages to facilitate essential commerce. Congress of humans brings impression, expression, suppression hence Delegation, Abdication, Power. Every man has his own Slave though he doesn't know him. Every man has his own Master also.

June 4th: I have taken to Fantasies. Was certain that I saw Father today with riding crop in the Harness Room. Later saw blood in the sky and am determined to control. Spent the day with Hawe overseeing the men cleaning the old fruit gardens. Much better in the evening. The bishop of Lannigan is to be in the town on Sunday it is said to defy him.

June [Undated]: Great heat from the fields and even river. Saw the other Scully boy and the girl today.

The air above the river was like blue water in motion. At the Observatory window he stood and felt he could hear the contented chuckle of water over stones. Then he saw the couple away below him on the riverbank. The other Scully boy and that girl. Young foals in pasture. Not walking but wading through the long rushes and the switch grass. Creatures of the river in their natural place. Her long black hair was tied back and she tossed it like a young filly as she made short runs, letting the clumsy, ploughing boy catch up with her before moving on again.

It is true then, Butler observed through his passionless eyes. It is true what the anxious schoolmaster had been saying to him for weeks now. These two are lovers.

'What can I do? What would you do, sir, in my place? There's no law on earth to say they can't marry.'

'Can he provide for her?'

'Is it Marcus? Marcus, is it? Oh, he'll make a home for her, I suppose.'

'Doesn't he have employment?'

'Aye, he's a learner over in the Tannery, if you can call that employment.'

'It is a trade.'

'Oh, it's a trade all right.'

They moved along by the giant elderbushes on the riverbank below Whytescourt, sunlight disintegrating about their heads in a shower. Dull beat of a hammer came over the water from the yards opposite and in the distance somewhere a saw screamed into wood and died, and screamed and died, again and again.

When the couple had passed from sight of Whytescourt Butler stepped back into the old dust of the room behind him, the dog Lincoln padding along at his feet.

He had asked Scully why, if the couple were free to marry, was there such a fuss?

'The people would use it against me.'

'Against you?'

'Against us! Against them!'

'How, may I ask if . . .?'

'You, sir, can speak lightly of the people. You don't have to live amongst them. You don't have to face their hostility. It's easy enough for you to counsel indifference ('Not indifference,' murmured Butler). But look at my situation! And that of my family!'

It was tiresome because there was little point in saying that no matter what the situation the principle remained fixed. Otherwise there was no meaning. Meaning rested on a fixed point. Even their priests understood that. The cross.

Butler opened his journal and sat down to write.

She lay back against the slope, hand held against the sun, watching the flesh of her fingers edge with pink. Everything, everything was burning away quietly in the heat, a secret combustion which only revealed itself now and then in the sharp crack of a stalk or the collapse of brambles deep within the heart of a hedge, a whole architecture of dry sticks coming down.

She struggled up on her elbows and under falling eyelids watched the commotion down at the water where he was trying to flush out waterhens from the shallows with a great, dripping branch.

'Marcus! Come here a minute, I want you.'

He paid no heed to her and she sighed, picking and biting a daisy stalk, sharp annoyance in her teeth. He could be such a child at times! There were times when she felt she could ...

'What is it so?'

He was towering over her, his head in the sun so that she couldn't see his face.

'Sit down here,' and she made room for him. 'Oh, look at all the poor primroses dying in the sun! Oh Laws, the heat of it!'

There was a constant, somnolent murmur of wild bees somewhere in the trees.

'Marcus ...' Softly.

'Hmmm.'

'Mrs O'Shea was telling me all about that brother out in Melbourne. She said she'd give us his address any time we wanted. I thought we'd ask Mama for the brown trunk because she doesn't use it any more. What d'you think?'

'Hmmm?'

'D'you think we'd maybe write to Mrs O'Shea's brother first? He'd get you a job maybe out there. I was looking at that advertisement again of the agent in Liverpool. You can save a lot on the boat by bringing and cooking your own ...'

'She keeps her things in it.'

'What?'

'Mama. She keeps her things in the trunk.'

'Well, she could put them anywhere else. It's little enough to ask for if we're going off for the last time.'

'That's a cruel way of putting it, Nina. About Mama.'

'Well, I didn't mean it to be cruel so. It's only that we have to face up to things, Marcus. We can't go on all the time acting like children.'

'Don't talk to me like that, Nina. I'm not a child.'

'Well sometimes you act like one.' It was the wrong thing to say and she knew this at once, biting her lip. 'Oh dear,' she cried, trying to laugh. 'Oh dear,' putting her hand over to run it through his hair but he turned his flushed face aside. 'Marcus, I know it's hard for you leaving Mama and Dada . . .'

'Isn't it hard for you too?'

'It's different entirely for me, Marcus, you know that. I don't belong to them. That's the truth.'

She had shielded her eyes to look at him and it chilled him: the certainty, the calm, the composed face.

'Marcus, you don't want to go and go back on it all, do you?'

'No one said I wanted to . . .'

'If we're to go in September we have to have the money down come the end of August . . .'

'I know that, I know that . . .'

'. . . in half one-pound notes it said. Otherwise we don't get that assisted emigration as they call it. I've got all the clothes marked out for us to take. All you've to do is to gather that money for the boat.'

'I'll get it, Nina. Don't fret.'

'Will you ask Mr Cody?'

'No. I'll be able to get it, Nina. I'll get it . . .'

'When are you going to tell Dada?'

'I'll tell him.'

'But when, though?'

'Ah, Nina! Just sit quiet a minute.'

She lay back again but this time stiff, staring.

'You mustn't mistake me, Marcus. Sometimes I don't think you think I'm in earnest at all. I think you only want to quiet me by saying yes all the time . . .'

'That's not true . . .'

'Sometimes I think you want to stay on in this terrible place.

Well I couldn't, Marcus. I couldn't.'

He saw that she had been crying without betraying it, great tears oiling down her face beneath the cope of her hair.

'Nina, Nina, please ... I don't want ... It's only that it's hard, don't you see. I wouldn't want them to think I was running away. I've gone and given my hand to Father Lannigan in this ...'

'I don't care. I don't care, so I don't. I couldn't care less about Father Lannigan or any of them. It's only us, Marcus,' she hissed the words fiercely. 'That's all that counts. Only us.'

His broad, reddened face was alight. 'I believe you, begod,' he laughed, shaking his head. He wanted to reach out and touch her but didn't. Her body appeared to quiver in the sun. To touch it was to lose her, as she was then, at that moment.

She dipped the hem of her skirt in the running water to cool her eyes, letting the sun scorch it off the skin. Oh the heat!

'You have to turn your back,' he cried. 'I'm going in for a dip.'

She felt with her eyes still closed the drawing off of each drop of moisture from skin into the air ...

'Nina!'

'Oh, all right so!' She gathered up her skirts and moved off, her hair untidy, her shoulders drooping, carrying her shoes, feeling the powdered, baked clay of the river path on her bare feet. She flopped on her knees again. 'Am I far off enough?' But he didn't notice her mockery. Marcus was one of the few boys of the town who would go into the water of the Big Paupers, a lazy pool where the inmates of the Workhouse were brought in the summertime for compulsory bathing. Beside it was a shallower pool called the Little Paupers and according to the town the whole place reeked from one end of the year to the other. 'Can I turn round now?'

'Not yet.'

'Ah, Marcus!'

She heard his gasp and the slide into the water and turned. He was in up to his belly, still holding on tightly to a large overhanging branch of a tree because he was really quite frightened of the water and wouldn't let go. She was amazed as she always was by the length, the long shaft of his body which ran like a white column of stone from the water-top up into the leaves of the tree. Whether it was the dark reflection of the water or the leaves about his shoulders, his whole body seemed to be mottled with running splashes of cold green colour, like marble, shadows whorling across his chest.

'Oh-ho!' He gasped, lowering himself down, slowly into the river, still holding on to the branch until all but his head and long arm was covered. This was what he called his dip and she knew he would never allow his head under the water.

'I'm coming nearer,' she called, teasing.

'Don't, Nina! Don't. Don't you ... Nina! Ni ...'

She laughed gaily and ran off laughing when he suddenly raised himself out of the water, a great cascading bulk, floundering and gasping and trying to splash water at her with his hand. But she was out of range in the meadow where she subsided, still laughing, below the level of the high grass. She lay there in a tumble listening to the ticking sounds of the meadow like a clock in the ground and thinking of Marcus. She wanted so much to go back to him and say ... that whatever happened she wanted him to be happy ...

In the muffled room of Whytescourt House Horace Percy Butler must have sat, stupefied, in the same heat. That entry for June in the journal in which he also mentions the figures of the young people on the riverbank was clearly completed later, with a different shade of ink and a renewed energy in the fingers. It is appropriate to give it here.

Whether man in great TRIBES is any different in MORAL HABIT to man in his private seclusion. For example crime and money only exist in a plurality.

Two items for our age: d. of a 7yr. girl in Plumstead (smallpox?). Her parents being of the sect known as Peculiar People they physically resisted medical ministrations. Item the second (all within one week) in village Charterhouse husband beat wife to d. before whole village on some minor pretext. Villagers shut their doors and observed spectacle through windows. The offspring, five, of the misfortunate couple ran from door to door appealing in vain for help.

Mr. Darwin wd. have it that LAUGHTER which now universally among men signifies pleasure ETCETERA must have been practised by our progenitors long before they deserved to be called HUMANS.

Simian Humour.

It is claimed that living organisms may now be evolved *de novo* in the glass bowl. At the two ends of MATTER and TIME, we approach the limits of our presumptions. No mystery, after all, perhaps, but a Heap of Chimistry.

Whether laws may be made for the whole body through observation of functions of the part. Witness the scale of life from private to public, from man to minute organism.

Whether societies, institutions, communities have properties, rights and obligations unknown to the individual. And then whether there be constant connexion in good ordinance between the valid decisions of the many and the rights, needs, obligations of the single individual. The true revolution is not made with guns but with the spread of one opinion over many which in time becomes the opinion to be destroyed again.

Today we carried Mother to the Bath-house with Miss Padst attending. She is wasting away to bones in clothes. After washing she had a seizure and had to be straightened out like a disused contraption ...

As the sun went down on that day in June 1872, Butler dozed in his Observatory, Bishop Nugent sat in the parlour of his Bishop's House in Kilkenny and Nicholas Scully set out from home to find his brother and sister because their father wanted them.

The bishop was consulting with his clergy as to whether he should go to the town on the following Sunday to confirm the children in the Augustinian Friary. Father John Purcell said it would be a test before the people. That if Lannigan were to intimidate the bishop himself then ... The priests argued this way and that, scarcely aware of His Lordship's presence. (How excited they were, like children, by all this Lannigan business! Even Monsignor Connelly, God bless him!) While he sat quietly watching, having decided long before that he was going to go anyway, whatever the danger. To tell nothing but the truth he thought this aspect of the matter a bit exaggerated. A mountain out of a molehill. Is it Willie Lannigan, Lord save us and bless us!

In the town itself the streets were nearly empty. A dog was scratching in the dust of the Cross when Nicholas stepped out of the house and walked down Quarry Road, knowing where he would find them. He could never walk anywhere in the town now without the feeling of forms lurking in doorways, windows quietly closing, curtains being lifted an inch. When someone passed, Nicholas, like everyone else in the town, would bow his head. You just didn't force another to meet your eyes; it was a kind of courtesy that grew out of fear and guilt. Only in the hours of violence did people look one another in the face, then, when your commitment was unmistakable, when you could not avoid being anything but what you were.

Just below the Tannery a group of men were plastering a wall and he had walked into them before he knew it. The Doyles. Ger and China and Jude. Georgie Doyle, a great gross figure spilling over his pants, paused effortlessly with a huge limestone block clasped to his stomach and called, 'Hey, Ger, will ya lookit who's here!'

He walked quickly past them with head down and it was only later when the fierce beat of his heart had slowed and they were well behind him that he really allowed himself to hear their obscenities, their threats and that hoarse laugh that came at some whispered joke about himself and the priest. He dreaded the thought of being beaten. Blood or pain. For a moment he thought they would ... Up against a wall.

Nicholas climbed a gate near the shallows of the river at the end of the town and saw Marcus and Emerine strolling along the bank below him, carelessly. He was still trembling.

It had been one of the happiest days she had had, oh, as far back as she could remember almost. They had just talked and walked and she couldn't remember from one minute to the next what they'd been saying. But it didn't matter. Now she was asking questions of Marcus about Australia, drowsy, wandering questions about the weather there and the people and the strange names there like Wagga Wagga and the man in the Tichbourne Case . . .

Marcus, who had never been beyond Kilkenny in his life, played the game well for her, building cities with houses as high as a steeple, streets flooded with curious people, great open spaces of land waiting for any man with hands and a plough to mark out his share. He opened the ground for her and shovelled up diamonds as big as the stepping-stones in the river. He . . .

And she listened. Knowing full well and much better than he the kind of game they were playing. She knew the rule of how it had to end and even while she talked happily she was already seeing bleak days of struggle to find work, to find food and a home in a strange hostile place . . .

'Oh Marcus,' she whispered, 'Marcus, I wish . . . I wish . . .'

'There's Nick!' Marcus stopped and pointed because his eyes were better than hers.

'What's he want?' she asked crossly.

The dark figure in the distance was waving both hands above its head. Marcus didn't answer but quickened his step which annoyed her still more.

'Can't you go easy?' she pleaded, complained. When Nicholas arrived back from the Dublin trip with Father Lannigan he had moved back to live with them again at the Cross. He hadn't said why but there had been some kind of row with the priest and he was there all the time now, much to Emerine's annoyance, hanging about the house doing nothing. She was frightened but couldn't say why. 'Marcus,' she whispered, trotting to keep up. 'Marcus, please . . .'

'What?'

'Marcus, I don't want you to say anything to Nicholas about what we said.'

'Said about what?'

'About Australia. About going off.'

He didn't answer at once, appearing to walk even quicker than before.

'Marcus ...'

'He's my brother, isn't he?'

'Oh, Marcus!'

'Oh all right so.'

They arrived at the gate where Nicholas was standing, Emerine trying to straighten her hair and her clothes because there was about them suddenly a certainty that their day had ended and that the other life was resuming again. All he said to them, standing there in his odd, offhand way, was, 'Can you come home? Dada is looking for ye.'

6 . *The Lawyers*

William Edward Lannigan was then about forty-four or -five years of age. Those contemporary descriptions of him that survive tend to exaggerate his height, his weight, the volume of his voice. More than once they speak of him as standing head and shoulders above a crowd. But in point of fact he was only five feet eight or nine inches in height. He didn't even stand impressively since one shoulder was markedly shorter than the other. It is true that his head, at least, was handsome, with that great lock of black hair across the forehead. He liked walking-sticks and owned a variety. In the good years he dressed well, even foppishly, with a taste for silks. There is some evidence that he was bronchial and he died, as may already have been mentioned, of pneumonia, in the County Home, in 1883.

When he spoke to the people he spoke roughly, even crudely, in the flat local accent with a vocabulary of the fields. But when he gave out a homily or read aloud his own correspondence (as he frequently did at this time in place of the Sunday sermon) or when he addressed what he considered to be his social betters, he always affected a cultivated speech, an elaborate grammar. Mr John Halton QC, who was in the defence team of the Cardinal at the trial, described him, in a memoir later in the century, as an imperfectly educated peasant of genius. There were others, including his own religious hierarchs, who saw only his arrogance, his cupidity, his blindness to the sufferings of others.

He was one of those men who, while their personal attributes may be weighed and measured with apparent ease (everyone quickly offering an opinion of them when asked) nevertheless still retain to themselves something which continues to surprise both enemy and friend. The reason for this is that before different people he displayed a different dominating quality – to one his pride, his greed, to another his passion, his faith, perhaps his insecurity, while to yet another his rashness or his

98

courage. Like all men who inspire great following or great rancour he had that capacity or, as it might be termed, imperfection, of offering to others a single quality in great measure, to each one, perhaps, the quality that one desired to find, so that again like many great leaders of men he was in part the creation of those nearest to him who fed him out of their own hunger.

It is true, at any rate, that there was a surface or perhaps more than one surface that hid surprising recesses in the man. Down there or back there (since this reserve, this secretiveness, had something to do with time, generation, his translation out of a hovel not two miles from the town into the respectability of the priesthood, his identity through his dead parents with their dead parents and a lineage of poverty, ignorance, disease) somewhere there a boisterous animal was caged. In someone less uncertain of his own nature this might have been turned to advantage especially when his case was taken up by men sophisticated enough to be charmed by the unsophisticated without needing to patronize it. In this well of half-hidden wildness the man's sardonic humour resided like an unkempt, unwelcome cousin. He once described his bishop, in the presence of the Cardinal and another clergyman, no less, as 'two half-farts that didn't add up'. He was also to describe him, however, elsewhere and at another time, as 'that simoniac ecclesiastic who has spent a lifetime in mendacious traffic'.

In the end he was a victim of the two styles. To be whole he would have had to opt for one or other style. Or perhaps to have opted for one or other style would have meant that he was whole. When he was virtually isolated and at bay he groped to find a connexion between either style and the needs of his own heart. And he couldn't. There was increasingly more and more for him to say and less and less value in the words and phrases available to him. Hence the great silences of his last years in the town which Nicholas Scully alone witnessed in their fullness.

But even in the beginning when words were his all, his mode of being, and while he put on and put off his fronts recklessly to suit the occasion or his whim, the priest was already driven to concealments and stratagems to mask the shifts and twists of his personality. In the literal sense he was a compulsive, expert liar but this had little to do with dishonesty in his dealings with others. He would himself be (and was) deeply shocked by accusations of dishonesty. In his own mind he saw his manoeuvres as right and desirable if they made matters easier, a little less troublesome for all. He knew that he had never knowingly subtracted from the material or moral possessions of any man. He prided himself on his diplomacy, even his tact, which he confused with persuasiveness. For a man who was so deeply embroiled in quarrels he was singularly fond of the word agreement. He never forgave what he called a betrayal. He liked each gesture of his to have a certain air of piety. In this way he had not yet come to know the essential fibre of his being that he was squandering and crumbling with each sleight, each shift and twist until, when it was too late, he realized that he had become a hollow man, sounding forth as resonantly as before, but in the end without as much as a scrap of conviction.

But at this, the height of his career, he tried to believe in his own claims to virtue. And sometimes he was troubled by knots of his own conscience while knowing that in any verifiable way he was doing right. Like his speech, his moral sensibility was divided, part of it self-righteous and confident, part of it threatening him with self-degradation. Otherwise how can one begin to talk of his strange, tormented attitude to money?

When they went to Dublin in May 1872 to confer with the lawyers, Father Lannigan and Nicholas Scully lodged with a Mrs Broe who was formerly a Miss Ashe of Kyle town. She kept a house on Thomas Street. It was a good stiff walk from there, crossing the river, to the stuffy, dust-ridden chambers near the Kings Inns where the consultations took place with Mr McAllindon QC and his tall assistant, Mr Houston QC.

'We must be in good time, Nicholas. And not let ourselves down in front of these gentlemen. They're Protestants, y'see. Masons.' He fussed over Nicholas' clothes, the black frock-coat he had recently given him, and bade him shine his shoes again. On the way the priest cracked his stick against stone and parapet to make his point and Nicholas, dazed by the congregation of people on the narrow streets, tried to keep up, tried to hold on to the large folio of papers that he carried for the priest. 'I suspect the Protestant whenever he starts on the Bible. Spouting. I can't stand that kind of Joe Holy. They think I'll do their dirty work for them. Not all of them, mind you. Only some of them. And – and they never see I see their motives. They think: oh, here's this clob of a priest from the back of beyond! He'll bang a few times against the croziers if we give him air! Oh yes! Well, boy, they don't know their man so they don't. Only the other evening I told Lord Desart himself at his own dinner-table, mind you, that I . . .

Nicholas remarked that some of the men on the Defence Committee, Mr McKinley for instance and Lord Clifden, were men of honour.

The priest really didn't seem to hear. 'They respect you if you stand up to them. Stand up to them. Not be afraid . . . not be cowed down. That's what has this country the way it is. With the English and the Protestants, I mean. Not an ounce of self-respect. Why we'd never have had Mr McAllindon there now (he's very famous, don't you know, at the Bar) we'd never have had him at all but that I went in to him myself. Over beyond in the Law Library there. I went in to him and I said: I'm Lannigan the Kyle priest. May I have a little of your time, sir?'

But when they reached the lawyers' rooms there was no one there and they were kept waiting for over an hour. By the time the two lawyers arrived from the courts the priest was fit to be tied and Nicholas feared the worst.

'Litigation, litigation, Mr Lannigan!' the little lawyer cried but in no way apologetically when he came in. 'Sit down, man. Sit down! Half the country would be at law and the other half in prison. I do declare. Good morning, sir! And how are you? Bring up the briefs, Mr Houston, bring up the briefs. Now, Mr Lannigan ye are going to tell us something of this encounter with your Cardinal which is the matter of your case. And we may put questions to you, Mr Houston and I, as to particulars. Sit down, man. Sit down. It does no man good to overstrain the limbs. Where were we now, Mr Houston? Ah! Yes! Hmm! Now – ah, ah, ah . . .'

Nicholas had never seen Father Lannigan so put down. The

frosty voice of the lawyer had cooled the room as if one of the dirty windows that scarcely let in the light had been thrown open to admit the wind. Father Lannigan sat meekly in his chair and recounted in a low voice how the Cardinal had intervened in the troubles of Kyle as the special legate of the Pope. How he himself had been called before the Cardinal in Dublin to answer charges of misconduct and how he had been finally suspended and the Big Chapel placed under interdict. He gave all this out with such flatness that Nicholas could scarcely believe it was he, the same man who an hour before would have tossed these same facts to explode like bombs around their feet. It was only when he told how the Cardinal and his Monsignor had tried to trick him into leaving the town that—

'And there had been no talk of this before?'

'None, sir. But now he wanted what the others wanted in the town. To get me down off my own altar and put another in my place. Well, I tell you . . .'

'And what did you say to this?'

'Well, I said, well my Lord Cardinal, I said, and who shall take care of my parish while I'm away? Oh, he said, we'll take care of that! We'll take care of that. We'll take care of all that, says he! Well, says I. Well, my Lord Cardinal, says I. That won't do at all. Am I to come this far and have to give in to the curates and the mob? Isn't this to say I was wrong from the very start? Well good morning to you, my Lord Cardinal, says I and I put my hand to my hat, took my stick in my hand and walked away. Not another word!'

'I see. I see.' Mr McAllindon paused in the act of writing. The small face like a sharp shopkeeper's now without the great wig. Considering gravely. Looking into the eyes of the priest but seeing also that scene in the brown, comfortless study in Eccles Street, the three clergy . . .

'Tell me. What did you say the name of yon other clergyman was, Mr Lannigan? With the Cardinal, that is.'

'Monsignor Doyle.'

'Former Vicar-General of the Archdiocese. Shrewd. Prominent in education agitation. Spent many years in Rome also. Author of articles in support of Papal Infallibility.' Tall Mr Houston had bent over the older, seated man to give this startling addition. Then he added, after but the slightest pause, 'Recently deceased.' He rolled all this out in his rich baritone, rolling the words out like items from a great store within his bony forehead and then his long body sprang back, switch-like, to its upright place. Fiddling with his cravat. Hardly appearing to listen.

'I see. Died. I see,' said Mr McAllindon, still staring at Father Lannigan.

'His henchman. His follow-me-around. Yes, your eminence! No, your eminence!' sneered the priest, breathing heavily through his nose. 'Yes-man. That's him!' Indignation wormed his lips but in a silence that lasted for some minutes while the two lawyers watched him, quite unmoved. It seemed to Nicholas as he watched all of this, appalled, that they were measuring their man and later, at the trial, he was to understand why, how destructive the priest could be to his own case in the witness-box. 'Monsignor Doyle,' the words finally came, spent, 'is one of those clerical gentlemen brought in from Rome to complete the papal conquest of our people. It's the last and worst invasion of all this god-forsaken island. Oh, they have their agents everywhere now. Priests and bishops. Men in newspapers, schools. They're nearly finished the business, don't you know. In twenty years' time no one'll remember how the Pope was once kept in his proper place. And they'll be surprised when the second Reformation starts again, wondering why it happened . . .'

'Quite. Quite. Now you must tell us as much as you can, without holding back, of this meeting between you and these reverend gentlemen.'

'Oh, I remember the scene quite clearly . . .'

'It was a kind of trial, would ye say?'

'I suppose that.'

'But ye claim there was no citation to trial, no formal procedure, so to speak . . .'

'Oh, nothing like that at all.'

'Were you accused?'

'Oh, he spoke of how I'd brought my fellow clerics into the common court. How I'd been suspended. How I'd ignored the suspension. That kind of thing.'

'Yes. And judgement was passed, would you say, by your Cardinal as a result of this ah-trial?'

'In my absence. Behind my back, sir! I wouldn't go up to hear it so they sent me . . .'

'Never mind that. Judgement was passed.'

'Oh, judgement was passed all right. Never you fear.'

'Now. Mr Lannigan. How would you say your Cardinal would justify all this ah-business as a just trial?'

'He wouldn't. He couldn't.'

'But he will!'

The priest shrugged and said nothing.

'Ye'll have to assist us, Mr Lannigan, with your opinion.'

'I am.'

'Not quite, Mr Lannigan. Not quite. Wouldn't you say, Mr Houston, that Mr Lannigan isn't being quite ah-candid as it were in his opinion of his Church?'

'I'm still a member of my Church, sir!'

'But expelled . . .'

'Suspended. I haven't been excommunicated.'

'Tell me, Mr Lannigan, do you really hope to stay on in your Church when all this is over? In the Roman ministry? What do you hope to effect, man?'

Again the priest didn't answer. Mr McAllindon let the silence grow until it choked the room. And suddenly from his corner seat Nicholas understood. This was the real trial, this menacing preliminary, and not the event that they were all preparing for. Here the priest was bodily in the dock and not just party to a libel action. In his excitement he even recognized in the little lawyer, withered skin and bright eye, an old adversary of his own.

He had found a kind of faith with the priest in the weeks before. If it hadn't a god in it at least it had the resemblance of an ideal. But as he lived close to Father Lannigan he had come to rest, more and more, in the humanity of the man himself. Tears came into his eyes as the priest remained bowed in the silence of the lawyers' room. He felt a deep hatred for the impassive gentlemen of the Bar who again, as it seemed to him, were calculating the resources of their client, coldly, even with contempt. Why didn't he speak back! Didn't he understand what they were trying to do to him! They wanted to take away the only thing he had left. The pathetic, clinging hope, the impossible dream that he could still belong. That even yet he could still win the right for each man to make his own way to God, for each man to discover his own god, and still remain part of the one communion . . .

At length, when the lawyer spoke, it was in a voice altered from the ambiguous charm of before. Each word was clipped into its appointed place, nailed down.

'Before, sir, you enter the witness-box you must come down on one side or the other. There must be no dallying. Either you approve of the character of your Church or you do not. Otherwise, do you see, you waste my time. And that of Mr Houston. And your own time, if you want to win . . .'

'When we are made priests,' murmured Father Lannigan, and in his consternation Nicholas couldn't make out whether he was defiant or humbled, 'we are priests for ever.'

There was another pause at this but Mr McAllindon had clearly decided to change the mood because he allowed an icy smile to cross his face.

'It's a matter in your favour, Mr Lannigan – don't you think so, Mr Houston – that your Church has such ah-strange notions of what a judicial inquiry should be.'

To which tall Mr Houston bowed low in agreement.

'They don't want me because I won't renege,' Father Lannigan had said that very first day. 'They're not interested in my case as it is. They want to make it into a case to suit themselves.'

And indeed, as Nicholas had already perceived, Mr McAllindon continued to harry his client like a prosecutor.

'Well, now,' the lawyer began on the second day, 'tell us, Mr Lannigan, how you answered the accusations of your Cardinal at this ah-trial.'

'I referred him to my nine grounds of objection . . .'

'You're what, Mr Lannigan?'

'The document I drew up. The boy has it here,' and Nicholas was ushered forward with a great flurry of papers.

'What is your name, boy?'

'Nicholas Scully, sir.'

'We've a copy of these already, I believe, Mr Houston. Now, Mr Lannigan, your point in all this ...' The lawyer fingered the papers without relish. The door creaked open and a tiny lady crept in. 'What is it? What is it? Can't ye see I'm in conference, Miss Greene?' The lady fled without a word and he continued on, testily, to the priest. 'It's that these papal bulls or whatever they are, forbidding one cleric to sue another in civil court ... that these bulls aren't effective in this country at all. Isn't that what you're trying to say, ha?'

'Yes. Not received.'

'Aye. As you say. Not received.'

'I say the constitution *Apostolicae Sedis* isn't received anymore than the bull *In Coenae Domini* ...'

'We must keep to the matter in hand, Mr Lannigan.'

'But isn't this what matters? Where the line of the law stops? And if it does at all? Doesn't it matter that a court in Rome can lay down the law to the court below there on the quays?'

'It matters all right,' Mr McAllindon was amused. He distributed his laughter parsimoniously around the room reserving most of it for Mr Houston. 'It matters before the Chief Justice. Eh-he, Mr Houston?'

'It matters before the Chief Justice, certainly,' and Mr Houston joined in the lawyer's joke. Resonant chuckle to high piping laugh.

'The courts,' Mr McAllindon laughed as if the joke was still in progress, 'are open to every subject of the Queen. Priest or bishop or not. And no rule or canon of a private society may interrupt the law nor deprive a subject of seeking redress for a temporal wrong before the courts. And that's what our Chief Justice will say.' Mr McAllindon concluded his laugh, swallowing noisily for several seconds. 'Well then! Now! Ye say that it was agreed between ye at this meeting to defer the matter to Rome?'

'Aye, it was.'

'But there was nothing about yourself leaving the town?'

'Nothing at all.'

'The Cardinal claims ye agreed to step down for a while.'

'It was said I might make a retreat.'

'A retreat ...'

'Aye. But I might make a retreat in my own house.'

'And is this customary, Mr Lannigan, in your communion, to retreat in your own house?'

'Oh, perfectly customary I would say.'

'I see.'

Mr McAllindon didn't believe him. The calculated pause fastened doubts on Father Lannigan that continued to trail along in the silence.

'I might make a retreat in my own house. Of course I might. There's no one to say I . . .'

'We'll take your word for it, Mr Lannigan. Now! This Monsignor Doyle. He's since died, hasn't he?'

'Yes.'

'So it's a matter of what you and the Cardinal say that determines how the court may judge this interview between you?'

'Yes. But I can tell you, sir, that many excellent divines will testify that a man may retreat in his own house . . .'

'We've passed on from that, Mr Lannigan,' said the lawyer drily. 'We're now talking of the fact that there are no living witnesses to what transpired between you and your superior. In other words much of your case will rest on whether the jury believes you or the other man.'

'I've never been called a liar yet, sir, to my face. My honesty has never been called in doubt by any man!'

'Your honesty, if I may say so, Mr Lannigan, is of less account than your credibility. You see, sir, in ways your case is simple. In other ways it isn't easy at all, for someone like myself, shall we say, to follow the rights and wrongs of it. The law likes clear lines, Mr Lannigan. Litigants oughtn't to be related or bound to one another by vows of obedience and the like. It makes for complication, don't you see. When you were made a priest, Mr Lannigan, you agreed to obey your Cardinals isn't that so?'

'I took a vow of obedience.'

'Aye. And you can't very well complain now, can you, when it's a burden?'

'I can complain, sir, against injustice . . .'

'That won't do. That won't do at all, Mr Lannigan. We have to answer the charge of how, if you willingly entered your profession, you may now turn about and throw off your contract. It's a maxim of the law, Mr Lannigan, that a man who neglects to speak when he might and ought will not be heard when he desires to do so. There isn't much sympathy, you see, for the man who puts on his own chains.'

'And what if the contract implies contempt for the law, the courts and justice?'

'But you don't say that at all, Mr Lannigan. You say you're still a Roman priest . . .'

'I say my present authorities are bending justice under the guise of Church law . . .'

'Hmm. Well. Well, we'll see. We'll see.'

'Are you suggesting, maybe, I give up the case? Maybe it might be better if you sent back the brief to my solicitor below in Kilkenny.'

The lawyer rolled his eyes in pantomime shock and Mr Houston smiled his support.

'Oh, no, goodness me, no. We're not suggesting any such thing. Sure we're not, Mr Houston? Not at all. It's only that . . . well . . . we have a wee margin. Not much. I'd say we're out in front, Mr Lannigan but it won't be easy to stay there, so it won't. And that's where this matter of credibility comes in.' The lawyer began to muse, almost to himself. 'Your Cardinal, now. A distinguished man, wouldn't you say? A respected man. Head of his Church and so on. Not a man to be dismissed lightly. The kind of man people'd believe in the witness-box. Whatever his evidence. Isn't that so? Ah, but then you might say there's another side to the coin. He has his enemies, your Cardinal. You might say there are people in this town that can't abide him. Nor what he stands for. You might say he stands for Popism in this part of the world. And many people don't care at all for Popism. No more than yourself, Mr Lannigan. Correct me if I'm wrong now . . .'

The priest had been trying to interrupt for several seconds, what the lawyer was saying clearly agitating him in his seat so that he twisted this way and that.

'Have you,' he managed to say at length, 'Mr McAllindon, any acquaintance with His Eminence?'

'No-o. I've served on committees now to which he made representation.' The lawyer answered cautiously, his eyes blinking like jewels. 'But come, man. Ye must not expect personal acquaintances to be of any importance in the matter. Let's say I don't know your Cardinal.'

'Who does?' The priest spat the words and stopped. He had been trying all along in this company to control the spasms of hatred which he felt for those who had injured him. In some way no legal victory seemed worth the final betrayal of his own, especially before men like these. 'Even those nearest him,' he whispered, 'say they've no contact with him.' He looked down gloomily at his hands. He felt suddenly without an ally who could understand his feelings. Ideas, yes. Feelings, no. 'He's a cold man right enough. I mean he's fond of using terms like self-discipline when in effect he's talking about the discipline of others. The need, that is, to emulate his own example.'

'But isn't that a Roman maxim?' Mr McAllindon pronounced the word Roman as two words and this raised the note of triumph in his voice, the face lighting up before Father Lannigan. 'Isn't that so? Isn't that so, now? Down with the individual. One Pope. One authority . . .'

'We've allied ourselves to unbelief,' he announced grandly to Nicholas that night when they were back in Mrs Broe's sitting-room and then, in a rush, the words tumbling out of his mouth, 'Oh, but did you see the crit of him across the table like a – like a – like a – I-don't-know-what? And that other lummox backing him up good-oh! Isn't that right, Mr Houston? Wouldn't you say so, Mr Houston? Oh, of course, Mr McAllindon! A fine pair of cross-fire merchants the two of them! Well, let me tell you, boy! They'll have to get up earlier in the morning to catch me on the hop. Popism how are ya! It'd be a nice how-d'ya-do if I handed those two a stick to wallop me with. I'd be the right galloping eddjit if I let the likes of those two run a halter on me, so I would . . .'

'We musn't forget,' Mr McAllindon warned the very next day, 'that this matter is secular, not religious.'

'The religious question is a matter for your own Church,' opined Mr Houston, without looking up.

'Precisely. Precisely,' Mr McAllindon rubbed his bony hands together vigorously, the matter settled. 'My service, Mr Lannigan, begins with the fact that you wish to sue for libel. And not before the fact, don't you see. You consider the publication of this suspension to be injurious and a source of libel, isn't that so? Isn't that right now?'

Father Lannigan nodded. But he really felt they were drawing further and further away from the real issue, the issue planted in the streets of the town like a diseased root which had sent him on this restless journey through the courts looking for . . .

He had gone to law as a man might go to his doctor. Liberty was being poisoned by certain members of his Church. He only wanted a treatment. It had never occurred to him that he would set in motion a deep antagonism between the institutions nor that he would be expected to espouse one above the other. The lawyer was beginning to sound like a manipulator of dogma himself, a priest of tort and not a dispassionate reader of a law above creed or faction.

Mr McAllindon went on and on about the case. Counts and Innuendos. Interest and Duty and Privileged Communication. But the priest hardly heard him at all. 'Your case,' they had told him at Lord Desart's dinner-table, 'your case clarifies the struggle of the last two decades between Church and State. You may help to restore that balance which the bishops want to topple . . .' And now here was this mean little lawyer trying to exert his own prejudices! If he didn't play the game, he was being told, he didn't have a chance. He was being offered a new baptism, a new orthodoxy. As exclusive and diminishing of the individual as the old! All that was changed was the institution. Tyranny was what men devised to make all men as much the same as themselves as possible . . .

'May I say something?' asked Father Lannigan but of the book-lined walls of the room, the tomes, the dead of the law while the lawyer continued in full spate . . .

'Of course, of course,' Mr McAllindon stopped short suddenly.

'All I wanted to say, if I may . . .'

'You may say anything, Mr Lannigan . . .'

'All I wanted to say is that the – the canons of my Church are not contrary to natural justice. If they were they wouldn't be the rules of God Almighty. Don't try to tell me, sir, that the State law is just and the law of the Church unjust. I won't hear . . .'

'Will you explain,' Mr McAllindon asked quietly, amicably, 'will you explain the law of libel, Mr Houston, to our friend Mr Lannigan here?'

'If the injurious statements made by the one person of another be true they are justified and cannot be the grounds of libel,' boomed Mr Houston.

'Point number one,' observed Mr McAllindon, encouragingly.

'But even assuming them to be false, yet if they are made by a person who believes them to be true and whose interest and duty it is to communicate them to another . . .'

'Very important this . . . interest and duty,' whispered Mr McAllindon.

'. . . whose interests in turn require that they should be so informed, the law, upon the grounds of public policy, regards such communications as privileged.'

'. . . privileged,' came the refrain from Mr McAllindon.

'. . . and will not permit an action to be brought against the person making them.'

'And that,' concluded Mr McAllindon happily, 'is what your priest, your Cardinal would have us accept.'

'He will claim privilege,' opined Mr Houston.

'It being his interest and duty, don't you see, as Papal Cardinal, to make known your suspension to the people of the town whose interest in turn it is to receive it . . .'

'It's an abuse of the law,' breathed Father Lannigan. 'Can't you see it's a perversion of the law by those who see themselves above it?'

'He will claim privilege,' Mr Houston's nagging boom.

'Damn his privileges!' shouted the priest.

'Mr Lannigan, please . . .'

The priest had jumped out of his chair and not knowing which way to turn was standing, trembling and enraged.

'Don't talk to me of that – that – that—Privil. Privileges! His and his likes ...'

'Mr Lannigan! Mr Lannigan!' cool Mr McAllindon leaned across towards him. 'We're talking about a legal technicality, man.'

'Privilege,' came Mr Houston's chorus, 'is a term in law to ...'

'A great injury has been done me!' It was as if, finding himself on his feet, he had only to reach out and pick up the rhythm of his old speeches before the people. His voice rose. His body straightened and he looked off through the walls at a massed congregation. The two men were clearly uncertain as to how to deal with this. 'After thirty-six years of active life as a Christian minister ...' Mr Houston became embarrassed and looked towards his colleague for guidance but the small lawyer, after the first shock had sat back and was letting the priest have his say. 'I am deprived of my living ... condemned without trial ... nevertheless ...'

He suddenly stopped. He saw the white face of the boy in the corner of the room and it stopped him like a signal, a wave of a hand. He wondered if he had said something indiscreet. This silence in the room waiting for him to act, to go on with his (what exactly had he said?) speech, statement or to stop. Well, to hell with their feelings, who were they anyway but two fellows he had employed, if they didn't like what he said they could lump it. And he sat down.

'I'd have less to say about your ... this is only a word of advice now, Mr Lannigan. But if I were you I'd stay away from personal tribulations and the like. The Bench is only moved by logic and good sense. And juries too ... in my opinion. Wouldn't you agree there, Mr Houston? I mean the plea of passion. That kind of thing. It doesn't, as they say, cut much ice in the well-regulated court-room.'

'You mock me, Mr McAllindon.'

'Eh? Eh?'

'You don't take me seriously, Mr McAllindon.'

'I take you seriously, Mr Lannigan. We take Mr Lannigan very seriously, eh, Mr Houston?'

'I know without knowing that there's a law somewhere ...

I don't know where ... a law that's been flouted in this treatment of me. That's all! I know it. I can be patient. I know it's
only time and I'll find that law.'

Mr McAllindon smiled on all, first on the priest and then on
Mr Houston, on Nicholas, on the cramped space of his little
room. He opened his hands, munificent and with the promise
of future gifts.

'But of course, of course, man! Isn't that what we're here
for? Isn't it? To find that law!'

At Mrs Broe's they shared the best bedroom. Each night by
the light of a single candle placed on the floor they undressed
on opposite sides of the room and then got into the two narrow
beds. The priest blew out the candle and the last sight of him
that Nicholas had was of a crouching, female-like figure enveloped in a great tent of a nightshirt, blowing and wheezing
close to the candle-flame on the floor. The beds were damp
which brought out the smell of use and there was a half-hour of
turning and creaking before sleep during which Father Lannigan gave out a decade of the rosary, HAIL MARY and Nicholas
answered, HOLY MARY ...

It had been the most humiliating day of all before the lawyers.
They had finally come around to the subject of money, that
half-covered accusation against the priest that caused so much
enmity ... What was behind the bishop's accusations that
he'd neglected his duties and turned shopkeeper? ... How
much ... from previous actions ... lower courts? ... This
Defence Fund now, Mr Lannigan, who ...? Could ye give us
a rough idea, approximate terms, so to speak, of your emolu-
ments before and after the interdict and suspension? And what
was all this about other clerics, curates, bishops, cardinals and
even an ecclesiastic over in Rome (whose name had escaped
Mr McAllindon for the moment) making money for themselves out of their benefices? Don't you think it's a bit tactless,
Mr Lannigan, to be making that kind of attack just now? ...

'You'll go on home tomorrow, Nicholas, on your own and
I'll come on after,' the priest had said on the way back to Mrs
Broe's.

Lying in the clammy room Nicholas knew he was being sent away so as not to witness another day like today, the stuttering, incoherent, floundering inability to answer the lawyers. He is like some kind of animal, thought Nicholas, innocent and caught, running this way and that to get out of the pit.

'You could get the boys assembled for the night I get back. There should be a fair-sized gathering.' He did not look Nicholas in the eye. And then, later, 'I've had word,' whenever he used his own pronoun, as now, the priest seemed to draw height and weight from it, 'I've had word,' he said again, 'from the famous Scotsman Doctor MacIntosh. Have you ever heard tell of him? Oh a famous man. He's coming down all the way to Kyle just to see me. He's going out of his way just to see me. Someone'll want to be there to meet him. Get Mrs Rowen to make up a room for him if he's there before me . . .' And later still . . . 'He's very well thought of across the water. It'd be better to be in with him than out with him. He might put a bit in the papers. Every little bit counts. Sure anyways there's little more for you to be doing here, is there? . . .'

Now in the darkness of the bedroom Nicholas lay stretched out, listening to the breathing and sighing of the man beside him. The priest had hardly spoken since they had come into the house. Another of those deep silences that Nicholas was beginning to know so well. With each revelation of the man's weaknesses, each shabby prop of self-esteem, each heavy attempt to patch up that frontage of his, Nicholas' feelings for him became more anguished, more unendurable.

'Pray for me,' came the voice suddenly out of the darkness and Nicholas held in his breath, cringing beneath the blankets, when he heard it. 'I need your prayers, Nicholas,' came the anonymous, spiritless thing across the room. It was possible that he'd been waiting for it (not just now as he lay in bed but ever since he moved in to live with the priest in Kyle; his secretary, God bless the mark!) this appeal that fractured all the careful privacies between them, as priest and layman or boy, since that was how he treated him, as a boy, their furtive undressing in the room, their turns at the ewer and basin on the washstand, the chamber-pot under the bed. He wanted to leap up and say: Now what is it to be, priest! You're only a . . .

'Do you hear me, Nicholas?'

'Yes, Father.'

'Eeeeh,' exhaling, collapsing sound through his teeth, of re-assurance or relief or just weariness. "I'm gone down in your estimation, amn't I, Nicholas?"

'Oh no, Father. Not at all.' Crimson, thankful for the darkness, Nicholas tried to stuff the blanket between his teeth.

'Young people are heartless.' His voice seemed weary, past caring but then it took life. 'It's them two fancy connivers that have brought me down on me knees. The great Mr McAllindon! It's just as well there was no one around to see it. That's all I say! I'm a weak man, Nicholas. Oh, I know they'll tell you Lannigan is a bully. That he's well able to handle himself.' The voice rose momentarily. 'Sure they were saying only the other night beyond in Lord Desart's that I could rise an army if I put my will to it. Ah but sure ... What do they know? What, I ask you, do anyone of them know?'

In the pause Nicholas hoped it was over. Tomorrow they would get up and go on as before, the priest back on his faulty pedestal. Nicholas stretched himself surreptitiously and waited for the city clocks to strike.

'Nicholas ...'

'Aye, Father ...'

'I meant it now. About saying the odd prayer for me. I've never felt the need of the help of God Almighty more than I do this living minute. Oh, I know He and His Blessed Mother are beside me when I'm in there fighting for what I know is right. It's different though in the nights. In the dark. The devil is loose then and God help me his temptation against the Holy Spirit is something fearful ...' There was a long silence and when he spoke again it was the voice of a man trying to cope with a persisting memory. 'I have the most terrible dread betimes, Nicholas ... But sure isn't every mortal man...? We have to renew our faith each day with the rising sun. Wasn't it always so even with the pagans? I often think ...' and Father Lannigan allowed himself a grim laugh in the dark. 'Though 'twould hardly pay me now to preach it ... couldn't you see the faces of them? ... No, I often think though, I really do now, that all religions are one and the same when all is said and done. Down there somewhere, down deep in the act of human faith, deep in the simple human hope that somehow, something better is going to arrive tomorrow, with the new sun...'

'I've no faith!' Sudden, shocking, Nicholas heard his own yell in the dark. When it was out he trembled violently and lay waiting for the priest to leap up or something.

'Well, Nicholas,' came the words, wearily, 'it'll all look different in the light of day.'

'I've no faith. I've no faith at all. I don't believe in anything any more!' Nothing could stop him now. He babbled, like a crying child, eyes smarting. 'How can you...? How can...? Something so rotten, so...! That makes such wrong and suffering in the name of virtue! How? How can anyone believe in a God who rules the world like a Roman Province?' It was a phrase out of a book but what matter. 'Anyway I can't believe. That's all.'

He calmed a little. He sat up in bed. He supposed the priest would now say get out or something worse, there and then, night and all.

There was a prolonged silence in the room while the mattresses in both beds creaked and whispered. Then he heard Father Lannigan out of bed, rustling and searching in the dark, for his clothes perhaps. And Nicholas shivered. A spark and the small golden flame of the candle wavered and swelled against the rich blackness. Nicholas looked over and saw this new, unknown face looking at him. Whether it was a trick of the candle or what the priest's tousselled head had become strangely youthful, softly illumined like an old painting with the suggestion of a sad smile on the lips. Oh Christ, Nicholas cried, who is this man?

'Cover your chest against the draught, boy,' the old voice, however, rasped as before. Nicholas lay back, tense under the blankets, looking up into the dimness of the ceiling. 'Now, son, say it again to me. What you just said.'

'Ah, what does it matter any more.'

'What is it, Nicholas?'

'Nothing.'

'Nicholas, Nicholas ... Speak to me as favour to me, won't

116

you?' The questing face suspended above the white nightshirt. 'You don't have to say anything if you don't want to. We all know that ... I haven't talked ... it must be for months now. Do you know this is how they've taken away my ministry? And not by their suspensions and what have you. They've silenced me all right. Sure the priest that can't talk to the single soul isn't a priest at all ...'

So Nicholas did. Telling a story of a boy out there, setting out but never arriving. Someone other than himself, a rare, delicate person put upon by circumstances, unearned misfortune. As he went on, dressing the story, he hated himself, he hated the priest for provoking him to it. It was all a mockery, this storybook of Maynooth, prayers, spiritual advisers. It said nothing of the reality ...

'I remember well the day your father said you wanted to be a priest. Do you know what I said, Nicholas? Do you know what I said to him?'

'No.'

'I said, well, he'll either make a priest or break a priest.' The priest tried to laugh but it didn't rise. 'It's what my own father said of myself, God rest him. We're like one another so, Nicholas.'

'I'm not like you,' raged Nicholas. 'I'm not like you! Whatever your faults you're good, you're innocent. I refuse to be ... innocent.'

'The greatest temptation,' mused the priest in a low voice, 'to the man who has lost his faith is for him to believe that he's unique. That he's alone. That there was never anyone like him. This is an old trick of the devil. It makes for awful pride. And just as easily it makes for awful despair. Oh, I know, you see, Nicholas. I've been through it all myself. Not once but many a time.' He sighed. 'Why do you say you've no faith left, son?'

'I just know.'

'You haven't become one of these new rationalists by any chance?' There was mockery, the hint of laughter, in the question.

'I know that much if nothing else. Religion was never meant to be rational.'

'That's so. It never was. *Credo quia absurdum.* And you

know, God help them, that's the tragedy of the materialists. They've been fighting a claim that never existed. They've been attacking a Church that's never existed except in their own minds.'

'But the trouble is,' Nicholas rushed in excitedly, 'if you can't use reason in your beliefs you have to believe what's revealed to you. What's told you. Why should another man have to stand between me and my Maker?'

'You're very proud, Nicholas . . .'

'Isn't that how you've clerical dictatorship?'

'Well, I wouldn't go so far as . . .'

'But isn't it true, Father? Why can't they just say that to the people? That Christ's teaching isn't rational and was never meant to be. That if you want to believe you have to take the risk. Or do as we say. We know! We're appointed!'

'There are good and bad men in the Church, Nicholas, like everywhere else.' Father Lannigan's voice was cautious and sad.

'Father, how can you speak like that after all you've been through!'

The priest gave a single sharp cry and half turned away.

'I have pity,' he whispered in a moment, 'for the poor and the ignorant. Oh, it's easy for us to talk about authority. But who has the right to take away hope from the ordinary poor souls of the earth? Hah! It troubles me every time I stand up there in the Big Chapel at home. When I know I'm taking away another brick of their house with what I'm going to say.'

'What does it matter,' muttered Nicholas stubbornly, 'when it's the truth that's at stake?'

The priest lay back, tiredly, and the self-confidence that Nicholas had begun to feel began to seep away from him.

'Who'll worry about the truth, Nicholas, when the poor come marching out of the cities? It's happening today in many parts. It could happen here if we take away their hope, their faith.'

'So it's better to leave them with a false faith . . . ?'

'I didn't say that!' The priest paused and after a great effort he carefully chose his words. 'The Church is the guardian of the One, True Religion . . .'

'There's more to it than that now, Father.'

'Is there now?'

'I don't think the Church and religion are always the same thing.'

The priest laughed shortly. 'Maybe we've had enough for one night, Nicholas.'

But there was no attempt to put out the candle and Nicholas sat forward in his bed with a wild exhilaration. His head swam with sleep and a kind of hysteria. It was this easeful intimacy with the priest that stirred him most, not least the remarkable fact that it had been inspired by his own admission of apostasy. He believed, now, that Father Lannigan was a great man, a man of great virtue. Who else would have talked to him like this, with such compassion, such insight! He wanted to offer himself to Father Lannigan in some kind of pact that would seal his feeling for ever. In spite of whatever he had said he knew he was Father Lannigan's man for ever, his follower, his accomplice even ... 'I just have to understand, Father,' he blurted out, 'the harmony of matter and spirit in the scheme of God!' It was his offering, his part in an exchange to create a bridge between them ...

'Why did you say that about the Church?'

'About it not being the same as religion?'

'Aye.'

'But, Father, don't you say it yourself all the time?'

'Maybe I do.'

'But why is it?' Nicholas cried brightly. 'Why is it that something that claims to be from God has to end up so ...? Why can't it be pure?'

'Because we're men and not angels,' replied the priest heavily. 'Don't you know that God works through the materials of the earth. Is it miracles you want every day of your life! Messages sent down from Heaven! Arragh, boy, have a bit of sense.'

Nicholas was wounded by this tone and remained silent for a while.

'I can tell you, boy,' and Nicholas knew by the way he shifted himself that the priest was about to pour forth one of his speeches, 'I can tell you the Church was never at its best when it carried on about miracles and cures and the devil knows what else. I never believed in the same miracles meself and

119

that's a fact! Aren't the ways of God closer to the things we see about us every day in our lives? I never went in for all this carry-on with saints' bones and the like. Oh, we have our holy places, I won't deny that ... but Almighty God isn't running around interfering with nature to keep our spirits up. No. if we can't believe in God in the seed and the branch and the rotting leaves then we may give up ... Sure, isn't that what the Incarnation is all about? He didn't walk in outta the sea one day or step down offa a cloud. Not at all! He was born like the worst and best of us in the belly of a woman. There's your spirit and matter for you! The Word made Flesh!

'I remember,' he said then, much more quietly, 'my own father in the haggard below one day at home when a calf was dropped. He made the Sign of the Cross with a sup of the milk on the cow's back and then he walked around the four of us shivering childer and did the same on our foreheads. If any priest can do more at the communion rail itself I never learnt it in my theology books!

'What is it Saint Paul says?' he cried, need and loss in his voice. '*The first Man Adam was made a living soul. The last Adam was made a quickening spirit.* Without Christ, son, we're living in a world where everything is alien to the spirit inside in us. With Christ, the Spirit is poured into all things. Even our own rotting bodies are made incorruptible. Faith is simple, Nicholas. Faith is simple! That's why the faith of a poor ignorant man is equal to that of Thomas Aquinas. In a way, I suppose, the people without books are closer to creation ... It's easier for them to accept something like grace, f'rinstance, because they know so much is working, unseen, to good production at the butt of a tree ...'

The voice lulled Nicholas. As it went on he even dozed once or twice, waking with a start to catch a striking line about this God-in-nature. All this and the nervous candlelight with its scattering shadows made it more and more difficult for him to retain a grasp on the reality of what was going on ...

'And what's death so? What's death if the immortal is in the mortal?' He shouted loudly at one point without any apparent connexion with what the priest was then saying.

'Death,' said Father Lannigan, taking his question without a falter, 'death is the beginning of the resurrection.' And later on he came back to this again because Nicholas came out of sleep at one stage as if cold water had been poured on his head to hear the priest intoning, *'Behold I show a mystery; we shall not all sleep but we shall all be changed at the last trumpet . . . this corruptible shall have put on incorruption and this mortal shall have put on immortality . . .'*

It was a strange night. When he remembered it the next day he was sure that some of it could only have been dreamt. The priest out of bed, for example, prancing about in his nightshirt but then having dismissed this as a figment of his tiredness or unsimple feelings for the man, he remembered with unmistakable clarity Father Lannigan standing above his own bed but no longer ludicrous because now the nightshirt made him look like a painted christ.

Nicholas remembered saying something about political priests, men more devious than any courtiers, the new money-changers in the Temple. He could never have anticipated the priest's reply.

Instead of defending the Church against the charge the priest gloried in it. He took on a new liveliness with the topic.

'Is it politics ye're afraid of? Sure, who says politics is evil? Hah? Isn't it the one human art that's indispensable if people are to live together at all . . . Of course no one says otherwise. If the Church weren't a political organization it might as well close up its doors altogether on the world and stick to meditation! I won't go so far as Pius IX and his Syllabus of Errors and so on. But begod we'd be very simple-minded if we thought the Papacy wasn't like any other government just because it deals in prayers and not water pipes!'

Back and forth by the end of the bed walked this shrouded figure of invective and expostulation. At times he seemed to lose the thread of what he was saying and then he was plunged back into the law case and the town, excoriating the curates and the mob through his spittle until the final insult was wrung from him. But he recovered from these asides without lasting effect to pick up his speech again on why it was not only accurate but even good to consider the Church as political . . .

'I'm not saying this is good or bad. It just is, Nicholas, be-

cause God works through men and the institutions of men ...
Oh, you may say, as my good friend Lord Acton says, beyond,
how about power and so on and so forth. I'll say this much and
no more about that. We may settle our arses on the ditch.
Because as long as things last and men be as they are the
Church will be as she is. When Christ enters the human he
doesn't outwardly transform it or anything like that but only
inwardly. Like some class of yeast, maybe ... Anyway, where
was I? ... Did I hear you say something about the individual?
Hah?'

Nicholas, melted into the bedclothes, had said nothing,
could say nothing, but the priest bore down on him with his
frenetic stare.

'Well, boy, I'll say this much about the individual! If it's the
individual you want to hear about I'm your man! No one has
suffered as much as myself in the cause of ... But I won't go
into that now. We'll leave aside that for the moment! ... All
that has to be said,' and Father Lannigan sniffed with a great
air of authority, 'is that there are two kinds of judgement, the
private that is sophisticated and the public that is diluted, if you
get me. Watered down to take in as many different views as
possible. Every political act is a public act and is *ipso facto* impure and that's the answer to your question. Why is the Church
government impure? Hah? Because it's only a weak sign of the
life to come, even at the best of times ...'

And later, it seemed much later ...

'To get out and be part of it! That's all that counts, boy!
I've no time at all for the ninny-jinnies sitting at home on their
arses looking into the fire. Your salvation is in what you do, not
in what's done to you. If there's any message from the Passion
of Christ it's that it's better to live and die for whatever is
yours than half live and half die all your life out of fear ... And
that's what happened at the Council of Trent. The periodic renewal. Every couple of centuries or so. Oh, we're ripe for it
now in the Church. And may God forgive me if I blaspheme
but I think I'm a weak instrument of it myself. That's what
keeps me going. That I play a small part in making Christ new
in a few men again ... The new man has to cut off the growths
about his heart; he has to remake himself every day. So 'tis

with the Church, you see, because it's no less human than the men who staff it . . . The Counter Reformation and so on. The Great Councils. Wasn't Paul himself brought in just when there was most need for him? . . . The Road to Tarsus . . .'

But the last thing which Nicholas remembered of the night was different to all this. It was of the inflamed face of the priest thrust down at him out of the half-darkness of the room. 'Get the boys together, Nicholas, when you get home. Pass around the word, first thing, that I'm on me way back. Get every one of them out and we'll show these . . . we'll show them, we'll show them who's who.'

Nicholas closed out the face and the voice. He could go and organize his own rabble! All that fine talk and this at the end of it. Well, he wasn't going to . . . And in this way he finally sank down into sleep, determined to be better than this even if the world had nothing better to offer.

It was the day after the trial of the O'Connor boy who had thrown himself in front of Queen Victoria with a Fenian petition. Father Lannigan was making his way to the station on his way back to Kyle after the final session with the lawyers. He bought a news-sheet from a ragged person on the quays and put down the two handbags to read the print in the darkening light. 'They're going to bate the poor fellow, Father,' cried the news-boy as the priest picked up his bags to cross to Usher's Island.

It was true. Baron Cleasly in the Central Criminal Court had sentenced the youth to prison for a year, with hard labour. With the added punishment that he be given twenty strokes of the birch. At the other end of the bridge Father Lannigan had to negotiate a large, collapsed dray, atumble with vegetables, and a dead horse. The smell was offensive and a swarm of ruffians stood ready to pounce, a little distance off from where the driver and his helper stood guard over their property.

He finally managed to locate a cab from all this confusion and began the journey up the river towards Kingsbridge Station. The damp evening was settling over the city more securely than night itself. Father Lannigan recalled the petition of the boy when the incident with the Queen had taken place. Albert or Arthur or some such name, O'Connor. He couldn't remember the details. The Queen driving in the Park. The pistols which wouldn't fire. It might serve in the music-hall as an act. And yet, as he felt the horse slide on the wet cobbles in front of him, Father Lannigan was deeply touched by the fate of the boy. The bizarre defiance. The innocence ... It had even excised the weight of doubt in his mind about his own case and the raw memory of the lawyers' treatment of him. This had reached a climax this afternoon when Mr McAllindon in anger had called him an equivocator.

Outside the cab on the oily surface of the river seagulls in great numbers were scavenging on the water, fighting one another in a fierce, natural act of survival. Father Lannigan watched the birds, dully, considering that nature never failed to provide a model of human society and its refuse on the water-top. He was deeply depressed. He had spoken at great length the night before to the boy but now he couldn't remember any of it. His memory was failing. That was it. His memory was failing on top of all the rest.

It was frustrating to be going back with such little promise of success. He didn't really regret the choice of lawyers, though, indeed, they could be a more pleasant pair of buckos. No, in this he had been well advised. It was the Law itself that left him disillusioned or perhaps not the Law but the process of the Law. Father Lannigan was too tired to decide which. 'The Law,' Mr McAllindon had said at one point, that very day, and he recalled the remark now with a new anxiety, 'the Law, Mr Lannigan, is not concerned with motives but with actions.'

He wondered if Nicholas had got Martin Donovan's wagon for the march through the town that night. He could hardly walk. The crowds would be huge and the feelings high among the people. When the boy had left the previous day he had been in a kind of temper. He might not attend to his instructions.

The Law is concerned with actions, not motives. Somewhere there, Father Lannigan felt with near despair, behind that axiom rested his own cause, beyond the reaches of human judgement, too deeply submerged in the motions of a particular, individual spirit for the public courts of this world to do it justice. Still he brightened up a little when he thought of the big crowds that'd be waiting for him at home when he reached the town. By the time he had arrived at the station he had already thought out the first words of his speech to the people. 'My loyal friends,' he would say, 'the Law is on our side . . .'

7 . Summer 1872, Continued

'What does he want us for?' Marcus asked grumpily when they were out on the road again with the river behind them.

'He didn't condescend to tell me. Do you think he'd tell me what was on his mind?' Nicholas walked on ahead quickly, not looking around.

'Marcus!' cried Emerine, 'I can't walk so quick!'

'Is it about us, so?' shouted Marcus, waiting to hold her arm.

'How do I know?' Nicholas threw the words back over his shoulder. He couldn't bear to see them, together.

He could hear her say, 'You mustn't tell, Marcus,' and his brother's grumbling answer, and turning about on the road he called, 'What's the big secret?' trying to smile but feeling a twitch over his face.

She took a deep breath and ran up to him. Her shoes were in a scarf that was knotted to the red cord about the waist of her dress and he had this sudden impression of a dance, her brown bare feet in the dust. She caught his arms and her warmth enveloped him. 'We're going to run away to be married, Nicholas. Aren't we, Marcus? Promise you won't tell anyone, Nicholas!'

'You've gone and said it yourself now,' complained Marcus, deeply unhappy at the whole business.

'Oh hush! You'll promise, won't you, Nicholas?'

'I – promise.'

'There you are!' To Marcus. And she held Nicholas with one hand reaching for Marcus with the other. 'Nicholas has promised, Marcus. Everything will be grand!' The chain of her hands joined them . . .

The Master stood in the front room and drew some considerable support for what he was going to say from the sight of all his family gathered about him. He liked the ceremony of all the family together and slightly less so the kind of occasions which made this possible – his monthly budgeting, arrivals and departures of importance or, as now, a particular announcement of his own which merited the attention of everyone in the house. Henrietta, who alone knew what was to be said, sat white-faced in the corner.

The Master began. He thought it advisable in view of the inflamed nature of the matter to hand and the unsettled relationship at present between him and his two older boys, to begin circumspectly by way of reference to Duty. How Duty was sometimes divided or apparently so and then it was a question of a man's moral resources to seize upon the right course. Sometimes, indeed, the world at large was incapable of perceiving the motives, the quality of a decision made by a man within the counsels of his own heart. Sometimes a man might even lose those nearest to him but he hoped and prayed . . .

Then he remarked how they were all now, except little Florrie (and here all looked in the direction of the glum little boy who was propped between the knees of Henrietta) adults. With adult responsibilities. And here the Master looked sternly at Marcus and the blushing girl. In fact it could be said that soon the family would be separated as each one made his own way in the world. The Master leaned over at this point and put his hand on Henrietta's shoulder but she was quite unmoved or rather she was not moved any more than she had been at the outset when she was already clearly but silently upset.

Eventually he came to the priest.

What had happened was this. Four months or so before, the Commissioners of National Education received a letter from District Inspector No 50, one Jude Hassey. Mr Hassey and Master Scully were friends ('colloguers', the priest called them) and when Mr Hassey came on inspections they had many whispered conversations in the corner of the classroom. The question was this: who prompted Mr Hassey to write the letter to the Commissioners informing them of Father Lannigan's suspension and replacement by a priest in the Friary? No one doubted that the directive had come in some fashion from Bishop's Palace and to there from His Eminence in Dublin. But Mr Hassey was a determined Protestant. So the priest had spent many hours of his time trying to decide if Master Scully, too, had turned to betray him, a go-between, a carrier of messages behind his back.

The truth was that Mr Hassey acted on his own initiative in a sudden realization of his function. On his next visit, to see that the Commissioners' dismissal of Father Lannigan had proceeded accordingly, the priest had him physically thrown out of the schools and his spectacles were broken and his lip split. (... *insolent transference from my management to that of the nominee of the pretender to my parish, and I hereby give you notice that if anyone representing you or acting as an officer of your Board shall be found in this school at any time after this date, he shall be summarily ejected from the room exactly as your 'impartial and efficient' inspector was treated on his last visit. Trespassers beware!*)

Henrietta tended Mr Hassey's wound and repaired the bridge of his spectacles with thread; ('the man is a lunatic, Mrs Scully. An absolute, a raving lunatic. I've never been so ... in all my life!') which did little to abate the priest's temper.

Father Lannigan continued to occupy the schools, more and more resembling a surrounded outpost in enemy territory. Master Scully and his two assistants, Miss Mary Ann Joyce (Category: First Division, First Class) and another lady, were paid by subscription of the loyal parents. A Parliamentary Sub-Committee was formed of members of the Defence Fund to pursue the action of the Education Board at Westminster. (– *No attention having being paid to my last several letters ... The petty spite of a clique at your Board at my having exposed before the public their mean subserviency to ecclesiastical dictation, will soon again be exhibited before the Imperial Parliament and the shameful way in which some men, who, neither born great nor achieving greatness, have had greatness thrust upon them, can misapply the money of the public, will become a subject of inquiry within the walls of the House.*) Later this year Mr Bouverie intervened on the Irish Education Vote in the Committee of Supply in the Commons with a censure against the Irish Commissioners imputing that as a lay tribunal they had acted wrongly, combining with the Roman Catholic Hierarchy to punish one of its ministers, that a State body like this should surely be outside the internal disputes of a private society such as the Roman Catholic Church. It was largely due to Mr Gladstone's intercession that this vote of censure was defeated, fifty-seven votes to forty-nine. The Prime Minister appealed to the House not to censure a Board which had conferred such services on Ireland for a first error in judgement.

But meanwhile the priest and his supporters continued to occupy the schools, united it seemed, at least until that day in June when Master Scully assembled his family together. What he had to say to them was that, after careful consideration, he had resigned his headship of Father Lannigan's schools ...

'Where are you going to, Marcus?'

'I'm going up to the schools.'

'Now?'

'Aye. This minute.'

'He won't be there, you know. At this hour Father Lannigan'll be left by now.'

'He'll be there all right. Didn't Dada say he was?'

'I'll come with you. Do you mind if I come up with you?' Nicholas hadn't seen the priest since their visit together to Dublin.

'Do if you want to.'

So they walked up the hill of High Street together. There was little to say. When the Master had finished talking to the family ('I told him of course that he had my moral support. But I couldn't stay on in the schools with the way things were. It's a big step, mind you, for all of us. It won't be easy to make ends meet. We'll all have to put our shoulder to the wheel, now ...') no one had spoken either.

The sun was going down over the river. People in the street were even shouting pleasantly to one another about the rise in the weather. All day wagon-loads of fresh hay had been going through the town giving the place a smell like newly-baked bread.

'If he'd only have the gumption,' Marcus blurted out suddenly, 'to – well – go one way or the other! But no – oh no!'

'He's afraid,' said Nicholas.

'I'm afraid. Aren't you afraid? Isn't everyone afraid?' cried his brother blearily. 'What has that to do with it?'

'Maybe he has more to be afraid of.'

'No one has more than anyone else in this town to be afraid of. We're all in it. It's only some do what they should do and some don't.'

'I don't think everyone can or has to act to be, I mean to be whole,' said Nicholas in confusion. 'What I mean is I don't understand, morally, what's the difference between people who do and people who don't,' he ended, his words in the air, un-attached.

'You don't know what you're talking about, boy.'

'Maybe I don't.'

Two town girls that the brothers knew came down by the shops and one of them asked Marcus if Nina was in or out. He didn't answer, didn't even seem to hear and the girls stopped to stare. Nicholas said nothing.

'What happened in Dublin with yourself and Father Lanni-gan?'

'Why?'

'I thought you were out with him now.' Nicholas didn't answer. 'I thought you weren't going to have anything more to do with him. Sure you don't go up to the Priest's House any more?'

'No. No, I don't.'

'Well, boy, I can tell you, I'm for him,' Marcus glowered at the pathway in front of them. They were both thinking of their father back in the house and of how his admission of with-drawal had sent them both off like this, the very opposite to what he could have intended, to the priest. They were both conscious of how so many of the Master's gestures towards authority ended like this. 'I couldn't stay in that house for another minute,' Marcus went on gloomily after a pause. 'It'll soon be all over and we'll be well out of it!' Nicholas knew this was half-guilt because he hadn't stayed behind with her, with Nina.

'It was probably my own fault. I mean the disagreement with Father Lannigan.'

'You're still for him so?'

'Oh, I'm still for him.' He wanted to be agreeable to Marcus. He could see the heavy pain in his face. He felt he knew what caused it. When the Master had finished his piece and no one said anything he had, finally, spoken again in a voice full of self-pity, 'That's all then. You can go out so.' And when they had all moved to follow Henrietta out, the father had called to the girl, 'I want a word with you, Nina. On your own.' Emerine had looked at Marcus but he hadn't offered to remain behind and it was in this way that Nicholas had followed him out and up the street leaving the girl grim-faced and angry behind, alone with the old man in the front room.

If he said anything about Marcus she wasn't going to answer back. The best thing to do was to say nothing at all. Having smoothed herself down she sat perfectly still, feet tucked in and hands neatly folded on her lap giving him what she called her lady-look, eyes wide and attentive and head periodically nodding.

The Master droned on. It was almost his speech before all over again but now he turned to the family, how much joy she had brought over the years to all of them, to Henrietta, to himself. She wouldn't remember it now, he was sure, but when she first came to them she didn't want to stay at all! Screamed her head off for days! The Master smiled and Emerine smiled back, warily. She sighed, deeply. Whatever it was he had to say it wasn't this and she wished he'd get to it quick and get over it.

'Do you ever go to visit them at all now, in the home, Nina?' he asked suddenly.

'I go in to see Sister Paul. Often. I was in only last month.' The colour went in her face and a hand jerked nervously across her breast.

'I'm sure you do. Oh, I'm sure you do, now.'

There was a long pause while he sat there, bent, in the corner behind the desk. She had no pity left for him, indeed no feelings of any kind. No one ever brought up the subject of the orphanage to her unless it was to offer her a hurt or a threat. She knew that from long experience. Some of them would pretend to want to know what it was like. More of them would pretend to be sorry for her. But it always came down to the same thing. They only wanted to show how different they were, how better-off they were or that.

But the Master had moved on to talk about the house. She looked with him and they both looked around the room while he spoke of how with the summer now he'd have time to put a bit of wash on the walls and a spot of stain here and there. They might even go into Kilkenny one of these days and get a stretch of material for the chairs . . .

What really amused her was that the Master never did anything like that around the house only giving orders and advice and tripping over buckets and everything while Henrietta and herself moved furniture and stood on chairs taking down cobwebs or painting the walls. As far as she could see he just foosthered around the place when there was anything to be done. Only for Marcus they might as well be alone in the house, herself and Henrietta!

When he said: 'We're a family of martyrs, don't you know, Nina. Everyone of us wants to suffer for something,' it was only to put her apart. When he said: 'I often wonder what'll become of us at all,' it was to leave her out, to say that she was free, she wasn't under the same danger as the rest of them, all the real Scullys.

'You don't give me credit, Nina, for very much, do you?' His look out from under the busy eyebrows was kindly.

She blushed.

'I don't mean, now,' he followed hurriedly, 'that I took you out or anything like that.'

'I was glad of the home, Master,' she said coldly.

'Asha, girl, don't say such a thing!' He looked off, out the window but to something beyond the street, beyond the town and Emerine began to weep, loudly at first but then in quiet gasps. He never even looked towards her. When she dried her eyes after what seemed like ages he was still frozen to the same stare out the window. 'I suppose,' he said at last, clearing his throat, 'it's time I told you about your mother and father . . .'

She was ashamed of herself for having wept.

'I don't want to hear of it,' she tried to make the words as bitter as she could.

'Well, they were both from a long way from here, Nina, and as far as I know they're long dead and buried now.'

'I still don't want to hear of it!'

'Not even if I have to tell you for my own peace of mind?'

'Not even.'

'Aren't you the hard person, Nina, on your own self!'

She felt empty of everything except the passion to come out of this without giving herself away. But no matter what front she showed he was determined to go on with whatever it was he had to say. 'Your mother,' he said and stopped with the weariness of the years passed rushing back in upon him, 'I suppose,' he continued again after the pause, 'she was what they call a woman of the roads.'

Emerine was so shocked that she half stood up but he motioned her back with a gesture. 'And your father was someone I loved very much, Nina, very much. These things change with the years ...' he seemed at a loss for words or unable to recall exactly what he had to say. 'I won't deny, Nina, that I – well, didn't approve of your arrival when you came into the world. I won't deny that.'

'Why did you take me out so? Why didn't you leave me where I was?' She was fiercely angry at a kind of bumbling in him which persisted in making the bad worse with every action of him. 'If that's what you thought of me. And of my – my mother.'

'Ah but sure I loved your mother most of all, Nina,' said the Master simply as if this explained all and she couldn't speak knowing that this time she was truly outside, outside the lives of these people who lived a long time ago. He talked of them so familiarly but it was all so far back that they might have been in a far-away country as far as it concerned her.

'If they're dead and buried,' she remarked coolly, 'what matter so!'

'Don't be so hard on yourself, girsha.'

'I never want to be owing anything to anyone—'

'But sure Nina, aren't you one of ourselves? Don't we love you like one of our own?'

'Deed I'm not!' She stopped short, biting her lip, afraid that she'd angered him but he only looked at her with a sorrowing watery look in his eyes, and she held the gaze without flinching.

'I think, girl, it'd be a good idea for you to go away for a while, altogether and maybe come back in a year or so.'

What was he saying? What was he saying?

'What do you mean, Master?'

'I think it'd be good for you to leave the house.'

'Where would I go, Master?'

'I was talking to them inside in the Laundry in Kilkenny – 'Twould only be for a short while, of course.'

'And what could I do?' she asked, tearfully.

'They give good keep.'

'But, sure, Henrietta—'

'Oh, I talked to Henrietta. She thinks it'd be good for a while, too.'

Nothing had prepared her for this. She half stood up with one hand out as if she had lost her sense of direction.

'Where are you going, Nina?'

'I'm going out to Marcus.'

'You're going no such where, miss! Not until I say you can.'

She sat down again, tightly clasping her hands together because they were shaking.

'If you have to be saucy don't be so in this house.'

'I'm sorry, Master,' she said woodenly.

'I won't abide it! I won't abide it!'

The thing to do, she was sure, was to recover herself and get out of that room, out of that house, as soon as she could.

'But sure, it's only all for the best, Nina. You know that. The way things are here. After a start things'll have settled down again and you can come back ... It's not as if 'twas for ever, now, is it?'

'Do you mind if I go out now, Master?'

'I wouldn't want you to go up near the schools now, girl, if that's where the others are gone.'

'I want to talk to Marcus.'

'And what is it you want to see him for?'

'To tell him.'

'Now, you're beginning to annoy me again, girl! I won't have it! I've had enough annoyance for one day!'

She took a deep breath. 'I want to see Marcus. That's all.'

'Marcus isn't going to change things. I can tell you that now. What's to be done is to be done.'

'Why?'

'Why, because he's my son, that's why! He'll do what he's told a while longer yet.' She smiled secretly aside at this and much of her confidence began to come back. Indeed she'd have turned on her heel and left, there and then, but for all that'd been said she still didn't want to hurt him more . . .

'They say children take after their parents.' His voice was sluggish as if it was making its way against a great, littered current. 'But the truth is stronger by far than that. Children imitate their own, they go down the self-same tracks, and seldom turn off. They make the same mistakes, over and over again . . . So the older you get the more you think you're seeing things appearing again out of the past as the children grow up around you . . . things you had almost forgotten, things best forgotten, oftentimes . . .' She didn't know who he was talking about for a moment and didn't even have much interest in his rambling, weary words until she realized he was talking particularly about herself. 'I won't have you do to my son what your mother did to your father.' It was the last crushing thing for him to say. But he had hardly said it and she received it than it became a compliment, even while the first sting of its insult still hurt. She didn't think of what he was saying about her mother, didn't want to think about that. She only thought: *I matter! They now know I'm no longer a child.*

'Can I go out now, Master?' She asked with exact politeness, even opening the door a little behind her back.

He said nothing and she started out. Then he called and she looked back. He was sitting over in his corner with dust rising like faint smoke around him in the last light of the day. No matter how often she and Henrietta cleaned that room there was always dust there.

'Nina,' he called. He looked so old, he looked so old there, sitting behind his desk, with the great thatch of white hair down over his eyes. 'Don't,' he said, 'please don't think I meant anything disrespectful. Of the dead.' His voice caught on the knot of the words. 'I loved them – both.' He shook his head from side to side. 'Sometimes, in those days it used to be the custom . . .' Whatever he wanted to remember wouldn't remain, the brief life of memory running down rapidly into silence. 'Your father was my own brother, Nina,' he whispered at length.

The words thrilled her. They tempted her to do something daring, something shocking. But she said nothing. She went out and closed the door quickly behind her before she would betray herself.

Opposite the school house they were lounging against a wall or gathered up into hissing, malevolent knots maybe ten or fifteen, men and women and young boys, they didn't have time to count because as soon as they appeared on the scene the two brothers were threatened. They ran the last twenty yards to the school-house door and when Nicholas put up a hand to pound on it a rock crashed against the wood beside his head. Doubled-up and shaking with terror he looked to his brother. But Marcus was upright, yelling back defiance at the mob and even bending to lift a stone.

'Leave them be, you – you fool,' he gasped, 'you'll only make them worse!' And then with both fists pounding, 'Open up! Open up! Please! Father Lannigan—'

'G'wan ya hoors, back to the Commonses!' roared Marcus.

'Come over here, you little fairy-man and I'll give you yer—' One of the women with her shawls flying had stepped out towards the centre of the road and all the others cheered.

'Go home and put yer drawers on ya!' jeered Marcus.

'Bejasus if I get me hands on you, young wan, I'll give you yer drawers! Ya little shit-face.'

'Go home outta that y'ould sow!'

At this point to the immense relief of Nicholas the door was opened and they were both pulled, roughly, inside. He could hardly stand up with fright. Two big men, both of them strangers, were guarding the door. One of them carried a crowbar as lightly as a sally-plant. These were some of Lannigan's Bullies, as they were called by the people, kinsmen and followers of his from townlands like Knocksolon and Carrig. They didn't look twice at the brothers but rolled themselves like great lumps of timber back up against the door.

Inside in the Female Infants something odd was happening. Seated in the big teacher's chair was Father Lannigan and round about him, like attendants, were several gentlemen, standing, Mr Proctor, Martin Donovan and Mr Dubby who owned the Medical Hall and others. In a corner at a table laden with account books and small piles of money were the two sisters, the Misses Johnstone from Hibbel Hall, long, snow-white creatures with identical large staring eyes under identical mops of curly matted black hair and heavy fruity lower lips that gave their faces a perpetually bruised and tender look. Miss Mary Ann Joyce, the Master's Assistant when he was headmaster, was rooting and rummaging noisily in a cupboard, only her skirts visible.

Father Lannigan sat collapsed in the chair. His face was drawn and instead of the collar he had an old woollen scarf wrapped about his throat. Mr Proctor was saying, in his high voice, 'I simply can't agree, sir. I cannot agree!' when the Scully boys entered the room.

At once Father Lannigan fixed Nicholas with his deep, feverish stare and shouted, pointing, 'He'll take it on! He'll take it on!'

Everyone paused to turn on Nicholas who stood quaking in the doorway.

'Really, Mr Lannigan, it would be quite impossible,' Mr Proctor pettishly tapped one of the schools desks with the cane in his hand.

'No!' roared the priest. 'You'll take it on, won't you, boy?' he appealed to Nicholas who didn't know what to say.

Just then Miss Joyce backed out of her cupboard, her moon-face all flushed, her arms laden with rulers, writing tablets, coloured cards and a variety of other teaching objects.

'Father Lannigan,' she twittered, 'far be it from me to complain but there are twelve good pencils missing from the press. Now, I'm not a body to go about accusing others in the wrong . . .'

'Just a moment, Miss Joyce,' Father Lannigan held her off with an outstretched arm.

'Mr Lannigan!' said Mr Proctor, the effort at patience

clearly marked in his voice, on his face. 'We had best consider the schools closed. Permanently. We will move the records of the Committee to Hibbel Hall. I shall make myself responsible for whatever valuables . . .'

'He's right, Father,' breathed Martin Donovan. 'I'll bring up one of the carts, after.'

Several people started to shout at once. The priest kept appealing across the stormy room to Nicholas who now understood perfectly what it was that was required of him: that he take his father's place.

'But there are no pupils any more,' Mr Proctor, exasperated, waved his stick over the empty desks, 'even if one should . . .'

'That's not the point!' roared the priest. 'It's the principle of the thing.'

Above the hubbub Nicholas thought he heard an increase in the shouting out on the street. Marcus had gone forward to talk to Martin Donovan and they had drawn into a corner together. Meanwhile the Misses Johnstone continued to look about them, dreamily, their long arms shaped like swans' necks, delicately supporting their chins.

'Father Lannigan! Father Lannigan!' cried Miss Joyce and perhaps because this was her room and she had some special control over it, the others relented. 'Do you mind, Father Lannigan,' she smiled a baby smile, 'may I say a word? Thank you, thank you! I don't want *anyone* to think me *troublesome*. Has anyone ever accused me of—? I don't think so! I really don't think so! But what's a body to do when one's back is turned and in an instant, in a flash someone has – has purloined your belongings!'

'Miss Joyce,' said Father Lannigan, 'you're dismissed!'

'Dismissed!' smiled Miss Joyce. 'Dismissed! How ridiculous!' Her fingers touched her cheek as if she were confirming that, yes, this was really she.

'There isn't any school any more,' answered Mr Proctor, but to the ceiling, his eyes uplifted, it being no longer possible to converse with those around him.

'Yes, dismissed,' repeated the priest, sourly, 'sacked!'

'Whatever can this mean?' Miss Joyce, still smiling but less fixedly, was appealing to the company. 'Dismissed! Nonsense! This is amusing. I must say this is very amusing indeed—'

'Amusing or no,' growled the priest, 'you're out. Take your – and go!'

In the pause everyone waited for it to end, all to some degree embarrassed by the priest's action. No one could think of anything to say, Mr Proctor standing in the centre of the floor clicking his tongue and tapping his boot with his stick.

Miss Joyce still retained her benevolent smile but two tiny points of scarlet had appeared high on her cheeks. 'Very well, then. I won't dawdle. Never fear. Please continue with your negotiations, gentlemen. Don't let my little efforts to get one or two— Don't let an old lady stop you – I'm very well, thank you very much—' But she scarcely moved from where she stood looking towards each of them in turn. 'Thank you, I'm perfectly well,' she said once more although no one had addressed her.

She appeared to be the only one not to hear the priest's growling command to the room at large, 'Will you get her to hell out of here!' But Nicholas, who knew Miss Joyce of old, saw the coldness behind the glazed smile.

'Is this,' she cried with one finger up as if she were teaching her elocution class, 'the reward of twenty years of full and faithful service?'

'Miss Joyce, Miss Joyce,' Father Lannigan, with a great effort, swivelled about to face her. 'You're aware, are you not, that Paschal Time has ended and that according to the General Council of Lateran a parish priest has to ensure that each of the faithful must communicate at least once, at least once, Miss Joyce in his or her parish church. You know this, Miss Joyce. You know it as well as myself. But when, Miss Joyce, when have you been to the communion rail of the Big Chapel in this time? When did you make your Easter Duty, may I ask? Or may I ask where did you make it, Miss Joyce?'

Miss Joyce had received all of this with what could only be called a girlish simpering. 'I am asked if I have performed my Easter Duty!' she informed the wall beside her, incredulous. As the priest turned towards her she had turned her back on him.

'And the answer is No!' roared Father Lannigan.

'And the answer is Yes!' rejoined Miss Joyce in a tinkling voice that was almost happy.

'Really, Lannigan!' Mr Proctor moved rapidly in front of the priest. 'I mean the situation is surely bad enough!' And he took himself off again to lean morosely against the wall at the end of the room. As if to confirm what he had said a violent crash of falling glass came from the far end of the building and women screamed in an adjacent room.

'Where?' roared the priest again. But everyone else had moved out of their situations and then stopped again, shocked, as people do who would like to leave but cannot. Nicholas sat down and held his head with his hands.

'Why,' he heard poor Miss Joyce, flustered, 'a body doesn't know what to do. One says one thing and one another and one doesn't know whom to acknowledge—' There was the sound of a door banging and she appeared to have gone out.

'Another betrayal!' He heard Father Lannigan in what sounded like triumph and the others all began to chatter among themselves. Either he is mad, thought Nicholas, or else (and this possibility presented itself with a rush like blood to the head) they were all locked in events which made the normal appear mad.

When, later, he raised his head he saw Emerine. She was just inside the door talking concernedly to Marcus. His first thought was of how she could have made her way through the mob outside. He got up unsteadily and made his way towards them as towards relief. But when he drew near it was clear that they were having an intimate talk so he stood off. He felt a need to protect their privacy, even and perhaps especially, from himself.

'If you don't, Marcus, I'm going to—'

'How can I, Nina? How can I? Now of all times!'

'All right so! If that's how you want it, so!' And she left, going as quickly as she had appeared, a wan face drifting out without a flicker of interest towards anything.

Before he could take this in he was swept back into the confusion of the school-room. It had been decided that the Misses Johnstone would depart, escorted by Mr Proctor since it was getting dark outside, bearing all the vital records in the school-house to Hibbel Hall. The two girls were at the centre of all this noise like animated paper decorations. But Father Lannigan continued to sit apart in a kind of stupor, gripping the side of his chair with clamped hands.

'She's going to leave us,' Marcus told him out of the corner of his mouth as he passed.

'Is it Nina?' he asked stupidly but Marcus had gone off to help with something.

It was at about this time, in the midst of all the din that Miss Joyce thrust her head out from the inner room and cried loudly, 'Am I not vouchsafed for in my testimonials?' Only Nicholas seemed to hear her and she withdrew herself rapidly with a look of immense surprise on her face. There was a chatter of female voices surrounding her so that, at least, she wasn't alone.

Meanwhile the Misses Johnstone had been cheerfully laden down with boxes, record books, canvas pouches of coin and a large wall-chart. ('Can I help, Pru?' 'No, I'm just— Isn't it absolutely?' 'Got to keep your skirts free!' 'Absolutely! You do look a sight, Cilla!') Mr Proctor pointed out things to be taken, things to be left, and at last they set out.

Nicholas watched from one of the windows. The warm dusk was shortening and it was already night beyond the town. They crossed towards Coal Lane where the carriages were waiting, Mr Proctor walking ahead and the girls behind rippling with giggles and small bird-cries. Like a single, cowed person the sullen mob of now about thirty or forty people, stood and watched. There were constables and militia on the street near the barracks and Nicholas thought he saw firearms.

'They'll take it from them. They'd take a lick of the boot from the Ascendency and be thankful for it.' The contemptuous voice at his elbow. Father Lannigan looked at the scene outside, his lip turning. With the old woollen scarf about his throat he looked less like a priest than ever. 'What's wrong with your brother?'

'What's wrong with him?'

'He's in there moping around like a goose.'

Nicholas didn't answer that.

'What do we do now, Father?'

'We gather up our things and get to hell out of here. Will you lookit that collection of misfortunates out there and tell me what's the use in anything any more?' Nicholas looked and wondered unhappily if he shouldn't go out and find Emerine. She might have ... 'When you see a gather of asses like that you begin to wonder, oh, you begin to wonder right enough. What is it, in the name of God Almighty that corrupts a crowd? I ask you!' He appeared to be searching the faces outside for someone. 'They began off ... I suppose ... maybe some of them anyway ... with the desire for right. Ah, but who knows? Isn't it the queer nature that we have! We have to live together because it's our nature and it's in living together that the worst comes out in us! Every animal in the universe makes a better fist of it.' He paused and exhaled deeply. 'Is that auld Jude Hennessy abroad there? God save us but wouldn't you think he'd be at home in bed where he belongs readying himself for his funeral! Aye,' he spat, 'if you stir any pot enough you're bound to bring up the bottom of it!' He grinned at Nicholas but Nicholas shrank from him. He was beginning to dread the rough manner of the priest; it was a kind of stigma that was belittling the cause they were fighting for.

'I had to sack her.' Father Lannigan spoke through pursed lips. 'She was adin there in the Friary behind my back, like the rest of them and playing kiss my arse and kiss my elbow to my face! I won't stand for it! I may have little left but what I have I'll hold! And them that stand with me will do so, boy, without half-measure or I'll do without them. I'm telling you that, now, boy!'

In horror Nicholas heard the voice rise, the familiar growing hysteria. He saw the priest grip the window-sill with such force that the frame might have come away. It suddenly occurred to him that somewhere along the line the priest had outpaced him, that he, Nicholas, had been left behind in the last headlong involvement, that he had failed the man if he had ever intended to follow him to the end because he couldn't rise to this kind of passion. He had begun to find the mad dash of words distasteful, pathetic, sad. Nicholas didn't want to think any more about it. He didn't want to unknot the few remaining ties with the priest; he dreaded there would be nothing left to replace them with.

'I'd better find Marcus,' he murmured at the window.

'We'll tidy up here, Nicholas, put a good bolt on the door and tomorrow we'll—'

'Yes, Father.'

The others were waiting. Miss Joyce had the help of two neighbouring women but instead of leaving at once she was apparently telling the two women of highlights of her career in the school. 'Not one red mark in my record book,' she was saying when the priest and Nicholas entered and at once she beamed and nodded in their direction. 'Mr Hassey always said, "Now for the prize-work, Miss Joyce, now for the prize-work!"'

'Don't you think we ought to go home?' Nicholas whispered to Marcus.

'We will when the priest says so,' his brother muttered.

'Young Lord Clifden,' Miss Joyce sang out from a corner, 'detached the balloon and behold! It flew up, up, up!' Her voice followed the balloon of the story rising higher and higher and she gave the same girlish tipple of laughter again. She was apparently describing that great day when Lady Clifden and young Lord Clifden had come to the school and had been treated to a demonstration of the Maynooth galvanic battery, the Leyden jar and the properties of hydrogen in a gold-beater's skin, by the Master and Father Lannigan. Miss Joyce, trembling with excitement, had held the various instruments.

This was finally too much for Father Lannigan. He was re-minded, perhaps, of the school's glorious days but at any rate he shouted crossly, 'That will be enough, Miss Joyce. You may now leave, if you will.'

'But, of course, Father Lannigan,' she cried over-agreeably, 'do excuse me!'

They all left about this time and Father Lannigan's two guardsmen put a heavy chain and padlock on the front door. To everyone's surprise the crowd had almost dispersed and those with the priest walked unmolested, apart from a few hoots, to the Presbytery.

It was on the 10th June that they dispossessed him of the

town schools and established the bishop's man in his place, a new curate called Foley, who without much enthusiasm, led a gang of men to the schools that night where the chain and padlock were removed and the buildings occupied.

8 . *Confirmation Sunday*

On the second Sunday in June when the town waited for the bishop to arrive to confirm the children in the Friary Nicholas got away and walked across to Whytescourt House. He was answering an invitation of Mr Butler to come and be interviewed so that he might be placed in a position somewhere ('I have a pending arrangement,' the letter had promised darkly) but the invitation was weeks old by now and the truth was that he wanted to be anywhere but in the town on that Sunday morning.

The priest had been put out of the schools on the Friday. All day Saturday he had sent his messengers through the countryside gathering support for a massive demonstration of hostility against the bishop on the Sunday. It had become too much. Nicholas felt he could no longer distinguish between the sides since each had given itself over to violence. He had slipped away from the priest's house, where he had been sleeping, when the morning's confusion was at its height. He couldn't go home. Since the departure of Emerine the place was a hive of unexpressed sorrow. So he went instead to Whytescourt.

They told him that Mr Butler was in the Blenheim Gardens and there he found him. A seated, diminutive figure away down in the middle of the descending tables of immaculate gardening. Gravel walks and glittering fountains. High box hedges. Carved, insolent fauns, more sinister with the stain of greenery all over their horned heads. Fat stone cupids wallowing in the green clotted pools. It was the showplace of the estate and Nicholas stood a moment on the heights receiving this human mastery of shade and growth; in the cool misted sunshine the whole place breathed out the spirit of the land's variety but under governance. There was someone, maybe a gardener, raking or spading at the far end and in this stillness he might have been deliberately put there, a delegate of years of endeavour, years of control, years of discipline.

'Come here!' Mr Butler's shrill voice came out of the distance and Nicholas ran quickly down the path to where he sat bending forward over a cluster of burnished purple flowers. He was wearing an old linen hat that was far too large for his small head; indeed his whole body seemed dwarfed by his clothes but this might have been because he also wore a wide, baize apron and huge gauntlets. Nicholas wondered if he even knew who he was.

'Look!' Mr Butler pointed at the flowers and Nicholas looked but could see nothing out of the ordinary. It was possible that he thought him a member of the household of Whytescourt. He framed a sentence: I am Nicholas Scully, sir, come to be seen . . .

'Heliotaxis,' said the gentleman, at last, crouched down. Then he looked up rapidly, suspiciously, the little dancing eyes behind the pince-nez. 'Do you know what that means?' Nicholas shook his head. 'No? Well, I won't tell you! Here! Sit down here, young man. Now! I've two questions to ask of you and the first is – don't answer until I've arranged myself properly – there, now! What is it that you want out of life? Eh?'

Nicholas felt like laughing at first but the gravity of the little man on the bench stilled him. He sat down as he was told and Mr Butler wrapped his green apron about his shanks, put down his gauntlets and lifted up his hearing piece. 'Well,' he asked of Nicholas with his eyes cocked to one side.

'I never—'

'Never mind that, please,' snapped Mr Butler. 'Speak out!'

Nicholas shrugged. Since the conversation was ludicrous already he could hardly make it more so.

'I want things – to make more sense. To have more sense than they do now.' He spoke sadly. He wondered what Mr Butler could make of that in placing him in employment.

'Yes. Yes!'

'. . . shape,' said Nicholas, disconsolately, looking around the gardens. 'Arrangement!'

'Ah – shape, yes.' Seemingly satisfied at this Mr Butler put down the hearing trumpet, picked up the gauntlets and leaned forward again over the flowers. 'Heliotaxis,' he pronounced each syllable as in a lesson. 'I shall tell you what it means. It means a property in certain organisms to bend towards the shining sun.' And he looked up at Nicholas, impishly. Then he stood up rapidly and sat down with Nicholas as before. 'Now,' he said. 'Here is my second question, young man. Why do you associate with that – priest?'

Nicholas didn't answer, couldn't answer this for some time but the man beside him continued to sit quietly, graven, with the instrument crooked to his ear. Nicholas quickly passed from resentment to unease. He would have liked to have been away out of the garden altogether which despite its spaciousness had now begun to exert a constricting, delimiting force on him like an enclosed room.

At length he murmured, 'Father Lannigan is a – a man of courage.' It depressed him that he could find no other attribute.

'He talks like a herd!' Mr Butler cut across him.

'Maybe – so, sometimes.'

'The man is a peculator!'

Nicholas tried, with great difficulty, to draw one simple thing from the jumble in his head. 'The man,' he said at last, 'isn't as important as what he stands for.'

'And what does he stand for?' Mr Butler demanded in his ragged, high-pitched voice. 'Shall I tell you? Nothing. Just nothing. He's neither for his Church nor against it.'

'He stands for – improvement.'

'Fiddlesticks!'

'. . . reform—' Nicholas looked about him wearily, at the flowers, so luxurious, so petted. Meanwhile, Mr Butler had taken a dibble and a packet of whitish powder from his apron pocket. He made a hole deftly in the flower-bed, poured in his preparation and closed it up again.

'What we borrow from the soil we must give back. More or less,' he said, patting the earth comfortably.

'Sir,' asked Nicholas with a certain strain in his voice, 'what am I invited over for?'

'When I die,' came the remarkable answer in the beaded voice, 'I shall rot. We can only leave behind an idea in

147

another's head. 'It's from this that we derive biographies, histories . . .'

'I thought,' remarked Nicholas wryly, 'I was sent for to be looked at for a post in Kilkenny.'

Mr Butler laughed in a high tee-hee and slapped his thigh. 'You've humour, my boy. I like that.' Then he ignored Nicholas altogether for several minutes. It was Nicholas who first heard the outcry from the town and he stood up, shielding his eyes against the piercing light of the morning. It was a noise of cheering somewhere deep within the walled fastnesses of the town but no human figure presented itself anywhere and the bridge was deserted as if nothing would ever pass that way again.

'What is it? What is it?' Mr Butler sprang up, irritated when he saw his stance.

'I think—' but Nicholas didn't complete the sentence because just then a great wave of human voices came rolling across the roofs of the houses and the river to where the two men stood in the deep garden. He stood with Mr Butler who by now had arranged his hearing device and they both stood, still, listening to that great wash of sound as it reached them and receded and reached them again as if a great ocean were stretched out before them.

'It sounds like a riot,' Mr Butler's voice cracked with disapproval.

'It sounds like a prayer,' murmured Nicholas but low so that his companion wouldn't hear. He didn't want the sarcasm of the older man. He was suddenly overwhelmed by the imminence of some violent action in the town and it was bound up in some fashion with the fact that this was Sunday. He couldn't make up his mind whether he wanted it to be a reverence or a desecration. He had even begun to regret having left the town when Mr Butler pulled at his sleeve.

'I can take it from the misfortunate. I can take the mad fury from the wretched. This I understand. Their violence gives them back their humanity, even if they never succeed in getting what they want. But what's this?' he cried wildly, waving his trumpet towards the town. 'Nothing is purified by this!'

Nicholas said nothing but sat down. The moment had

passed. All that came from the town now were the sporadic yells and cheers, the usual, contemptible idiocy of the mob. The great, resonant voice of before that had seemed to come out of the ground was gone.

'— Why don't you tell them? Why don't you tell your priest to tell them? Tell them to march for something worth the beating?' Mr Butler was screeching in his ear, hopping about from one foot to the other.

'Do you mean the poor? Or what?' Nicholas was a bit tired of the performance.

'I mean the dispossessed.'

'If they came to your gate, sir,' he cried, colouring deeply at his own temerity, 'you'd bang it shut on them.'

'I'd open it wide,' shouted Mr Butler demonstrating with his hands. 'I'd carry out the silver with my own hands. I'd say: This is yours. Go on and do the same to the next.'

Nicholas laughed shortly.

'You don't believe me, sir—'

'No.'

'Damn your impudence, sir.' And Mr Butler danced about but instead of some rash action he simply put the trumpet to his ear and listened again to the town.

Nicholas stood up to go but the man held him, in silence, with an outstretched arm.

'Sit down here, my boy.' And Nicholas sat down again, feeling perfectly stupid but what was there to do? 'Now,' began Mr Butler, exactly as in the beginning, 'this question of shape. You realize, of course, don't you,' and he smiled at Nicholas, his face wrinkled like a walnut, 'we put our own shape on the world. We create ourselves each day and if we have the desire we may create what is about us. Some men will have a shape that is beautiful. There are others that want a shape that is moral. These are absolute terms, of course. There is nothing of quite such purity in the world. We are composed and our compositions are composed of impurities. But we have to have our absolutes, nonetheless.' And he smiled engagingly again as if he were talking of sweet biscuits. 'What, what, Mr Scully, would you say,' and Nicholas heard a condescension in the voice, 'what shape does your priest want to put on his world?'

'I didn't know you were all that interested in what went on in the town.'

'And who, pray, told you that?'

'I suppose, my father.'

'Your father—' But Mr Butler didn't go on with that. He began to tidy up odds and ends about him as if he would leave but he didn't. 'A man came the other day,' he started haphazardly, 'a man from the town came to the kitchens the other day – or so they have told me – saying that he starved. He said that since he would follow neither party neither baker would give him bread. Do you think,' Mr Butler raised his head, 'the story likely?'

Nicholas nodded.

'I find it a moral story,' the gentleman observed. 'You see I would have a moral shape to my world!' It was apparently a joke to smile at. 'I am very interested in what happens in the town. I am very interested in what happens to you, young man—'

'To me?'

'Certainly. To you. To all of you!'

'Why?'

'I am a scientist. Or at least I believe in progress. Which is the same thing. Answer me this now! Explain to me the brutality of religious conflicts.' When he asked his questions Mr Butler sprang forward as if a bolt of energy had been shot through his body. Nicholas shook his head slowly. 'It's like throwing bones from a window for the dogs to fight between themselves on the streets. I mean your priests!' cried Mr Butler sternly. 'On both sides. They're both accountable! Can you settle anything by inciting people in the streets?'

'Sometimes I think it's the people who rouse the priests—' Mr Butler just glared at the interruption.

'It's an abuse.' He stamped his foot. 'It's an abuse of the people. Feeding them this dreadful poison. Do they want to exhaust the matter by factions? Is it because they're afraid of reason? Is that it? To argue their position?'

'The people want it as much as the priests. I mean the fighting and—'

'Fiddlesticks!'

'When a doubt is put on what they believe,' Nicholas persisted, 'when they think that all might in the end be wrong, they think to survive by the fire of—'

'I will tell you—'

'—holocaust.'

'What is it that makes religious factions so – so savage? It is because its hatreds are based upon mindlessness. That's the answer to my question.' Having disposed of this Mr Butler jumped up suddenly and put out his hand. 'You are to come back some other day, young man. Good morning!'

'Good morning!' murmured Nicholas deeply embarrassed. He shuffled his feet and turned away.

'How is your father?' Mr Butler called after him.

'Oh – he's – he's unhappy.'

'Unhappy is he?'

'Yes. He's not very happy at the moment.'

'I see.'

'Yes.'

Mr Butler looked quizzically at the town across the river. Then he waved Nicholas off with a gauntlet held in the air and that was all.

The benches had been removed from the back of the Friary Church to make extra room. They had been standing there packed tight since early morning waiting for the bishop. The friars and Father Foley came out to the altar rails now and again to exhort them to prayer and to remind them of the bishop's arrival, that he was coming all the way from the city to talk to them and bring them word from the Holy Father himself. The people listened passively to this, hushed and tense and when left to themselves again they remained in their places, their dark, expectant faces turned towards the tabernacle. Once or twice they moved restlessly, not singly and weakly but all together in a swelling wave like wind over high grass.

Outside, the bishop arrived and looked worriedly from the carriage window. The street (the New Line, wasn't that what it was called?) was empty. A few old papal flags and bits of coloured paper hung limply from windows opposite the Friary gate. Inside the gate itself (barred, he noted, until the three carriages, his and the two carrying the Kilkenny priests, actually came to a halt outside) was a great mass of people and some priests. He saw Lutterell there and didn't like it at all. He saw old Canon Dempsey who ought to know better than be there at his age. But then he realized he was only five years younger himself and he drew up the collar of his cloak. Some of them stepped out into the street looking up and down as if expecting trouble. Well, if Willie Lannigan could cause that kind of commotion, maybe they ought to think the whole business over again!

He remarked to Monsignor Connelly who had shared his carriage that the situation was clearly worse than they had expected. Barricades no less. Worse than Paris.

But then they were upon him, many hands reaching for his hand, faces and lips jostling to wet-kiss his ring with an urgency he had rarely experienced before. The eyes of Michael Nugent misted. In all his forty odd years of ministry he had never been able to subdue the emotion which simple piety aroused in him. It was, and he was fond of using the word to other priests, like the one, big happy family. He would have sunken down there on the flagstones of the Friary yard with them to call upon God's succour in these terrible times but that he didn't think it would present the right appearance. As it was he swayed a little and someone called loudly to the mob to stand back. Stand back and let His Lordship pass. And the cry was taken up by several others even those almost on top of him.

He couldn't rid himself of the sight of the dead town at his back, more so since the gates clanged shut and chained behind him once more: the sight, that is, of those lifeless windows and barred doors all the way from the bridge to the Friary, no carts, no horses, no asses, no stray dogs. Monsignor, who had witnessed the occupation of Rome, said he had never seen the like of it.

They had left the Bishop's Palace that morning in better spirit having just had the latest mad letter from Lannigan. Everyone said it made out once and for all that the man was mad. The younger priests couldn't get over it. But he knew his

Willie Lannigan and he laughed outright at the beginning of it. (*Right Reverend Sir — It has been announced more than once in the Friary Chapel of this town that you would administer the Sacrament of Confirmation to the children of this parish in that Chapel but I hereby inform you that I will not allow you to administer that sacrament to any parishioner of mine, except in my church and on my presentation of the subject ...*) They had gasped when he had got that far in the reading in the Palace study. Father John Purcell had urged that it be published at once, to show the people what kind of man they had to deal with. This hero of liberty! But wasn't that just what the boyo out in Kyle wanted! The name in the papers. Besides the less the people had of his ideas the better. It wasn't in the papers you could answer the 'violation of canonical rights of the parish priest'. Turn him out of the town altogether then, they cried. He had to smile at this! Didn't they know you couldn't brush the likes of this out of the door. It was a hard fact, and God help the people, but it had to be settled here in the town, on the streets, between the people of the town. Letters from Rome were all right in their place but if the town wasn't cleaned of every scrap of Lannigan's notions they'd only be plastering the hole in the wall. The people'd have to pay for it. Until every follower of the man'd have come back there'd be bones to be broken.

Inside the Friary a choir of children's voices rose in praise of the God of Love. In the yard the bishop's party had hardly made any progress through the crush. At one stage it even seemed that someone might be hurt. 'Can't some of them move out on the road?' he asked loudly but no one heeded him. He was not, in fact, feeling at all well. Indeed hadn't been feeling well in himself for the past week ever since that last chill of the bowels. He believed this pushing and shoving could do little but harm and he tried, in vain, to see a passage over their heads.

What had deeply upset him in the letter, but he hadn't said this to anyone else, was the threat. (*If it is your duty to come to confirm my children in the Friary Chapel here it will be my duty to conduct my congregation into that chapel and prevent you from violating the canons of the Church ...*) There was always that bitter black blood in the Lannigans, long before this fellow arrived on the field.

To his sudden annoyance he observed that Monsignor Connelly had in fact worked his way through the throng and was now actually entering the Friary door. Well! It was incredible! They were saying around him that it wouldn't be long now and suchlike but this, this departure of Monsignor Connelly without as much as a word in his direction. Well! He'd often seen this in the man before. Not selfish, exactly but self-protective. Something about his height, perhaps, because he was very small.

No, really what had been upsetting was not so much the physical threat (whatever he was he wasn't afraid for his own skin) but that taunt about martyrdom. (*Do not however flatter your hopes* – no, not quite that – *do not however flatter your burning zeal for martyrdom with the expectation that the slightest injury will be done you* ...) Oh, he knew where this had come from! He remembered the row, years ago, when they were both teaching inside in the College and Lannigan mocked him for his friendship with his superiors. 'You'd have yourself canonized, Mick, if you only knew the Pope well enough,' he said. Everyone had laughed in the priests' refectory. He had a cruel tongue, Willie Lannigan.

They had at last begun to move and Bishop Nugent felt sufficiently at ease again to raise his hand in benediction above the unkempt, rough heads about him. These, he thought, are the people of the earth. It's for these that we do all as He did. (*Do not fear for safety while among my people. My people have been taught by me to respect the Law* ...) As he walked the last few steps to the church door, Bishop Nugent prayed three times: first, for the people who pushed at him and plucked his sleeve, that they might understand, then for himself and his priests that they might avoid error of judgement, finally for his adversary up the hill at the other end of the town that he might, at last, emerge from the dark corner into which he had pushed himself.

The throne had been placed beneath the orange and purple window of the Holy Innocents. He rested one hand on the ornate skirt across his knees and the other on the curly head of the cherry-faced acolyte at his feet. The ceremony was nearly at a close and Michael Nugent was drowsy in the perfumed, incense-laden air with its whirls of sun-dust above his head. As he nodded, the high mitre almost toppled from his head.

'Let me make clear to you what has happened in your parish!' The well-developed voice of Father John Purcell rang out from the top step of the altar. Bishop Nugent himself never gave sermons any more; he always had one of his young men, one of his clever-alls, as he called them, speak instead in his presence. In this way he could have said to the people what had to be said and still be above the saying of it, as it were. Besides, he liked this other voice that was directed as much at himself as at the people; it offered him a consolation that as time passed became more seductive.

'Listen to my words that you may be assured in the truth and let you pay no heed to the several agents of the Lord of Lies himself that pervert the truth daily. I refer, of course, to the newspapers.'

A capable man, was Father John Purcell if a bit inclined to overvalue his own judgements, now and again. Hah! So he left in the bit about the papers!

'... *The Times* and that most stupid of British papers *The Standard* as also the Dublin rags *The Mail* and *The Express*...'

When they went over the sermon together before leaving Kilkenny he tried to get him to ... 'Don't you think, John, you could skip the papers bit?' But no, not at all. Going on about how it'd get back to the editors as if they were waiting with their tongues hanging out beyond in London to hear what he had to say! Did he think it was up in the Tivoli Theatre he was!

'The Vicar of Christ ... divinely appointed centre of our unity ... suspended and removed the late pastor of this parish, William Edward Lannigan ... now most terrible opposition against Our Holy Father himself ...'

The preacher paused and drew the people into his hush with a brief gesture towards the seated bishop. They looked towards the old man who sat bowed and frail but nevertheless awesome in his strange, impressive vestments and in the unfamiliar powers of his blessing.

'It is being said,' Father John Purcell summoned each and every one of them to witness, a new briskness in his voice, 'by what wilful persons I don't know, that these unhappy disturbances are the results of a private quarrel between your former pastor and His Lordship, our bishop.' The people gasped and the old man seemed to raise his eyes to them momentarily. 'His Lordship has asked that I say, once and for all, before the Eternal Judge here present on this altar, that this is not so. His vindictiveness to His Lordship's own person gives our dear bishop real pain.' The people nodded in sympathy and the old man replied to them with several kindly, rapid nods in return. 'But explain it no one can. I can't. His Lordship can't.'

Well, now! That's going a bit far. He was always one to exceed his instructions, the same Father John Purcell. Didn't he know as well as most that Willie Lannigan believed he ought to be bishop himself! Oh, but he came up against someone who put him in his place. And who would do so again. Another clever-all, the same Willie Lannigan. All brains and no wisdom. He couldn't keep a parish going without ructions, never mind a diocese ... The bishop who ruled well ruled himself first. They thought it was all the gift of the gab, that if they could only make a big show of themselves the people would follow. Indeed and the opposite was true; the more the people saw of you the less respect they had for you ...

'The question then is simply this ... is the authoritative sentence of the Pope to be set aside? Are we to see a conventicle of Satan set up in your midst? ... Whosoever shall willingly and knowingly assist at Mass in that house now darkened by the shadow of interdict, himself commits a grievous sin, is witness to an appalling sacrilege and, as far as in him lies, acts out once more the part of those who mocked Christ crowned with thorns. Did you spit on the Dying Face on Calvary you would have committed no greater infamy than that committed daily, weekly by your own neighbours ... He who knowingly and willingly accepts the ministrations of this suspended priest at his dying hour receives, not God's assurance, but the seal of his own perdition. Your dying neighbours, my dear people, are being ushered to their doom by this unlawful priest...'

Well, it all sounded very impressive but he wondered if they followed a word of it. These young priests had all the right words in the right places but sure the people wanted plainer bread. The more he thought of this the more restless he became. When they finally gathered around the throne, a procession of chanting figures in chasubles and surplices coming to conduct him to the High Altar, he stopped it all. There was a hurried consultation and then considerable excitement inside and outside the sanctuary. The bishop himself was going to say a few words! His Lordship was going to speak to the people!

He spent a few minutes standing in silence at the communion rail, which was as near as he could get to them without their overwhelming him in a crush, his gently moving hands quelling their excited chatter. His face was kindly and understanding and his words, when they came, were old, well used, worn and inefficient compared to those of the preacher before. He increased this effect by frequent, aged stumbles and pauses as he spoke, appealing to them for patience with his manner and drooping figure.

'My dear people,' he began, 'my good people of Kyle,' and with a fatherly wave of his hand towards the confirmed children, 'and, of course, our own little angels. I won't keep you all much longer. I'm not a talker. When the good God was handing out the blessings He didn't give me the gift of the gab, so He didn't!' The people rustled at this, a nervous laughter. 'All I wanted to say. All I wanted to say to you was ... It's the reason I'm here. And it's this: don't be too hard on the misguided people who've been following Father Lannigan up to now. God help them, they know no better. If they come back to the fold, all will be forgiven them. The God of Love is always willing to receive those who return to Him. Isn't that so? Isn't that fair now?'

There was a murmur of relief at this through the crowded aisles of the church. They appeared to be repeating something from row to row and he gazed intently on the massed faces, trying to read them and conjure the right words.

'So will you go out from this church today and say to all the people of this town: it is time the trouble is over. It is time to come back to the Grace of God. I think,' turning now to his very attentive priests, 'I think, Fathers, we can say, can't we, that for the next week we'll all be waiting, with love and forgiveness in our hearts, to welcome back those who've been in the wrong. Won't we now?'

He turned back to the people and they sensed, some of them at any rate, the stiffening in the frame, the hardening of the voice.

'No one,' he said in that low, ancient voice, 'no one can expect more. Sure they can't? And once that week of forgiveness is up, dear people of Kyle, after the next seven days, it will all be up with anyone who stays with the priest. Next week,' and the whole congregation seemed to draw itself in in horror at his words, 'we will, we must, harden our hearts for ever. We must shut our ears if we cause pain. We must drive out of this town, once and for all, the Reds!' It was at about this point that there was a disturbance at the back of the church but he continued on without a break in the dry, level voice, to the end. 'It's for you, the people of this town, to settle this matter yourselves. No one else can. Fathers and mothers! If a child of yours is a Red you must put him out of the house! Sons and daughters, if your father is a Red you must leave the house and live with a neighbour. Because from this time out there can be no mercy on the enemies of God . . .'

The drums came as he ascended the altar surrounded by his attendants. At the first beat and boom the body of the packed, sweating people in the Friary stood up like one unsteady, lumbering giant, a growling sound running down through the throat of the building. Again the beating of the barrel drums but nearer now. Rum-Rum-Rum. Women in the front pews began to cry in high, wailing voices and stretched out their hands to where the confirmants still knelt at the altar rails: the girls in white veils, the boys in serge suits, all garlanded with bright red confraternity ribbons and medals of the Virgin.

The children alone were unaffected. Some of them stood up, the better to see or be seen, still believing themselves to be the centre of their confirmation morning, mistaking this sudden interest of everyone as fresh admiration until they found themselves being roughly snatched away. And then they, too, heard the barrel drums coming down High Street. Rum-Rum. Rum-Rum. Rum-Rum.

The bishop had half-turned in his ascent of the altar steps, crosier in one hand, together with the priests and friars presenting a tableau of indecision in the blue and amber light of the sanctuary. His face was flushed and the thick whorls of skin about his eyes were crimson and raw.

A single man's raucous cry came from the back of the church. 'The Reds is coming, Father!' Through the door at the back came shouts, now distant, now near, now scattered, now more frequent and then a great babble of cries was added to by those in the church. And still the bishop hadn't moved. He had not even fully turned as if the heavy golden cope from his shoulders to his heels had immobilized his aged body, twisting his turned neck with the strain.

Rum-Rum, went the drum. Rum-Rum, Rum-Rum. They must be at the Cross by now. Turning into the New Line. Maybe even outside the Friary gates! It was then they heard the stentorian voice, at some distance but still unmistakable. A solid flow of words above the revolt of shouts and cheers. Every adult in the Friary recognized it. Each one could, and immediately did, add a figure to that voice, could and vividly did see the mannerisms of that square, jutting face, imagining the neat frock coat, perhaps the long cloak, the upraised blackthorn stick. For a while they all listened to the voice outside like cowed and frightened eavesdroppers.

It was the children who best remembered the rest of it, remembering it as old men and old women and still telling it to their children who in turn were to tell it to theirs, and in this way the day lived on, not in its full meaning but in a single moment of stillness as the two mobs faced one another on the street.

This was how it was told: What the children saw as they were passed back from hand to hand over the heads of the crowd. Because outside the Friary, when they were hustled out, the yard was packed tight and outside the gates the street was packed tight for a distance of about fifty yards with pale, determined men, far more than when the bishop had arrived. As the children were hand-passed over the heads of the men they could see up to the end of the New Line to the Cross to where the Reds were gathered, an equally massive crowd of men, men from the countryside with their pitchforks, hurley-sticks, bill hooks and spade handles, and the drummers beside them but silent now. A distance of a hundred feet separated the two crowds and each crowd was fronted by a line of men, unbroken and as straight as if a chalkline had been run across at their feet from footpath to footpath.

It was as if an agreement had been arrived at to remove the children first, passing-back, passing-back, passing-back, passing back over the heads in that prolonged silence because afterwards, long afterwards, some of these children would claim that as they reached the back of the crowd and were lifted down to women who moved them away out of it, that just as they came down from the hands of the men they felt the tightly pressed crowd beneath them being swept forward from beneath their bodies in a rush as one would pull a rug from under a person, to topple him.

When Nicholas arrived at the Cross a few people and one or two policemen stood about in dazed groups as if they had witnessed a killing. All down the New Line he could see the litter of the stampede, abandoned sticks and other weapons, a coat with a sleeve torn off, a squashed barrel drum in the centre of the roadway. He stood watching while the bishop was assisted out of the Friary, a frail, bundled figure being lifted into the carriage. Columns of angry men formed up on either side to conduct the vehicle in safety to the edge of the town.

9 . *November 1872*

Here are three stories of that November as the town still preserved them, nearly one hundred years after the event.

The Story of Mag Mullally

There used to be a woman living below on the New Line where the Council houses are now. Her name was Mullally and she was dim-witted. They say she had a house full of children and no two having the same father. They say her children's children are still living in the town but with their names changed.

At any rate, this woman was living in a half of a house down on the New Line when the business with the priest was at its worst. He had once read her off the altar of the Big Chapel for whoring. They say he had also tried to drive her out of the town. Be this as it may, she hated him. At this time all the riff-raff of the town were against him because it was plain to anyone with eyes in his head who was going to win. And there were pickings to be had on the winning side.

This same woman would do anything for a glass of malt and maybe a rub of the relic into the bargain! They got her out one night and filled her with whiskey. She never went anywhere without a streel of children but they got rid of the children this night. They had to half carry her up the hill of High Street she was so footless. When they knew he was out of the Presbytery three or four of them dragged her into his house and pushed her in under one of the beds. Then they gathered in the darkness down there where the laurel bushes are today fronting the chapel. And waited their beck.

It wasn't long till he came back. Maybe from devotions inside in the Big Chapel. When he went into the house he soon found your woman, because she was stinking. Of course he lifted her up by the hair of the head and pelted her out. No sooner had he opened the door than they all jumped out from their hiding places yelling and screeching to wake the dead. Shouting that now they knew what he was up to! Getting his hole on the quiet. Wait'll the bishop hears about this!

The Story of How they Desecrated the Big Chapel

There used to be a pub near where the cinema and Bank of Ireland are today. It was run by a family called Delany. It was very popular because it was near the Big Chapel. When they had filled up, of an evening, they'd go over there in crowds and yell in at him through the chapel railings.

One bad winter's night they went over in a gang with ladders and stripped the roof off the chapel, about ten square yards of it and how they did it in the dark is a mystery. They picked a spot over where he'd have to stand on the altar at mass. The rain went down in bucketfuls but to the day he left the town he never lifted a hand to fix that roof. He said mass in hail and rain and sunshine without as much as a glance at the open sky above his head.

When they had finished that bit of work they went back to Delany's pub and filled up again. And it was that night or the night after or the night after that, that they went back over in the darkness to the Big Chapel porch and pissed in the Holy Water Font. Twenty or thirty of them in turn.

The Story of the Dancing Figure in the Vestments

They say that on certain nights a figure of a half-man, half-woman, dressed in the priest's alb and chasuble, is to be seen in the chapel yard, dancing and shaking. Many people have said they've seen it. No one knows what it means. A parish priest of some years ago had a mass said on the spot because he said it was a tormented soul. People say it must go back to the troubles of the Big Chapel.

It was a cruel November. For the first time in living memory the flooded river came into the streets of the town. Its icy blank water brought with it a strange sickness of the mouth and throat that laid down half the households in River Street and killed several children. The people called it White Spots. It was probably diphtheria which was endemic in the town later on, at the beginning of this present century.

At the Cross a group of charitable Protestants had set up a food kitchen but in spite of the widespread hardship it was unfrequented. They said it was a souper kitchen all over again, that it was a tool of Lannigan to sell children to the Protestants. After one wild night of high wind the canvas shelter used by the ladies was found blown down the Quarry Road and the whole enterprise was abandoned.

The people drew themselves in against the black cold of the gathering winter and against something less perceptible, a feeling, a fear, that the town had been cut off, abandoned to some malignancy within itself. There was even talk against the bishop, that he had let them down, that he had left them to their own devices. The priest was still up there in the Big Chapel and nothing it seemed was going to shift him. It didn't matter that hardly six people got into the place on a Sunday, it didn't matter that the place was more ruin than proper chapel, he was still there. Wasn't there anything at all to be done to rid the town of him?

He had virtually no supporters left in the area. He himself confessed to Nicholas that he knew very well what was afoot: they wanted to humble him in the town by working the people against him until he was finally on his own. It didn't matter how much he shamed them and their Pope in the eyes of the world; the victory they wanted was here, on these streets and in these houses. They knew, His Eminence and his cohorts, they knew damn well the world at large didn't matter if this small world was taken away from him. He had nowhere else to go but the Poorhouse. Well, they would have to prove that no man had the courage to stand alongside him. When that happened, he cried, and not a day before, he would take his leave. They would first have to show that his parish was dead on him!

It might have been this that kept him at home that November while the libel action opened in Dublin with arguments on the pleadings before the Court of Queen's Bench. He wouldn't be needed anyway until the trial itself. Meanwhile he made his plans for the Monster Poster Meeting, as he called it, which was the central event of that month, the fiasco, the absurd tragedy that put one ending to the story of the Big Chapel.

Nicholas was now living like a vagrant. He was to be seen at odd hours, crossing fields in the wet or pacing through the streets of the town in a rapid nervous walk, carrying a long ash staff and all wrapped up in his black frock coat, a pack that held most of his belongings hanging from his shoulders. No one seemed to know what he was doing with himself and if questioned he could scarcely have explained. At night he slept in the Presbytery or in a groom's room over the stables at Whytescourt, apparently with the consent of Mr Butler. He kept himself rigorously clean, spending a half-hour each morning washing and brushing before setting out on these devouring, inexplicable walks that got him nowhere except back and forth across the landscape. His face had taken on a burnt, ascetic look from exposure to the wintry air, his hair had whitened and now almost reached his shoulders.

In conversations with the priest he argued incessantly about Action as if to abstract in language the impulsion that seemed to drive his own body along so vehemently. The priest had little patience with him, being far more interested in talk about his Poster Meeting, of the great crowds of supporters, of the party due from Westminster. He had little time for a schoolman's discussion at ten o'clock in the morning of the moral shade of an involuntary or voluntary act. He grabbed a volume from a shelf and hustled the melancholy Nicholas out the door with it, shouting after him that he go and find his brother and do something to earn his bread and butter.

The people called him the Priesteen Scully and laughed at his odd habits. His contacts with the priest didn't even seem to affect them any more; they told ludicrous stories about him, of how he would strip off to the waist in the pelting rain, of how he was once found lurking, peeping in the windows of his own home at four o'clock in the morning, of how he stopped a mob coming in from the Commons one Saturday night and swore he'd go with them and do what they would do if they could only explain to him why they did things as they did. They just stood gawking and guffawing at him, a lean insistent figure in black in the middle of the roadway. His support for the priest,

164

then, if it was support, was made harmless by their turning him into a figure of their yarns. Every time he appeared a nudge or a wink from one to another was enough to put him safely away.

But Marcus was a different matter. Marcus they feared and hated. Since the girl had gone away he had given himself entirely to Father Lannigan. It might be said that but for his forcefulness the few dwindling supporters of the priest in the town, people like Martin Donovan and the Dubbys, would have crept away. He was out first thing each morning checking the Big Chapel. After the defiling a police watch was put on it but the men were unreliable. They didn't like being there. Father Lannigan wouldn't hear of cleaning the excrement out from inside the door, not to speak of repairing the roof and windows.

When he had made sure that Father Lannigan was still alive after another night he would rush off, riding one of Martin Donovan's cobs around the countryside handing out the priest's startling appeals for help or bringing messages of one kind or another to and fro between the gentry houses in the locality. He was attacked at least once, out at Ballyline Crossroads, escaping without a hurt. And still he swaggered through the town daring them to act, to do what they'd like to do but hadn't the courage!

He slept at home. Since Emerine had gone away he hadn't addressed one word directly to his father. And he answered his mother, when she had the need to talk to him, in grunts. There was a wild enthusiasm about everything he did for the priest; it was half a matter of grief because he now believed he had lost Emerine for ever and he couldn't understand how simply she had gone away. It would have been so easy, as he saw it, to defy his father and still stay in the house. He hadn't understood her at all when she appeared to want something more from him. She cried: 'You'll have to show now, Marcus, before the world, that you love me.' He stood wretchedly in front of her unable to speak. It was past his understanding that anyone could still doubt his love for her, especially Emerine herself. So she's gone away. He put it all down to the strangeness of women.

He walked the streets of the town like a man bent on attracting the whole weight of hatred for the priest on to himself.

In a matter of weeks they had lost all their children. Just like that! Only little Florrie was left to them now. She put her hand down the boy's arm while she stood at the bedroom window, looking out.

'Look out and tell me if they're at the Cross yet,' the Master called querulously from behind her in the room. He was still sitting on the bed.

There were three men out on the Cross, standing in the wet. They were putting up posters for Father Lannigan's meeting. She recognized the two from Whytescourt, Mr Hawe the land-agent in his shiny coat and hard hat and Logan the handyman.

'They are,' she answered.

The third was her own Marcus Antony.

'Fat lot of good it will do them,' fumed the Master. Having got out of bed he hadn't got as far as his shirt and the galluses were trailing along the floor behind him. 'Who does he think is going to turn up to a meeting in ... a meeting, I ask you! ... in weather like this?'

It was raining again, a sly secret drizzle. She could see the matted hair of her son's head, soaking. He was standing on a box hammering up a poster. The paper was curling under his hands with the rain. They were saying to her in the town that she had a lot to put up with, that she had her own cross to bear. She answered that while she had her health, such as it was and no one could say it was good, she would go on being a mother and a wife to all of them, whatever their differences. She would have to leave down a dry shirt for Marcus in the kitchen. He'd take it without a word in her direction. There was no reason on earth for him to treat her like that. The other thing they were saying, Mrs Fincheon and others, was that she deserved more of her children.

'What are you dreaming about, Henrietta?'

'Am I dreaming?' She laughed weakly and drew Florrie into her thighs.

'Yes, you are. Dreaming!'

'Well, I was thinking, Master, of my father ...'

'Your father?'

'Yes, father. I was thinking what counsel he'd give us now. I mean if he were alive. If he were here with us in this very room.'

The Master considered her in silence for a moment.

'He'd advise you to abide in your own house with your own husband!' He had blurted out the words.

She could hear the dismay in his voice.

'He wouldn't think it needful,' she said reprovingly, 'to give me advice like that.'

'Well I'm sure I don't know what to think! I've one son abroad on the street there and another God knows where he is. Is it any wonder I can't believe anything of my own any more?'

'Whist, Master! To hear you talking you're the only one ever to have suffered in this house.'

'I've had my share of it!'

James Florence started to bawl at her feet and she lifted him up. 'Poor Florrie,' she whispered in his ear and he stopped. He was a dead weight in her arms but she continued to hold him even after the ache came into her shoulders. He was seven years of age and only a big infant. She had given them all this much love and where had it got her. 'You're breaking my arms, Florrie,' she whispered again. 'Will you get down?' He stood down and in towards her body once more, his dry eyes wide and staring, his thumb sucking away in the corner of his mouth. To think they had once thought he might make an engineer! Poor Florrie!

'What're we going to do, Master,' she asked unexpectedly, 'about Nina?'

'What do you mean what'll we do with her? Isn't she well taken care of?' Then, after a pause, bitterly, 'She's the only one that's safe out of it all.'

He looked at the long figure by the window and the boy beside her. Not one of them living had taken after her. She stood erect with that stillness that he envied. All three of them were like himself. Bags of nerves.

'I wonder.'

'What do you wonder, woman?'

'I wonder if we did right to send her away.'

'I'm sure of it!'

'I'm not so sure of it, Master. Would Marcus be out there now on the Cross if she were still in the house?'

'Would you have them carrying on together on top of everything else? Is that what you'd want? Is it?'

'No.'

'Well, then!'

'There would have been,' she said levelly, 'other ways to separate them.'

He waited for a sign from her. All through their life together he acted upon the signs of surrender that she gave because most of what she actually said persistently contradicted him. And before she conceded to him he always had this moment of fear that a rash word from her would upset the whole balance of his world but his gentle Henrietta, as he thought of her at these moments, never seemed to let him down. A downward look or a smiling nod from her and he would seize whatever it was he wanted to do, with a renewed vigour now since he knew she would be beside him. But this time, apart from a certain stiffening of the lines of her face, there was nothing.

'After all,' she said, looking down into the street, 'we owe her a bit more than that.' One day, she couldn't place the time exactly now if she tried, the girl had become a stranger to the family.

'We'll pay whatever we owe to her! Is our friend Hawe still out there?' he called irritably, all in one breath.

'He is.'

'And the handyman with him?'

'Yes.'

He said nothing at all about Marcus Antony.

'You know, of course,' he cried, 'this is all in aid of bringing strangers into the town so as he can show them what those louts have done to the Big Chapel? He's lost as a priest, the same Father Lannigan! He ought to be a travelling Novelty Man, with a tent of tricks for fair-days.'

He gave a whooping laugh at his own sally.

'I wrote to Cousin Hilary in Thurles,' she announced abruptly and as she expected he caught his breath suddenly.

'What for? What did you go and do that for? What call had you to do that?'

'Now don't go and get all angry, Master...'

'Why wouldn't I get angry? Why didn't you...?'

'I just thought if they had the room we might all go over there for a while...'

'Not on your life!'

'All right so, Master. All right.'

'We'd be a nice sight all arriving in on top of them.'

'We won't say another word of it!'

'Anyway, woman, my duty is right here.'

'All right so. All right!'

'Here with my own...'

It would have been the last straw if he had had to turn to her family. This she knew. It would have been a sign that he had failed in everything.

'I really think, Master...'

'What is it?'

'I think I've failed them all as a mother.'

'Don't be talking rubbish, woman!'

'Well I think that, anyway.'

She leant down and kissed James Florence on the forehead. He always smelled of perspiration, day and night. He looked up at her vacantly and she wondered unhappily what was going on in that mind. She kissed him again, impulsively. 'Poor Florrie,' she whispered and his dark, passive childness was a comfort to her because she knew it would never reject her although she knew too, with disturbed instinct, that its attachment to her wasn't of need but something more tentative, moments of shelter for a little person who was locked away, most of the time, in his own mind.

'I'll always have little Florrie anyway.' She spoke loudly and to the child. 'Won't I, dear?'

He didn't answer but continued to suck his thumb furiously.

'Don't do that, child,' she commanded in a low, irritable tone, catching his wrist in her hand. He shook himself free and began to tug busily at the window curtains.

'I wonder what we'd all be like if there was no Father Lannigan!' Down on the street the three had moved on towards

River Street. Mr Fincheon was standing in his doorway looking after them, wiping his hands in a rag. She couldn't restrain
the bitterness in her voice. 'We'd be different to one another at
least. We'd be more like a Christian family and ...'

'Is there a shirt to put on me?' the Master interrupted.

'Not until the rain stops. Can't you wear what you wore
yesterday?'

'It was the same the day before,' he complained. He spent
most of each morning of his life now simply getting dressed.

She swayed against the window-frame, the colour even leaving her lips and she had to reach out a hand to support herself.

'What's wrong with you, Henrietta? What's up with you?'

'Nothing. Nothing at all.'

'Aren't you well or what?'

'I'll be all right. I'll feel all right in a few minutes.'

The Master started to mumble as he always did when he
wanted to say something but wouldn't.

'Is it anything I've said so?'

It was so typical of a man! He had to put himself into the
middle of it no matter what it was. Would it never occur to
him that, for once, he wasn't on her mind!

'I wasn't thinking of you at all, Master.'

'Maybe you're feeling a bit under the weather?' he asked,
maliciously. 'Maybe it's one of your spells again.'

It was his way to hurt her. She smiled and let him see her
smile, strained and suffering.

'As a matter of fact I haven't been feeling too well at all,
lately.' She spoke resignedly without blame for anyone.

'I haven't been feeling too well myself, either.'

'Well that makes two of us so, Master, doesn't it?' She
caught a brief reflection of herself in the window-glass and she
brushed a hand across her forehead. 'We're just getting old, the
two of us. That's all. Maybe it's time the children got out from
under us.'

'You keep saying that! What do you keep saying that for?
There's none of them ready yet to stand on his own two feet.
No matter what they get up to that's a fact.'

'Indeed and we're just an old couple, Master, now. Left to
ourselves.'

'Who says that? I'm not old. I'm not a bit old. I've never felt better since the day I gave up the teaching.'

She bent down again over the child.

'Will you come down with me, Florrie, and help me tidy the house? You can give me a bit of help. Will you?' She didn't expect an answer; she was only excluding her husband behind her back.

'They're not going to let him have a meeting just like that in this town. Does he think they're going to stand by idle and with all that's happened while he has his followers in?'

'To tell you nothing but the truth, Master, I couldn't care less at this stage what he does, the same Father Lannigan.'

'And what about your sons? Would you have ...?'

She made a curious, weary gesture before her face.

'We haven't a penny in the house. Have I to go around to Bulmer's and the Hall again this week begging for bread? Can't you understand, Master, how it humiliates me?'

'The whole town is near starving,' he muttered, not looking at her.

'Is that what you'd have me do?'

'There are others worse,' he shouted.

'Well,' she said, with that dignity that never failed to defeat him, 'well, at least you'll give me credit for knowing better once upon a time. I thought I'd never come down to this. I never thought we'd come this low, I'm sure. I was used to better in my father's house.'

'Am I to blame for it?' he demanded frenziedly. 'Is it my fault if ...? Oh, certainly. Oh, of course. It's always my fault!'

'No one blames you, Master.' She sounded as if she had risen above it all but at the same time she contrived to emphasize the immense pain by which she had earned this calm, this remove.

This infuriated him still more.

'Why don't you go yourself to Thurles,' he sulked, 'yourself and the child there?'

'My place is beside you, Master. You know that. Wherever you are.' There was nothing new about the words, he had heard the same many times before, nor about the tone, gentle and soft, but he could draw no comfort from any of it.

'Go if you want to go,' he snapped.

She drew the child with her and moved towards the door. 'There's work to be done downstairs. Whatever else happens that has to be done. Come on, Florrie. Come and give your poor Mama a hand.'

'If you'd talk to them maybe they'd come in off the street. They won't listen to me, Henrietta. Either of them. It's not as if I haven't tried.'

'Aren't you coming down?' she asked, completely ignoring what he said. 'Or will I bring up a bite to eat later on?'

The Master didn't answer at once. He was thinking of why he hadn't noticed before, the blanks that littered all their talk together, even the most intimate of it. He believed it must have been like that from the start. It was only the break-up of the family that was bringing things out into the open. They had a kind of freedom now, the way couples kept their love talk for when the children were out of the room. He felt tired all over again as if the day were ending and not beginning.

'Anyway, Master,' she went on through his silence, 'don't you think it's a bit late now ...'

'What way late?'

'I mean late to think we could ... stop them from ... keep them at home.' She had almost said 'save them from the priest'.

'Do you remember, Henrietta,' he appealed to her severe composure as she stood by the doorway, 'don't you remember at all the way we used to talk about them when they were small ... Marcus and Nicholas? I never thought ...'

'Don't. You'll just torment yourself, Master. What's the use ...?'

'I never thought it.' He shook his head doggedly.

'Well, there's really no use in going on about it now.'

'What time is it so?'

'It's near eleven.'

'I'll be getting up.'

'No. Rest yourself there where you are. I'll send the child up later with a bowl of something hot.'

'I'll rest myself so.'

'Do that.'

172

He lay back like a big, featherweight doll across the un-made bed. She looked at him. His eyes were closing. For a moment she thought she'd pull the quilt over his feet but his eyes suddenly opened again as if they had seen something frightening when they were closed.

'Oh Jesus have mercy on us!'

'What is it, Master?'

'What is it,' he replied wearily, 'but the life we're all saddled with.'

After a little while he called her name.

'Yes, Master.'

'You're still there?'

'I am. You know I'm here. What is it?'

'I was wondering ... what do you think? What your father ... what would he say if he was here with us now?'

'Oh, I don't know, Master, I'm sure.'

'Yes, but what do you think?'

She never thought of her father at all now except in likely quotations, as from a pulpit. But suddenly he was with them there in the room and she wilted. She knew that no one and nothing in the town would escape his condemnation because he would see it all as a failure in grace. For her father sin was like a ravenous plague that could decimate cities.

But he would reserve his strongest condemnation of all for herself because she had once, in a pale orange dress and with a blue bow in her hair, rejected his warning about Catholics and even welcomed his rejection of her as his daughter, running down an avenue bright with lilacs to where the young Master had been standing, waiting for her, hands deep in his tweed breeches, a sturdy confident strut in the way he moved to-wards her. Her father used to call her Hettie.

'I couldn't begin to think, Master,' she murmured, weakly.

He raised himself up, painfully, almost to a sitting position.

'They've no respect left for their parents. Any of the young people. That's the root cause of it all! The way they go on ... I don't know what the world's coming to. If they only had to go through what we went through when we were their age. It's too easy they've had it ...'

'Why do we always have to blame something outside ourselves?' she asked. 'It's never ourselves that's to blame. Oh never!'

'I don't know what you mean.' He sank back again on the bed. He wanted to stop her from saying any more. 'Leave the door open a bit,' he whispered, 'when you go out.'

'I failed to love them enough, Master, any of them,' she directed the words at him in a singing voice. There was something in the vigour, the enthusiasm with which she spoke that contradicted what she said. Whenever she spoke of her own faults like this it always seemed to cast her being in a more durable, iron substance which disappeared again in the soft, ordinary motions of her life. 'If I'd given them enough love nothing could ever have touched them.' She was brusque and impatient but whatever was her object it wasn't, as her words claimed, herself. 'I know what I'm facing for it!' she told him, with satisfaction. 'I'm no good and never was, Master, and that is a fact. I suffer every hour for it.'

The Master said nothing to this. She stood indecisively on the landing of the stairs, waiting for something from him. 'Well I'll send up something to eat in a while, Master. Come, Florrie! Come with your poor mother!'

'Don't close the door,' he called in a muffled voice from the bed. 'Leave it open after you.'

He heard them go down the stairs and then the comforting sounds of their movements in the kitchen below. She talked to the child all the time in a soothing undertone but he couldn't hear her words.

Horace Percy Butler spent the late summer of 1872 in Dublin having treatment for his ears. There is an amusing, mordant passage somewhere in his Journals of about this time in which he bequeaths two tattered, punctured ears on a plate to the Trinity Medical School, 'to confound the teacher and divert the apprentices'. When he came back from this latest adventure with his doctors he became even more of a recluse than before. His outings with Scully had long since ceased; they had seen very little of one another throughout the summer and when he was first informed of the Master's death he simply asked the messenger, 'What age was he?' But the death later affected him greatly and he was truly outraged when he heard of the meaningless way in which the man had died.

The Journals do not become of interest again to the narrative of the Big Chapel until early November. Throughout September and October there is nothing, not even the observations of cloud formations and rainfall with which he filled pages of the early Journals when he had nothing else to say. Yet in between these blank pages, like a forgotten book-mark, is the one recorded communication between the priest and Butler, a hastily written note from the Presbytery (*Dear Sir, My resources are virtually exhausted. I am hemmed in on all sides by my enemies and am I being presumptuous in assuming that they are also yours . . .?*) plainly asking for money and the support of Whytescourt for the forthcoming Poster Meeting. Butler had scrawled across the top the one word, BEGGAR.

When the Journals resume in November it was as if he had never been absent from his watching post across the river from the town.

November 10th: Colchicum Autumnale, Dickenson 46.3. Consult Prior. So little time now to consult anything. My desk is in chaos.

November 11th: Down again yesterday in the stables where Buckley was giving out food to the wretched of the town. They say they would have to go as far as Kilkenny to buy bread. Mother carried down on the settle bed to speak to the people in the yard. Splendid sight! She spoke to them of the need of moral earnestness and obedience to the Law ETCETERA. While they continued to ravage the bread in their hands. The charitable societies of Dublin and Belfast are sending food.

November 12th: More rioting last evening in the town. Ten more constables but as I told Proctor this could hardly put back Time. Mrs. Wilfird Frenche coming back from Kilbracken waylaid by mob. Kept her head. Splendid woman! Shouted that she would not be put upon by communists. And they allowed her through of course. She saw their faces, blackened she said, with burnt ash or something. Mother complained again that the young men, the Buckleys and others, were going over to the town after dark. Said I must speak to the men in the yards and remind them of the propriety of this house ETCETERA. The excitement has revitalized her. Remarkable. I replied that I cannot, in conscience, dictate how a man may act in a matter beyond my comprehension.

November 15th: Proctor called again to ask if I would join the supporting list of the priest. Urged that it was our struggle too. I asked, what do you mean. OURS? Knowing what he meant. He flushed. He said at least if I did not attend Christian service I should at least recognize this threat from Rome. I said I did. He said the priest was unable to support himself now that his congregation had been almost drawn away. He said the priest was in poor health and would need assistance if he were to pursue the case against his superiors after Christmas. I gave Proctor ten shillings and a further two shillings for the Scully boy who is the priest's companion.

November 16th: A man drowned today in the flooded river. It is said he was a vagrant. The American Army sergeant is still on his Great Walk from Gretna Green to London's Guildhall carrying his flag. As a species we are capable of the most elaborate tomfooleries.

November 17th: Rumour that the Earl of Harrow, Mr. Hooper, M.P. and other gentlemen coming from London for Lannigan's meeting. Lannigan it is said is in correspondence with Earl Russell and the Prime Minister.

November 18th: Universal elemental perturbation. Reported that here and abroad continuous gales and high seas. Also remarkable examples of telluric electricity. Mr. Jenkins called in the forenoon and said that his brother reported a shipwreck near Waterford. Piteous sight. The wretches died before the eyes of the locals on the cliffs.

Four blacks and eight white men but all foreign. Kitty the blue bitch has made a remarkable, a remarkable recovery. Instructed Kelly to put her back into the kennels. River rising in the Bottoms. Saw a haystack today in midstream caught by the broken boom of the mill. They say the peasantry in Knocksolon are in dire mishap due to the inclemency. And being in dread to enter the town as they have kinsmen of Lannigan amongst them. Mother sent Mrs. Bradshawe and two of the scullery help with loaves to the Commons cottages. The Almanac has it that our earth was to have been swept by the disjecta membra of Biela's Comet yesterday. Spent last evening in the Observatory with father's telescope. Ugly dark sky. A redness over the town. No stars.

November 19th: They barricaded all entrance to the town so that Lannigan's supporters couldn't enter there for their meeting. I threw open the drawing-room to Lord Clifden and his party who came in from the Kilkenny road after five. Later in the evening a large group of young arrived, McAllisters, Hennerberrys and others and tea was served. To the south of the town John Freemantle with Colonel Fitzgibbon and others were prevented from entering. Word came that a party from Hibbel Hall stopped at the end of the New Line. There was talk of forcing the barricades with militia. Cooler counsel prevailed. Fears were expressed for Proctor and others who were already in the town for the meeting and were cut off. A short while ago Colonel Fitzgibbon crossed the river with a detachment of the cavalry from Fethard. He said he has orders not to force the town. He has been in communication with the townspeople and agreement was reached that the town would be cleared by morning. People then began to leave for home. Mrs. Bradshawe informs me that eight bottles of whiskey, six of claret and two of Madeira have been consumed by our GUESTS. It is an hour past midnight of this absurd day. Word has arrived that Scully is dead.

platform with steps had been put up in the middle of the

Cross and around and about this throughout the wet, cold day were gathered the priest and his few supporters. Ten chairs had been arranged on the platform and Father Lannigan had a piece of paper in his hand indicating the seating arrangements of the distinguished visitors who were never, in fact, to arrive. A special table with adequate supply of paper stood to one side to accommodate the gentleman from *The Times* of London and his Press colleagues. When the rain became heavy it was covered with tarpaulin.

They should have known at once what was to happen. They should have seen that there was a plan of some kind. The streets had been thronged all morning but far from hindering Father Lannigan's men the townies seemed to delight in the spectacle. In the beginning the town youngsters even played around the base of the platform and people passing shouted mockingly but not menacingly at Marcus and the other helpers. Marcus and Mr Dubby and the others looked at one another in disbelief. They had been prepared to fight off assaults while waiting for the meeting to start.

The hour was fixed for three. But long before this it was clear that something had gone wrong. No carriages came through the streets and as the hour passed crowds of Schismatics, many of them drunk, started to block off the mouths of the streets letting very few people through. They yelled and screamed at the small band of Reds now left about the wooden erection in the centre of the Cross.

Marcus shouted to Martin Donovan that shouldn't they at least get the women out of there to safety but the big, gentle carter only shook his head sorrowfully and nothing was done. Marcus tried to persuade old Poll Dwyer to walk over to his own house. There was no certainty that they'd be allowed that far but the old woman violently refused to go anyway. They all stood close together for protection as the rain came steadily down. Mr Proctor with his son Jonas then tried to escape but the mob stopped them as they were going past the Friary and turned them back.

They were ringed now by the gangs of Schismatics and every so often a stone would come hurtling through the rain to crash against the wooden platform. There was a strange stillness

about the little group, no talking but Marcus could hear someone behind him, old Michael Bergin he thought, heaving and
spitting with a racking cough.

No one had moved when Father Lannigan strode down
High Street, bare-headed, his forehead shining in the rain. He
was surrounded by a group of fierce-looking men with Nicholas limp in the middle of them. Along with his Bullies he had
gone and hired another three or four toughs from the Commons just for the day and what upset Nicholas was that these
same fellows had fought for the bishop in the Confirmation
Sunday riot of the summer previous. But Father Lannigan
didn't seem to mind. Nicholas walked down the hill of the
town trying to keep step with these dirty, whiskered giants feeling the anticipation in their bodies, in the wooden clubs that
they carried, in their fists swathed in old leather gloves. As they
walked they even called jocularly to their friends in the crowd.
All was fair now; they'd take whatever was coming to them;
they were hired by the priest for the day.

Father Lannigan marched at the head of this column oblivious of everyone and everything, it seemed, but his destina-
tion, that square, rough platform at the foot of the hill with his
few, drenched followers around it. Something of the old sheen
had come back into his face but the skin had an ivory pallor to
it and deep, purple patches surrounded his eyes. He had taken
fresh pains when he dressed and he wore a new waistcoat that
Nicholas had never seen before. As always now, he wore
around his neck a woollen muffler in place of the roman collar.

The people moved back to let him pass and even the roaring
stopped as they came out on to the Cross and marched over to
the platform. Nicholas had the impression of a trap opening
and closing again and indeed the crowds moved in behind them
cutting them off from High Street and the hill.

What struck him most of all and in a particularly unnerving
way was how well he knew most of these people in the crowds.
They had been around him all his life as much as the streets
and stones of the town. They looked across that space of pelting rain proclaiming their names by their faces, reminding him
of some ordinary humdrum life that had been forfeited by all
of them when the priest had moved and they had been forced

179

to choose. He had an aching sense of loss for all of them. How many of them could ever know, understand ...?

'Lannigan,' called the dishevelled Mr Proctor as they came up, 'the streets must be cleared at once!' He appeared to have been dipped, in all his elegance, into a river.

'They've closed the roads on us!' cried the priest, ignoring Mr Proctor. Some of the women came forward and kissed his hands.

'Well, then,' Mr Proctor appealed. 'May we not leave peaceably?'

The noise of the crowd rose up again and it was scarcely possible to hear what was being said under the platform. Mr Proctor took Father Lannigan aside. Nicholas could hear hymn-singing from the direction of the Friary while over in a corner of the Cross the mob was bellowing out Nation ballads. Above all came the chant: 'We've stopped the Prods! We've stopped the Prods! We've stopped the Prods from getting in! We've stopped the ...'

'It's bad!' Marcus mumbled in his ear.

'It's mad,' he answered curtly. And then, 'Is Dada all right?'

They both looked across at their home. As far as they could see the crowds were particularly dense there. People were at the windows of the Inn and there was a scuffling at the Inn door as if someone were trying to get in or out. But there was no sign of life at all from the windows of their own house.

Marcus shook his head and these were the only words between them until after their father's death.

The priest looked about him with a quick, fierce eye and rapped the yellow, washed timbers of the platform beside him with his stick. He called to them all as if they were a bedraggled choir about to sing.

'Let us pray,' he shouted above the uproar, 'let us pray, my friends, in this hour of ...'

Some of the women knelt down on the streaming road and one or two of the men unbared their heads to the pouring rain.

'Almighty God, look down this day upon these Thy just servants gathered here despite the hostility of evil men ...'

Even while he prayed with closed eyes and face uplifted his

strongarm men were trying to provoke a fight by taunting the mob opposite. They banged their clubs on the ground and gave out strange animal cries through their teeth.

Mr Proctor was livid with anger and fear. He caught Nicholas by the sleeve and pointed at the priest.

'You must stop him. You. Scully. Do you hear? The man is quite insane. I can't ...' Nicholas tried to shake him off. He was himself almost sick with terror but Mr Proctor persisted, pushing his face with its sodden whiskers into that of Nicholas. 'My support ends now! Do you hear? Take my name off the list! At once! At once, I say ...' His son Jonas was at his elbow: a pale doughy face, a fur collar, a young balding head.

Nicholas turned his back. He tried to rub the rain out of his eyes with his sleeve but it was useless. He felt his body loosening with fear.

There was a sudden commotion in the crowd opposite in Lower High Street, just outside Fincheon's shop. Something or someone was being manhandled through the press of men and women on the street; there were shouts and one or two odd, raucous laughs.

'Look, Father!' Martin Donovan pointed and the priest stopped his prayer.

What he saw, what the others saw, was his one-time sacristan of the Big Chapel but now follower of the Popesmen, Jimmy Reilly, the small alcoholic little man who had spent all his years as far back as anyone could remember in a perpetual, amiable, rocking haze of drink, protected by the priest from that one tipple too much until one day, without a word to anyone, Jimmy had taken himself off and asked for a job down in the Friary. After a week there they had put him out, drunk. He was now a befuddled clown who was brought along by the mob for sport when anything was up.

What he saw, what the others saw, was the little sacristan with a priest's alb and chasuble, a bright green in the rain-light thrown haphazardly over his head so that the sacred clothes dragged along in the mud, tripping him up. When they saw him at the Cross he appeared to be fighting his way out of the enveloping, suffocating vestments, his arms flailing about while the young townies pushed him from side to side. When he fell to his knees they righted him again and pushed him on.

'Oh, good God!' cried someone in the little group at the platform.

The priest looked at the spectacle sorrowfully but said nothing for some time. Even some of the Schismatics, Nicholas could see Mr Kirwan prominent among them, were trying to stop the young toughs who were around the sacristan but they were unable to do so.

'They've forced their way into the Big Chapel,' Father Lannigan turned to those about him. 'They've managed to get into the sacristy. Let no one move. They mustn't move us at all costs. They want to shift us!' He relayed the words without emotion as if he were seeing something beyond their sight. When he turned away he said in a whisper, 'Poor Jimmy, God help him!' and Nicholas caught his grieving look across the heads of the others.

There was uproar across the length and breadth of the town now and people were running into the Cross telling of what was happening on the outskirts. How the Prods and the English had been stopped in their tracks! They had at last removed the vestments from the drunken sacristan and some women carried the grimed, wet alb and chasuble away in a guilty movement while Father Lannigan stood watching.

'We'll stay here,' he called to his followers, 'all day if needs be. They mustn't get the better of us. No matter what. If we stick it out . . .'

The rain had eased a bit and the two sides were seen to settle down to wait but the youngsters of the town still ran around the beleaguered group with the priest, pelting them with stones. Mr Proctor and his son sat morosely to one side on a step of the platform but everyone else seemed to cling close to the figure of the priest.

When it began to get dark the first house was fired.

They had kept the vigil with the priest all throughout the afternoon. He had prayed with them and once or twice he had led them in hymns in competition with the mobs in the streets. There was little real attempt to move them although once, when a gang led by the tailor Freely and the Doyles threatened them, crossing the clear space almost to the platform, Father Lannigan had had the men link arms with the women within the circle. The mob then moved off. There seemed to be some controlling element in the crowds, the same control, perhaps, that had decided to blockade the town, a control that had decided on attrition, on a slow wasting away of support from him, here where everyone would see, on the central stage of the town's happenings. There was about the crowd, at times, the character of spectators sitting down in rows on the street, on the pathways, passing drink from hand to hand while they watched and waited for some final act that would isolate and bring him down. But when the light started to fade they began to burn the houses.

The first to go was Mrs Rowen's. As each building went up a great cheer came from that quarter of the town and a group of runners came swiftly into the Cross and up to the priest and his people.

'Hey! Hey!' they shouted, with great merriment, singling out someone by name. 'Lookit your house burning down! Hurry up and get your water.' As each of the seven targets was fired, all within the one hour, the small body of people drew closer together; no one knew whose turn was next.

His example had helped to calm them in the beginning because his sister's shop was the first to go. When they came running into the Cross, a crowd of men and boys, some of them hardly old enough to know what was going on, he stepped forward to meet them.

'Let ye not come any farther! That's as far as ...'

They stood milling about in front of him not knowing what to do.

'My men will be here from the country any minute ...'

They gave a derisive laugh at this, some of them pointing to the mobs blocking the streets and at this he showed a slight break in his calm. He turned about on his heel several times, turning the same blank look on enemy and friend alike. He lifted a hand and let it flop in a curious gesture that might equally imply stubbornness or defeat.

'Her house is gone up, riverence!'

'Your shop is burning, riverence!'

'Your shop is burning.'

He turned back quickly to his own people who had been watching all this, clutching one another.

'My sister,' he said quietly. 'Thank God, she wasn't there.'

The other houses went quickly from then on. The Bergins'. Martin Donovan's stables and hay sheds. A cottage belonging to a relation of the priest who wasn't on the Cross at all. Poll Dwyer's little shop.

'Poll Dwyer! Poll Dwyer! Yer shop's gone up!'

The others gathered around the little old woman to protect her. She was sitting down on an old coat on the ground between their feet where someone had put her. At first she didn't seem to follow what was being said but then she began to rock back and forth crooning to herself, lost to them and to their sympathies.

He continued to say, 'We must stay together. We mustn't leave at all costs. I know it's hard. But that'd be their victory, you see.' But already a definite arrangement had been arrived at to bring off the women into a nearby house. As he watched this, the first truce ever between his own women and the women in the crowd (the whole movement was carried out with sudden, ostentatious charity, a display of blankets, hot tea and a great deal of womanly condemnation and commiseration) he turned, gruffly, to Nicholas. 'We mustn't let the rot set in. We must stay here until it's time for the meeting to end. It's now or never, boy . . .'

'The women had to go,' said Nicholas nervously.

'Oh the women had to go. The women had to go. I grant you that.' He started. Mr Proctor and his son and one or two others had moved off down the New Line accompanied by several constables who appeared to have materialized out of the ground. When this happened there was a general relaxation throughout the Cross with people getting ready to move off home. 'Wait,' shouted the priest wildly. 'Mr Proctor, Mr Proctor,' he called off after the retreating figures.

'Maybe it's time,' someone whispered tentatively behind the priest's back.

'It's not time! It's not time at all! Wasn't the meeting supposed to go on till seven at least? Hah? And they know that, so they do! They all know that. They know that as well as you or I.'

He flung his hands about. Nicholas and the others looked dumbly at one another. What was there to say to this? When you thought you had given everything to Father Lannigan he had that knack of coming up with a demand that no one in his right senses could ever have expected. It was nearly seven o'clock but who could have thought that he had set this target in his mind all along?

As the crowds moved off the Cross some of them stood to gape at the priest and his remaining few. It was all over and there they were now: weren't they a sight for sore eyes! And yes, that's Master Scully's two young lads there now and, oh, yes, old Dubby. He was always vindictive against the Church, the same Dubby. And look at the contraption himself had built to sit the Prods on! Who built that for him now, I wonder! Not the Doyles, I'm sure. Oh, begod, you can be sure of that! The Doyles'll take it down though, quick enough, as soon as his back is turned . . .

Father Lannigan stood helplessly for a few minutes seeing his remaining strength draining away with each trickle of the townspeople that passed. He felt himself being annihilated by this relentless normality spreading itself over the mob in this ooze of harmless curiosity. He tried to stand up higher to search the crowds for his true antagonists, the Kirwans, Doyles and the others but all that met his eye were the inoffensive shopkeepers, bootmakers, labourers, carters and journeymen of the town, many of them with their wives and children and he saw what it was that separated him from them. He was a man who could only live and be himself at an extremity, out on some dangerous edge of life. It was this bloodless, gormless army that'd finally defeat him if he allowed it; they would crush him if he wasn't careful under their ability to reduce everything to this mediocre dribble of half-interest, half-dismissal. He craved the attention of those that hated him with a passion; while he had that, he had life . . .

What happened next happened with such rapid, brutal force that it seemed to end as quickly as it began. At one moment the priest was above them all on the platform giving out one of his wild harangues. Then, as a cloud over the sun, the very face of the crowd appeared to change and darken and a mass of furious men surrounded the platform, lifting it up out of its foundations.

Nicholas felt himself being swept up and then swung sharply to one side. Like a great cartwheel he and his section of the packed crowd began to revolve, slowly at first then in a spin. He couldn't be afraid of the faces about him because they too were terror-stricken. He remembered thinking that his feet were off the ground when they struck the houses of the Cross. A shudder and a groan ran down through the press of people and someone near Nicholas was screaming, 'My hands! My hands!' when he saw that he was only four or five feet from his own hall door. In a panic he began to fight his way towards it when the wheel reversed and with another spin he and those near him were hurtled back into the centre of the Cross again. With each slide of bodies people were going down, going down under the feet, screaming.

Then, quite suddenly, there was plenty of space free and he found himself shaken but staggering upright, clawing his way past dazed people, trying to find his way to his own home again.

He heard a cry, 'There's one of the fuckers!' and a stick cracked across his shoulders once, twice, three times. He didn't even raise his hands. He could hear the dull welt of the stick against his wet clothes but there seemed to be no pain. He remembered thinking: *As long as they don't hit my head, I mightn't bleed.* But then he collapsed completely.

When he came to he was being held by many hands somewhere on the pavement outside the Inn. They appeared to be holding him so that he might see what they were doing to the priest.

Father Lannigan was out on the street. As he stood there, motionless, with hands straight down at his sides, confronting them in contemptuous silence, there was something pristine and inviolable about him; the rain that had reduced everyone else to sodden misery had washed him, clarifying the lines of his body, even the creases of his clothes.

They had cleared a space in front of him and into this a gang of drunken toughs had dragged the woman Mullally. Nicholas croaked a protest in his throat because some of the men were those same that the priest had hired only that morning from the Commons cottages for his own protection. Everyone watched the scene in a hush and there was about the whole encounter something of the intent, noiseless deliberation of a dance, the narrow concentration on the movement of limbs.

She was drunk and very frightened and made several, gasping efforts to escape between their legs but they blocked her off with their knees. They taunted him with her as they would goad an animal with bait, whispering secretly to him across the space between them. He had become as still as stone.

But then they were off in an uproar up the hill of High Street pulling the woman along with them and the priest started to follow, slowly, steadily putting one foot down before the other in a measured step. The crowd rolled in towards him but seemed to recoil again at his feet.

One woman with her hair flying had pushed herself to the fore. She was the sister of the farmer Ryan from Killineck who had been jailed for assault at the last Assizes. Her shrill cry could be heard above all the rest.

'Don't touch him! Let him pass!' she screamed, almost in the path of the slowly moving priest. 'Don't handle him. Ye'll be marked! Don't strike him. Ye'll be cursed so ye will! Don't . . .'

Nicholas shook himself free. A man tried to support him, saying that he'd be all right now but he was never to know who his helper was. Everyone about him seemed to be very shocked by what had happened on the street. There was much tut-tutting and turning-up of eyes. Although he was dazed his mind was angrily demanding how they could expect to disown what had happened now when they'd contributed to it an hour ago? They were all . . .

His father suddenly came out their front door at a run. His clothes had been thrown on him this way and that and Nicholas who hadn't seen him for weeks was deeply overcome both by his own negligence and the self-neglect of the old man himself. He started to say something when the Master rushed past without as much as a glance in his direction.

For the second time that day everything suddenly picked up speed and ran headlong to a violent end. At one moment the Master was crying to the people about him, 'Let my boy be! Let him alone!' and then Nicholas saw Marcus half propped up by a gang of young fellows, a terrible wound on the crown of his head and a scarf of thick, red blood about his neck and shoulders. The Master fell. At first Nicholas was certain that no one had touched him but later the more he thought of it the more he believed that he had been struck.

Marcus lashed out at those around him with the last limp blow left inside in him and someone whispered in Nicholas' ear, 'Your father's dead!'

He remembered the kitchen thronged with people and far too many men trying to get up the narrow stairs with the Master's white head hanging down between them. He had a moment of fierce revulsion because they were all great enemies of the priest. Beside the stairwell Mr Kirwan the publican stood mournfully with his hat held to his breast announcing to all, again and again, the facts of the Master's death. His mother was nowhere to be seen.

'Get out! Get out!' Nicholas yelled but they only looked at him out of their abundant pity.

He staggered off out to the lavatory in the yard and in the damp, dark little shed he vomited and shat alternately, for what seemed like hours, into the small hole of the wooden stool. He thought of how often he had relieved himself here in this darkness as a child with someone calling from the house and the whole steady beat of the known and the familiar about him. The smell from the pit underneath had the smell of all of them. This is what it was to die, to go back into a denominator, to be sacrificed to a new fertility. He thought of his father and of the strange, divided intimacy between them and he was filled with grief and guilt at whatever it was within himself that had made him such a failure as a son. Then he wiped his eyes in the darkness on his damp sleeves just as he used to when a child.

Horace Percy Butler began to turn the telescope in his study from the heavens to the town, from a perusal of the stars to a nervous, unwilling and frustrated (since the line of sight was limited anyway) examination of what was happening in the town. He could scarcely see parts of the streets but at times he thought he saw all in some impossible penetration of brick, being in this fashion confident that he had seen (two days after the event and despite the obvious intervention of high houses and roofs) the scuffle before Scully's door, the carrying of the dead body of his friend or at least companion indoors and the pause in the quarrelling that followed this, a pause of recognition, mourning, shame.

November 26th, 1872: Observed people on the roofs over near Moore's Lodge. Much shouting. Stopped when the militia arrived. They marched across the bridge as the rain came down again heavily in the darkness. I could make out their arms and the mounted officers. Tomorrow they will bury Scully. Can I bring myself to Kilbride Cemetery? Mother will certainly disapprove if I do.

November 27th, 1872: Today remained in bed. Quite unable to move. An immense lassitude, no will to go on, to get up and go on. Increasingly difficult to do anything worthwhile. Baffling impotence, a blank wall between self and action, self and enthusiasm, self and affection. Everything for the needs of articulate life must reside within. No external dependencies. Spent the day reading Stanley's ARNOLD.

November 30th, 1872: They say the roof has been stript from his chapel and other far greater enormities committed within the precincts of the place of worship. And all of this in the name of one christ or the other christ. The number of people residing in the Vatican is 3,000 and it consists of 50 separate buildings, with 14 courtyards and 12,000 rooms.

10 . *The Marriage*

They came and told her in the deep, flagged washroom of the Laundry and she took off her apron, folded it, put it aside, unpinned her cap from her hair and placed it neatly beside her apron and then she wept because he was the only father she had ever had.

'It'd be as well for you to stay on here until it's all over with,' they told her but she had already, secretly, decided on what she wanted to do not just for the rest of the week but for the rest of her life. So she kissed her friend Molly and the rest of the girls in the Laundry goodbye and went back to Kyle that very day because she knew, with a kind of amazement at her own possession, that there was no one left at home now who'd dare tell her to stay away.

Everything, everything had changed so much in so little time! It wasn't only at home where they looked at her like a stranger and everything was overlaid with the politeness of the dead-house. Marcus was running a fever from his head and they persuaded him to lie down in a dark room while she bathed his head with vinegar. He said nothing but she didn't care. She had passed beyond the need of words from him. Henrietta had come out of herself with the excitement and the sorrow. She sat all day in the kitchen with a high glow on her cheeks surrounded by mourning women exchanging whispered condolences with them like words of flattery. Florrie was boarded out somewhere in the town and Nicholas, when he appeared, was but a shadow.

But it was the town itself which shook her most. She wasn't long home when she saw that nothing like this would ever happen there again. Something at least had come to an end with the Master's death. The place was filled with military and gentlemen from Dublin with documents asking people questions. But it was the people themselves who suggested an end by the way they went out of their way to show to the Scullys that all was forgotten now, that it was all over now with the priest and wouldn't it be better, in God's peace, to make the town a fit place again for Christians?

A committee of them, Mr O'Brien the apothecary and some of the big shopkeepers like Mr Kirwan and others, was standing in the Scully kitchen discussing details of the funeral, giving one another support with manly coughs and flourishes of handkerchiefs, when Marcus staggered down the stairs and told them that Father Lannigan would bury his father in Kilbride Cemetery. There was an awful moment and then panicky consultations but then they turned, united, towards Marcus and said of course, Marcus, of course, they'd see it'd be done, they'd give their word to it and wouldn't he go back now and lie down and leave it all to them. And Mr O'Brien led him back upstairs again.

She would never forget the funeral. She was in the first carriage with Henrietta and Florrie and the townsmen were in the second carriage. One or two people joined in, walking, after the funeral left the house (in some kind of strange compromise it had been decided that the corpse would not be taken to either church) but they were few. Up in front, behind the hearse, walked Marcus and Nicholas with the priest between them. The whole cortège stopped momentarily outside the Big Chapel and then moved on again and she wondered what the gentlemen in the carriage behind would make of that.

'What have we stopped for?' cried Henrietta, fretfully. She sat with her back to the hearse so that Emerine had to tell her what was happening in front.

There were militia all along the street but no onlookers. When they passed the Big Chapel and the top of the hill the horses started to trot, the walking people would have turned aside at this point, their duty fulfilled and the priest and the boys would have sat up with the hearse driver for the mile-long journey to Kilbride.

'They stopped at the Chapel.'

'He might have spared us that!'

'It's a custom.'

'Don't speak to me of customs,' and Henrietta started to cry and Florrie followed her, a strange, deep-voiced bawling for a child of his age.

Emerine shrugged and looked out the window.

The funeral stopped again, abruptly, when it was still some distance from the cemetery gates.

'What is it now? Oh, my goodness, will it never end . . . ?'

Emerine raised her veil and put her head out the carriage window. Father Lannigan and the boys stood before the stationary hearse looking off towards the cemetery. A line of men, standing shoulder to shoulder, had blocked the entrance.

'It's nothing, Mama,' she said, trembling, withdrawing her head.

The men from the other carriage, Mr Kirwan and the others, ran past, their top hats askew and their walking-sticks in the air.

Henrietta started up. 'What are they doing to him?' she screamed. 'What are they doing to him?'

'Don't, Mama!' she tried to get the woman to sit down and the carriage swayed with their movements. 'Sit down, Mama. Please!'

When she looked out again there was great coming and going on the roadway with Mr Kirwan and his friends acting as go-betweens. Father Lannigan took no part. He stood aside, hands by his side, his face pale and set. Marcus did all the talking and she could see his bandaged head bobbing up and down.

What, Emerine's head drummed, *what have I come back to?* Up to this moment she had never doubted her strength to carry herself through but suddenly a great hole yawned in front of her and she wanted to cry out to Marcus.

Just then the carriages started again and they moved in past the gates with the sullen men standing about making no effort to stop them.

Henrietta asked, feebly, that she and Florrie be let stay in the carriage and everyone was happy to agree so it was drawn up as near as possible to the open grave and she and Florrie peered out, two fugitive, bluish faces, at the ceremony of burial.

Emerine was moved by how old Father Lannigan had become. He looked like a man who had come out of a long, wasting sickness, some part of his physique worn away for ever.

His hair was wild as he stood above the grave, an old purple stole on his shoulders but nothing else of his office about him.

Marcus stood rooted at the very edge of the hole looking down into it until it had been covered in. The only one to show emotion was Nicholas and he wept with abandon, his face turned away. At a distance that suitably conveyed their ambiguous engagement in the proceedings stood the townsmen, hats in hand. Emerine walked over to stand beside Nicholas and took his arm and he gripped her.

When Father Lannigan stood, finally, with the fistful of clay in his hand he paused a moment before letting it slide through his fingers to fall on the coffin in the grave. She thought she detected a curious smile on his face as he stared down at the remains of the Master, a look of fellowship, of secret sharing, of peace. She was to remember the scene vividly because the only priestly functions that she could remember Father Lannigan carrying out in the last years in the town were the burial service for the Master and the service that married herself and Marcus.

Later on when she tried to put a shape on those last, nearly five years in the town they resisted her like softly dissolving butter between her fingers and all she was left with was this blend, this running together of everything into the one, drawn-out moment. The days went so quickly, the days went so slowly but never at a pace that she could recognize from her old life when they were all younger, oh so much younger! It was like holding your breath for a long, long time and knowing that the seconds were spinning past but that you were holding them back at the same time because you could almost count them, one by one . . .

Today was the wedding day, that startled spring day when everything was broken up like glass into crystal-clear fragments (the closed group of them around the altar rails with only a rag of its cloth left, or their walk back down High Street, she still wearing her white shawl, the town grinning and the young fellows dragging the feathers and the tin cans along the road in front of them). But today was also the sleepy menstrua while the baby grew inside in her and she watched herself swell with a stealthy contentment and in this she was never more separate from all of it, Marcus even, because she knew she was nursing towards certainty inside in her, as securely as the growing egg itself, the belief that she alone knew what had been at stake in the town all along. And today, too, was the angry day they walked out the door leaving her with the baby, Nicholas and her Marcus, the sameness of them, oh, the sameness of them from behind, the same squareness of the head, the same breadth of the shoulders and she knew that one of them at least wasn't coming back.

She had sunk down into that lapping, drowning motion, observing herself with intent curiosity and a kind of easeful helplessness, during the first year after the Master's death. She might have crept into a corner of the house so little did she impose herself on anyone, working quietly in the kitchen with Henrietta or on the crochet of the white shawl which she alone seemed to know was for her wedding. She stirred only when Marcus thumped in or out but he was still only a giant figure above the line of her vision. When they came in sessions, Mr O'Brien and others, to persuade him to go back to work in the Tannery having arranged it all with Mr Cody she watched, brightly, from her corner as they slowly drew Marcus back to them, for the sake of his father, they said they were doing it and sure anyway Father Lannigan had been asked to submit and he was going to and was going to be put away into a home with the nuns, maybe. And while they were at it and no offence intended shouldn't something be done too about Nicholas the way he was going round the place like a . . . ?

When they were alone he asked her if he should take back the job and she said yes, flushing darkly, and he went back to work that week. She thought of how he must have been thinking of her all that time without saying anything and her heart sang.

Then, suddenly, when the year of mourning was up she shook out her hair and put away the black dress in a drawer. She rolled her sleeves up over her arms and all her actions became animated again. Within a week of her transformation she and Marcus had decided to marry. What matter if they couldn't leave the town now, wasn't it only right that they should make a go of it here especially after all that had happened? That's what she said to Marcus. But she was convinced in her own mind now that the meaning of their marriage had its meaning only in this house, in this place, that the display of it was nearly as important to her as the thing itself. So she also said to him that it might be the only salvation of all of them. She saw that he didn't understand. At the time he said nothing at all about being married by the priest and in the Big Chapel so she went around for days with her head filled with how they'd make a world of their own inside the four walls of the house. But then she seemed to slip back again into the old, sleepy rhythm of those years in which the wedding, when it took place, even the birth of the baby when it happened were only incidental awakenings, brief moments on the surface of a deep dormant pool.

She awoke out of it all when she left for the factory job in England. As she handed Mrs O'Shea the child and the bundle containing the sachet of mementos (driven out not so much by the new hostility around her or by the unwillingness of many to give her housework any more as by the conviction that she had to get out and go living free because only she seemed to know that what was being trampled on here wasn't simply just a few people but some part of life itself) she said, 'I'll come back when my husband gets out of prison, Mrs O'Shea.'

But in those first weeks of the marriage they used to lie on for ages in the big double bed of the front room upstairs while the first light came in the curtains from over the Cross and she nearly always said but without a whole lot of worry in her voice, 'You'll be late for work, Marcus. Mr Cody'll be raging!'

He would roll up her shift up over her thighs and waist and breasts so that she could feel the full hard length of his body against her. She giggled when their skin stuck together. When he raised himself up over her by his hands she took hold of his thing because she knew he liked her to but never without being overcome by a kind of terror. It was like having a separate, live, trembling creature between their bodies.

It was on one of these mornings that she broke off, abruptly, and said she was afraid.

'I'm afraid. Of Nicholas. Do you listen to me, Marcus?'

On one elbow she lay, her body from head to back to buttocks arched like a bow beneath the sheet.

'Why? What'd he do?'

'Nothing. He did nothing.'

'Well, what's wrong so?'

'It's he's always in the house, Marcus. I can't turn around but he's behind me.'

'Arragh, Nina!'

'Please, Marcus!' She touched his arm. 'I don't know what I'm afraid of ...'

'Is it Nicholas ... Nicholas?' And then to her silent, bent head, 'Nina, we can't put him out of the house. Is that what you want?' She shook her head still without raising it. 'Anyway he's only here during the day.'

She didn't want to say that that was the only time she was left on her own. There was something in Nicholas that reminded her of all the pain and fear in the town.

'Marcus ...'

'What ...?'

'Ask him to ...'

Marcus squatted before her on his haunches, the hair like black moss on his legs, in a great arc under his belly. He dipped his two large hands under the sheet and lifted her breasts out as he would two apples, need and curiosity together on his face

'Who told you?' he asked hoarsely. 'Who told you first about men, Nina? Was it Mama?'

And then when the terrible row took place when Marcus found Nicholas in the middle of the night crouching on the stairs while they were in bed and threw him howling out of the house she knew that what she feared and hated in Nicholas was what she feared and hated in the town, the poisoning of everything that was trying to live naturally ...

'Was it Mama that told you?' He was sweating and his hands were hurting her breasts.

'Yes,' she whispered, closing her eyes. Men, she decided, sinking down, should only be told what was good for them. If she started to tell him about Molly in the Orphanage he'd get weak. And as for Henrietta ...

'I'd like a word with you, Nina, if you don't mind,' Henrietta had said a couple of weeks before the wedding. They had had so many 'few words' together that Emerine was sick and tired of them. It had been decided that Henrietta and Florrie would leave for Thurles the day of the wedding. 'To give you the house to yourselves, for a little while anyway,' was how she put it smiling bravely and sufferingly at Emerine. As with all her concessions and gifts it made Emerine feel as if she were heartless and greedy for what was not her own.

'Oh, you don't have to stir, Henrietta.'

'No, no, you don't want us around at a time like this. We'll be all right, won't we, Florrie love? We'll manage.'

'All right so,' said Emerine sharply. She decided that from then out she'd stop being over-polite about that one's feelings. The more you gave into her the worse she got! When she came back home from the funeral everything had been different. She and Henrietta had shared the length of each day together. She believed things had started to change between them when she moved towards Marcus again. The declarations of suffering of the older woman began to get on her nerves after that. She started to call her Henrietta and not Mama any more.

But this particular encounter was unlike all the others. Henrietta led her into the front room downstairs and took down the window shutters. This was a surprise because the room was never used since the Master's death.

'I suppose, Nina,' she turned with smiling resignation, 'you and Marcus are going ahead with it?'

Emerine breathed out heavily. 'Yes, we are.' Since they had spent nearly a week past discussing details of the wedding she couldn't see the point of the question.

Then she started off about the death of the Master and how they always looked upon her as their own daughter and all the rest of it and now that the Master was gone to his eternal reward it was left to her to speak to them both, herself and Marcus, about what was in front of them and the big decision they had taken. And so on and so forth. And about Married Life. She repeated this phrase several times, Married Life and then looked sideways at Emerine and said, 'I suppose, Nina, you know what I'm talking about?'

'No, Mama, I don't.' In her bewilderment she forgot to call her Henrietta.

'Well, it's about yourself and Marcus.'

'Yes?' Emerine waited expectantly and then suddenly saw that Henrietta was deeply embarrassed. Her sharp, pointed face had a slight glow to it and she was sitting stiffly in her chair not knowing what to do.

'Oh I know what you mean,' gulped Emerine, blushing. What she wanted most of all was to get her out of the embarrassing situation.

'Oh you do?'

'Yes.'

'Well that's different so.'

'Mrs Dawson talked to me!' Emerine smiled out slyly from under her hair at the older woman, appealing to her to see the humour of it, but Henrietta sat coldly staring at her.

'Mrs Dawson?'

'Yes. The other day when I went up.' What she wanted to say, really, was that nothing she or Mrs Dawson or anyone else had to tell her would tell her much more than she knew already and anyway what was the mystery of it, a man and a woman, wasn't it nature? How scandalized the two of them would be if they met the likes of Molly in the Orphanage and heard her talk about men and so on! It was queer the way people could go half through life and through so much and still not know half of what was happening around them.

But all Henrietta said, by way of closing the matter, was, 'She's a good person, a good, good woman, Mrs Dawson. She's been very kind to myself when I haven't been too well. Will you pass me that knitting, Nina, in the basket in the kitchen on your way out? I think I'll sit quietly in here for a little while. It'll be good for me the quiet ...'

Marcus used to say that he learned all about it from watching the bull up on the cows down in Riley's and that he used to think it could only be done when it was a woman's time, like a cow's. 'You'd be in a nice state,' she told him, boldly, 'if that were so!' He grabbed hold of her, rolling her about in the bedclothes until she screamed, laughing, 'Stop! Stoppit! I'm smothered, Marcus so I am.'

When he was out of the bedroom she would stand in front of the big mirror looking at the way all the points of her body ran into the dark nest between her thighs. She thought of Molly, her one bosom pal in the Orphanage Laundry and wondered what she was up to now!

Molly used to arrive late and last into the laundry-girls' dormitory of a Sunday evening after being out with some fellow all day by the Castle. She'd stand at the foot of Emerine's bed, a huge mountain of a girl with brilliant, cascading red hair, stretching her hands over her head, gasping, 'Oh God, Nina! I love men so I do!' How they laughed together! Molly never talked about walking out with a boy or of being courted or boyfriends or anything like that. She'd always say with a throaty laugh as she set out that she was off 'to give it to them' as if she were dishing out punishment or something like that!

For a long time she had a respectable solicitor, a Mr Donan, standing out under the street-light every night looking up, lost, at the dormitory window. A married man too and a Protestant and past the age when he should have got sense! Molly used to wave her drawers out the window at him for devilment. It was Molly who told her all about men in great, gulping, giggling bouts of conversation with their heads half under the blankets so as the nuns wouldn't hear and have conniptions ... She never thought then that she'd come back so soon and marry him ...

'Bring up your basket, child,' Mrs Dawson commanded when she summoned her up to the house on High Street. 'I wish to discuss your impending nuptials.'

Mrs Dawson's sitting-room was one of the few places of enchantment from her childhood, the luxuriant flowers on the wallpaper, the high, polished sideboard laden with knick-knacks and curios and leather-bound photographs (of cousins in India, Mrs Dawson said) and all the beautiful pieces of china. Everything in the room was bright with polish and laden with the mingling, rich, strange smells that even seemed to follow Mrs Dawson about as she walked. Emerine sat dazed on the edge of the sofa almost afraid to put her hand on the deeply embroidered flowers of the antimacassar.

'Tea!' called Mrs Dawson sweeping into the room like a duchess with a silver tray and tea service in one hand, a plate of steaming scones in the other. 'Sit, child,' she boomed at Emerine who had scrambled up nervously. 'Today *you* will be served!' She poured two cups of tea with a flourish and produced a glass of brown liquid which she placed beside her own chair. When she handed her teacup to Emerine she added sternly, 'Minton!'

'Thank you, m'am,' whispered Emerine trying to stop her hand from shaking.

'My husband, the late Mr Dawson, was presented with the service by his appreciative colleagues. I hope you think it pretty, child.'

'Oh, I think it's lovely, Mrs Dawson. I do.'

There was a silence while Mrs Dawson sipped the liquid from the glass and took a large draught of tea. Emerine put her cup to her lips but she was afraid to hear her own mouthfuls and put the cup back again untouched.

'Tea!' Mrs Dawson creased her lips and sat into her chair. 'It is well known, child, in China that new tea exhibits the narcotic quality in a high degree which is exceedingly injurious to the nerves. Chinamen *never* drink new tea! It requires age to evaporate the unwholesome, volatile oil.'

'Yes, m'am.'

'Drink up, child.'

Emerine drank, perspiring around her nose.

'It has come to my knowledge,' said Mrs Dawson, 'that you're to be married by that,' the pause allowed her to purse her lips, 'priest.'

'Yes, m'am. He wants it.'

'Who wants it, child?'

'Marcus, m'am. My intended.'

'You know of course that the man is a lunatic?'

Emerine hung her head. She didn't want to go into all that again! After the row with Marcus over Father Lannigan she had sunk back into the drift, the flow, the way life eddied about her these days so that nothing much mattered one way or the other because they'd be carried to where they were going ...

'That his what he calls his church is a sty? That he's locked himself up in there in that house? A veritable lunatic I am reliably informed.'

'He's writing a book.' That's what Marcus said. Father Lannigan was writing a book.

'And what, pray, is in this book?'

'I don't know, m'am, I expect his informations.'

'Men!' Mrs Dawson exploded. 'Men! Men! With the exception of the late Mr Dawson I have not met one who has caused less trouble than he ... Politics! Trickery! Knavery of all kinds! We weak creatures,' she roared at Emerine, 'weak as we are have to mend the world that men destroy. Men ... Oh!' She took a noisy breath and then said more quietly, 'Men are generally dispensable and don't you forget it, child, especially during childbirth and in all matters having to do with female apparel which brings to my mind ... Are you adequately provided with clothing, child?'

Emerine told her all about how she and Henrietta had cut out the dress from a pattern in the *Emerald Ladies' Journal* and were going to make a jasmine head-dress with forget-me-nots and cornflowers.

'And what, pray, is the length of the dress?'

'Down to the floor, m'am,' said Emerine demurely.

'I am glad to hear it. Only the other day Mrs Johnstone said to me over tea in the Hall that some enterprising, I can hardly call them ladies, in America are determined to give a death blow to crinoline but of course realize that some equally witching attraction must be substituted and their notion is very short dresses *à la* Buy-a-Broom-Girl, disclosing much leg and very high ankle boot, something perhaps in the style of a balmoral ...'

Mrs Dawson paused to replenish her glass somewhere outside and Emerine rapidly emptied her teacup and replaced it on the tray. When she returned she took up the subject of Father Lannigan again, how it was generally felt that it would be better now for everyone if he were put away, how the dragging on of his law case, for over two years now, was a scandal and a reflection on the town.

'I'd prefer not to talk about it, Mrs Dawson.' She had had enough of Father Lannigan for a lifetime.

'You could always, child,' Mrs Dawson stared at her with wide eyes, 'be married in the house of God.' Emerine knew she meant the Protestant Church.

'Oh, I don't think so, Mrs Dawson,' she whispered.

Mrs Dawson tweaked her nose once or twice and taking a pretty lace handkerchief from her sleeve she blew into it with a loud, trumpet sound. She then sat a moment staring at the carpet at her feet.

'I was not myself,' she said huskily, 'blessed with issue. Mr Dawson and I,' she dabbed one eye with the handkerchief, 'enjoyed every other felicity but that of generation.' She turned on Emerine abruptly. 'Are you aware, child, of your natural functions?'

Emerine sat up straight with a shock.

'I beg your pardon, m'am?'

'Has your mother ... has his mother,' Mrs Dawson was extremely agitated as she tried to cope with Henrietta, informed you about ... life?'

'Life ...?'

'Yes, life,' Mrs Dawson shouted. 'There is a false delicacy in these matters. I do not see why we should not attend to our private functions as we do to our public. It is all a matter of loose clothing, moderate exposure to air and regular movements. I have little patience, child, with those of our sex who would put modesty before cleanliness. Be that as it may, I have asked you a question, child?'

'No, m'am,' Emerine felt herself sink into her chair. 'She didn't say anything.'

'I thought as much.' Mrs Dawson was satisfied. 'Your mother ... his mother is a Christian woman. She is upright, charitable and was a good wife to her late husband but she is a nincompoop and that is the plain matter ...'

Emerine tried hard not to smile. She tried to stare at one point on the rosy wallpaper, feeling slightly faint because she didn't know what Mrs Dawson was going to say next.

'Marriage,' Mrs Dawson announced with the air of conveying a divine promulgation, 'is the price we have to pay for lubricity and hankerings . . .'

Molly used to say she'd never marry 'because 'twould take the jig out of it.' After only one week Molly had organized a fellow for her and they all went walking out beyond the Black Quarry, Molly and Jack and she and Michael, hand in hand, and she was never so frightened in all her life. All along the road she tried to take her hand out his but he held on like a vice. Molly was in a kind of sleepy stupor and didn't seem to notice her at all and when they reached the Meadows she and her fellow disappeared altogether and her fellow leaned over and whispered in her ear, 'Is it afraid of me y'are?' She could have fainted!

She was like that the first couple of months in the Laundry, afraid of her shadow, ready to jump out of her skin if a fellow spoke to her! A bad case of the Shaky Marys, Molly used to say with that gurgling laugh of hers. All the screaming, high-pitched girls in the Laundry had the Shaky Marys according to Molly and several of the nuns too, if they only knew it! There was only the one cure for it and God help them many of them were going to die without ever getting it! When she couldn't help laughing in return Molly gave her a hug. 'There's hope for you yet, Nina,' and she gave one of her big, smothering laughs.

Maybe she was only waiting all the time for something to happen so that they'd be still able to go to Australia in September. But when August came and went her heart gave up. The only one to come and see her in the Orphanage was the Master. No Marcus. Once Mr Butler of Whytescourt came and asked many questions about the Boiler Room and gave her a shilling. The Master told her that things had quieted down again in the town and that there was promise of a good harvest and that maybe she could come home for Christmas. Little did he know! On his last visit before he died that November he asked her to give up Marcus and they sat in silence for a long time on the bench by the Convent drive while she couldn't answer. He gave up waiting after a while, stood up and took the stiff goodbye which he had for all his children, a hand on the arm, a word as he walked away.

'But why do you want to go back to that place for? Is it

because you love the lad?' Molly asked in the darkness between their beds.

She couldn't say anything and she began to cry because how did she knew what love was? If it was only going back to what she knew, then there wasn't much to life. It had to be more anyway than what she had been used to. All she had to her name was this fierce resolve to be free to be herself and not have people doing things for her because of charity. That was Marcus. He loved her for herself, she knew that. She could feel it in the way he stood beside her. But she loved them all, she really did, the Master and Henrietta and Nicholas and Florrie. The one thing that killed her, though, the one thing she'd never understand was why they sent her away. Was it because they didn't think her good enough or what?

'Nina, you want your head examined!' Molly burst out hoarsely. 'Don't you know you're on the wrong side of the fence and always will be as long as your name is known to those around you?' She was transformed by the bitterness, all the bubble had gone out of her leaving her cold and distant. 'We only get what we take in this life, that and no more...'

'I can't believe everyone's as bad as that, Molly.'

'Mary Mother! One fine day you'll wake up sorry and sensible, Nina.'

'Well, some people mean what they say to you. And I believe them. You have to believe in some people.'

Marcus said it was because of his fight for the priest that they couldn't run away.

'Don't talk to me about priests!' Molly waved her arms about. Emerine said it was strange the grip he always had on the family, Father Lannigan. 'They're all the same, priests,' said Molly. 'Why should it be us and not some other family?' cried Emerine miserably. 'Every man-jack of them's the same,' swore Molly. 'It's not badness they hate at all though they say it is when they're preaching. It's nature they hate! And the way the world is and the way men and women are. That's what they hate! And if it comes down to it it's themselves they hate most of all!'

It was strange how things that Molly said used to come back to her months even years after because this was what she was to repeat more or less to Marcus that January when Michael was born and Marcus couldn't bear to look at the blue, pinched lip of the baby because he shouted that it was the priest-curse on him as the people said it was, on him and on his breed for having had anything to do with Father Lannigan. When he sat for days above the crib without saying anything and she thought she'd go mad she kept saying to him, over and over, that it was only nature and nothing to be afraid of, that the baby was their own and that it was truly some terrible thing that made him want to give up his own flesh and blood because when Marcus first saw the deformity of the lip he went crazy and wanted to hide it away altogether so that no one could see it. When she had managed to bring Marcus around to his senses she then remembered Molly . . .

'Why, child,' Mrs Dawson asked when she paused in her tumbling lecture about marriage, 'why do you want to marry him?'

'Why, m'am,' Emerine blushed, 'because I love him, that's why.'

'Love,' grumbled Mrs Dawson as if she were picking up the word itself, folding it and putting it away in a drawer. 'Love! You'll have to give me further reason. We are not, I trust, inhabitants of the penny serial.'

'And why,' asked Molly as they came to an end of everything else in the dark dormitory, 'do you want to bother marrying him for?'

She didn't make a proper reply at all to Molly but started off about all the things in Marcus that she couldn't stand, how he wasn't too bright and she was always having to tell him things and he wasn't too clean either, how he hadn't too many civil words in his head and was always picking his nose and would fly into a temper if a body told him how to mend his manners, how when he'd get a hold of something he'd never let go even if his life depended on it, how once when they were all small he got lost in the dark and there was terrible trouble and when they found him at last he was sitting in a dyke in the fields minding a collie bitch that had caught herself in a burrow and how suspicious he was of anything you said if he hadn't thought of it himself at the same time. And as for this business of the priest ... If Marcus said his prayers itself she could understand it. It was only that he was taken in by the words of the priest and once he had given himself to someone Marcus would never go back on his word ...

Molly laughed at this and gave her a big shove with her elbow. 'Go on outta that with you Nina! You're mad about him so you are!'

So they sat on for hours after in the dark while Molly talked about all the fellows she had ever known and how happy they all had made her but Emerine heard a loss in her words and secretly, deeply, she was very glad that she had only had the one, that whatever Molly said it must be like dying a little to lose someone like that.

She was someone to remember, Molly! For all her wildness and terrible stories Emerine used often feel that she herself was the woman and Molly the big, tumbling child. It was that nothing seemed to change her, ever. And what were facts anyway if you didn't feed off them? Molly might as well be a slip of a girl for all the effect her life might have had on her. Only pain. Only when she became bitter, which wasn't often, did she become a woman, Molly.

Thinking about all these things years after used to help after the baby was born and she went through the terrible months with the world closing in around her and she wanted to scream *Let me out! Let me out!* She'd made no effort in all those years to keep track of Molly but she liked to think of her still free as the wind, still moving through her hordes of fellows as a breeze through corn. When she found how quickly she exhausted the first love for Marcus, so bottomless it once seemed! and how she had to draw more and more from reserves within herself she wondered if this was the kind of love which someone like Molly could never know, the love that had to be discovered from painful closeness to a person, the love that came out of regret and pity and fear ... They said to her that she was only a bit washy after the baby and the shock of the disfigurement but she knew it was more, she knew that her choices were all, finally, ended, that she had to survive now on what she carried with her or not survive at all and it was like the knowledge for the first time of her real name.

In the worst hours towards the end before she left the town altogether she used to think back to when she could have escaped out of it all and what kind of courage it was that had kept her going because then as now Marcus didn't seem to share the deepest hopes she had for both of them. Especially that day he came home and said they were going up that night to the Big Chapel to settle the wedding with Father Lannigan.

'You can't . . .' She started and then sat down weakly.

'What'd you think, Nina? Did you think we'd be married below in the Friary? How could you think such a thing, Nina?'

'I didn't think one way or the other,' she said, her voice shaking. Which was true. All she had been thinking about was of a curtain coming down around them to blot out the world.

He talked about Father Lannigan's trial then and all that was at stake. She didn't understand a word about the same trial and she didn't think Marcus did either. But men were like that! They liked to think they were busy about everything but the things that really counted!

'I don't understand a word of what you're saying,' she said to him and he stopped, furious.

They had to go back four times before the priest would agree to marry them, each time the scene in the Presbytery the same: the gaunt figure of the priest standing above the table that was littered with papers and Nicholas in one corner with head averted.

'What do you want to do to us? Why, Marcus? Why?' she wept.

'You said yourself . . . didn't you, Nina? You said it. You said we'd show them all. That be getting married we'd be . . . we'd be an example to them. Wasn't that what you said? Hah?'

She nodded. But this wasn't what she meant at all.

'Well, we'll show them all right! We'll show them that Father Lannigan's still a priest . . . We'll show them by getting married above in the Big Chapel!'

'That's not what I meant at all,' she whispered.

He hadn't understood so she began again at the beginning by saying that what they had between them was private and didn't need anyone else, Father Lannigan or the Pope himself, that it was for themselves alone, that what she meant was that in seeing them together and their love for one another maybe people might come to their senses as to what was really right and wrong in the world ...

'I only want, m'am, to marry him, that's all,' she said simply to Mrs Dawson. 'I think ... we think we can make something between us to spite what's happened.' She took courage at the silence of the old woman who sat with her bird's eyes blinking at her, sipping her drink out of her glass. 'We only want to make a home. Isn't that all that counts? That people can go back to living in their own homes? Wouldn't that save what's left of us? Oh,' she asked tearfully, because something in the old woman's eyes held her, a deep, plunging look that rode down into her heart, 'don't you think ... do you think there's any chance for us at all, Mrs Dawson?'

In answer Mrs Dawson swept out of the room with glass in hand and returned with it brimming and carrying under the other arm a large leather case. This turned out to be a beautiful silver cutlery service which Mrs Dawson plumped down on the table and, emptying her glass, began to select four knives, four forks and four of each kind of spoon from the case. This was not (she informed Emerine with a fierce look) a wedding present since she had already put many things aside for them but it occurred to her now (and it was always good to act upon one's impulses if one could be assured of one's integrity) that they might well do with some tableware to begin with. The rest could follow. The knives and forks and spoons spun and clattered in her fists and then suddenly she slammed the case shut and thrust the whole lot into Emerine's nervous arms.

'Take it! Take it!' she yelled, tears streaming down her face. 'What am I preserving it for? I have no one left. Who is there to have it but the jewmen! Take it, child, all of it ...'

'Oh, Mrs Dawson, I can't,' stammered Emerine.

'Do you mean,' Mrs Dawson as suddenly had become dry-eyed and accusing again, 'you are unable? Do you mean you're incapable? Or what? I dislike, child, all pitty-patty talk. Say exactly what you mean and avoid the deceptions of scullery help! Always take what is offered to you unless you believe it's unworthy of you ...'

'Yes, m'am,' whispered Emerine and Mrs Dawson embraced her almost driving all the breath out of her body.

Nature! That was it it was Nature they were destroying sure enough and Molly had been right all along. Even Mrs Dawson when she finally got around to it couldn't talk about it as it was but had to call it 'our natural functions' (as if it was natural for her) and 'their limbs of desire' and 'our seat of passion' (as if we sat on it to hide it)! She had to say that much for Father Lannigan he was hell-bent on dragging everything out into the open whatever the consequences and that was why they hated him so much. They were really afraid of what he might drag out next.

When they stepped out on to the street after the wedding Marcus held her hand tightly and said, 'Don't look at them. Look straight ahead!' She walked down the hill terrified but proud too to be seen as his wife in front of all of them. They must have had the young lads waiting with the scut of feathers and the rattling cans. It clattered along the road in front of them with the young fellows jeering bringing the whole town out to the windows and doors to watch. Without raising her eyes she could sense the whole place grinning, just one big mouth with immense lips rolling back from huge teeth but she wasn't going to be frightened by it because how could you be frightened by people who were afraid to appear themselves but had to send young lads to do the dirty for them.

It was the same with the filth they had made in the house and the dirty words scrawled on the walls although Marcus wouldn't let her see what they had done in the front room upstairs but she could guess because he had to throw out all the bedclothes and her nightdress and they spent the first few nights in her old room down under the stairs where they crept into one another and she felt she was taking him into the safety of her own ...

Was there anything worse than people afraid to be themselves? Was there anything in God's name worse than people afraid of what other people might think of them?

When they had finished in the Chapel Henrietta had one of her attacks and had to stay on in the sacristy until it was time for herself and Florrie to go to Thurles. Nicholas stayed with her and Emerine wouldn't mind but that they'd planned to have a little breakfast, not much, together in the house after the wedding as a small celebration.

'Child!' confessed Mrs Dawson tearfully, 'I will not be able to come to your church to see the wedding! You must understand my standing in the town . . .'

'Oh, I understand, Mrs Dawson,' said Emerine, calmly. 'Don't give it a minute's thought.'

'I should love to see you marry, child,' gasped Mrs Dawson, 'you will make a beautiful bride . . .'

'Thank you, m'am.'

'. . . but I shall never understand! Why, why you associate with the . . . the infidel . . .'

'Infidel or not, m'am,' said Emerine grimly, 'I'm going ahead with it. Because my Marcus wants it.'

'Yes,' said the old woman, looking at her anew and she rushed out of the room once more and rushed back again laden with curtains, crockery, cooking utensils, napkins, and a great variety of household objects all of which she heaped on Emerine.

'Oh, Mrs Dawson, please . . .'

'Take them! All of them, child.' In the midst of everything else she had contrived to carry back a bottle with her and she was now refilling her glass, splashing the liquid all over the place. 'And I wish you long life.' She waved the bottle above her head. 'Long and happy life!'

Emerine sank down into a chair in the middle of all the debris not knowing whether to laugh or to cry.

'Hold, child,' yelled Mrs Dawson suddenly, fixing her with a pointed finger. 'How do you propose to wear your hair?'

'My . . . hair . . .?'

'Yes . . . Hair!'

'I don't know, Mrs Dawson.'

'Up?' asked Mrs Dawson dramatically. 'Or down?'

'Up, I suppose,' answered Emerine desperately.

'Not, I trust, the chignon!' Mrs Dawson glared at her.

'Oh, no m'am, I don't think so.'

'I should hope not,' Mrs Dawson was in some way satisfied.

'Curls we know, frizzing we know, false long locks we know, even,' she conceded, 'the frontage may be capable of *some* explanation but who,' she bellowed, 'who can explain the chignon?'

'Yes, m'am,' Emerine murmured warily.

'How any Christian body could wear an appendage to the back of the head, a hideous bump far more monstrous than nature's own deformities assembled from the masses of hair bought by jew-merchants from Polish maidens or taken from the reeking scalps of South American caciques, yes, or cut from their screaming offspring and sold for drink, yes, drink! by wretched mothers of the London purlieus, oh! Hideous! Hideous! Behold!' waved Mrs Dawson at some unseen field of action, 'the decline of our sex! We are become the instruments of male tyranny, child.'

'I wouldn't go so far as that, Mrs Dawson,' said Emerine stoutly. She didn't want to get into argument with her in this state, but still!

Mrs Dawson took a deep breath and focused unsteadily on Emerine. She put out a hand and Emerine felt the soft, pudgy fingers against her cheek.

'You will ... you will ... you will be beautiful, child, on the Day!'

'Thank you, m'am,' said Emerine, bashfully.

But still and all she couldn't help feeling that the very least she could do would be to come to the Chapel door to see them getting married ...

Suddenly and quite without warning Mrs Dawson's face began to collapse. Starting somewhere about the forehead the flesh, old and pink, began to crumble and Emerine watched in horror while all the lines became like jelly and soft wet tears poured down the cheeks. It was so unlike, so much more horrendous than all the weeping and wailing of before that Emerine half stood and reached out her hand to the old woman.

'Oh, Mrs Dawson, what's wrong?'

Mrs Dawson gripped her hand tightly but was unable to speak for several minutes. Her eyes burned away fiercely under the sting of tears and she shook Emerine's hand this way and that, mute and stricken. Emerine could even see the front of

her blouse darken as it wetted under the tears that poured down
her throat.

'Mrs Dawson, m'am . . . please don't, m'am . . .'

'Ah, child!' the old voice was hardly audible, 'child, we are
the only flowers of the earth! If we don't attend to ourselves,
where, where are the blossoms? What's left? Where is the
brightness in the world. . .?'

'Yes, m'am,' said Emerine, crying herself now and not
really knowing why, knowing only that there, surrounded by
all the jumble of the wedding presents the old woman was
trying to tell her something, something wonderful and sad at
once, something of which she had only a dim perception . . .

11 . *Nicholas Scully*

'In a few months' time,' Mr Butler cleared his throat, 'your father will be one year dead . . .'

'Yes, sir,' said Nicholas.

'The time . . . the time has passed quickly . . .'

'Yes . . .'

There was a long silence while the carriage moved gracefully on high, oiled springs through the green, summer countryside, the spreading, dipping trees brushing its sides and roof. Yes, thought Nicholas, that was why we've gone down, something in Dada's character. He couldn't quite think of what it might be. Nothing heroic, certainly not, something commonplace even, like stubbornness. And he didn't even have the courage to act upon it himself but had left it to his two sons like a legacy . . . To my sons Nicholas and Marcus I hereby bequeath the full consequences of my desire to be . . . independent . . .

'In those days,' Mr Butler shook himself again, 'in those days,' he said, referring to the Master, 'we sometimes went to the Archaeological Society. Perhaps a young man like you would not be interested in the Archaeological Society? Eh? Shall we just take a drive into the country?'

'Yes, sir.'

So they took the road towards Ballyline Cross and the rich, leafy foothills of Ballingarry. It was the first Wednesday of the month of August and Mr Butler had arrived unexpectedly at the Presbytery to invite Nicholas out. Father Lannigan hadn't liked it; he said to Nicholas darkly in the porch that he suspected the influence of 'that atheist'.

But Nicholas went and as he sat in the luxurious, flowing movement of the carriage he began to wonder why. Because if there was anything certain left of all the thoughts that afflicted him it was the simple wish to do nothing to hurt Father Lannigan. 'I won't be long, Father,' he promised.

In the carriage he inquired politely about the burglaries at

Whytescourt House and Mr Butler became very excited and said the ruffians were lying low but that he expected them to return. He said he would be ready for them. At this he shifted his small body about on the rich upholstery and looked very fierce.

Clip-clop went the horses' hooves on the thick carpet of dust on the road and Nicholas noticed how the people cowered in the ditches as they passed. Mr Butler had been asking questions about the town and were the people hostile now and who was living in the house? Did his brother have employment again?

'What of the girl? Does he intend to marry her?'

Nicholas wilted at this as if he had been lashed across the face.

'I believe so, sir,' he said, at length, the words like raw food in his mouth.

'And your priest will marry them?'

'He doesn't want to.'

'Why doesn't he want to?'

Nicholas shrugged.

'Maybe he's afraid.'

'Afraid?'

'Oh, I don't mean for himself,' said Nicholas in a rush. 'For them. Father Lannigan isn't afraid for himself.'

Mr Butler sniffed. 'It's a courage I cannot appreciate.'

'Courage ...' Nicholas whispered. And stopped.

'Yes?'

'Nothing, sir.' And he tried to sink back into the rhythm of the carriage, floating on air away above the irregularity of the road below. What could be said about Father Lannigan's courage? Here, of all places! That he had the courage of a saint? Or a simpleton? That he'd leap into the abyss? That he'd face the possibility of ultimate failure with...

Only the night before the priest had crouched in the parlour, pounding the table as he roared at Nicholas, 'Certainty! Certainty! Certainty breeds prejudice!' Nicholas had been saying that people needed certainties in this life, thinking of the gaping pit that he found himself, everywhere. 'Certainty is the end of growth, boy, the end of life! And that's the meaning of death to have our understanding flooded with perfect Light! Don't talk to me of right and wrong, boy, because no law in Heaven or earth can ever get over the fact that men are incapable of a perfect judgement. Ever!'

Nicholas smiled at this because the priest was clearly thinking of his own trial and its disastrous result. He always had a way, Father Lannigan, of converting theology to suit what had happened to himself the day before! His God was his accomplice!

Across the August meadows to the glittering carriage came that voice, rising and falling, laden with its own mission and Nicholas surrendered to it once more . . .

'In the next world, Nicholas, things might be different but down here to live is to change and to be perfect is to change often. Where'd your science be, boy, if it wasn't for the uncertainty of man before all things, the heat of the fire, the motion of the air and the seas. We fulfil ourselves through doubt, son. It's through darkness that we find our way and this is the way too we stumble to God.'

It was then that Mr Butler remarked about the anniversary of the Master's death and they both looked into a field where a line of men were saving late hay, turning up the glistening green side to the sun.

'I find it difficult,' Mr Butler cried, 'to relate the peacefulness of the people now . . . to what has happened.'

'Yes.'

Two women appeared on a headland in the meadow, their fat arms bare to the light, carrying cans of drink to the men in the field.

'Energy,' said Nicholas thinking aloud. And then he blushed.

'I beg your pardon?'

'I mean, sir, I've learned,' he gabbled, 'that there's a . . . a momentum in the mass . . . beyond the control of any one . . . person . . .'

'You mean politics?' Mr Butler swooped towards him like a bird with Conversation Tube erect.

'I mean, I don't know a force or something,' he stopped and looked embarrassed at Mr Butler. Why, he wondered, did the man take such an interest in him? People said he resembled the

Master but all he saw in the glass when he looked was that big-boned, big-eyed head with its lank white hair that filled him with fear and, often, disgust.

'You must continue,' Mr Butler pressed briskly. 'We must express ourselves. We have to seek to find the words. There are words for everything, young man!'

'I can't, sir,' said Nicholas, trembling, because how could *he* ever understand perched high above the road under the rich red tassels of his carriage curtain and his gilt Ormonde crest...? It was easy for *him* to say, talk. 'We have to make a choice, sir. Don't we? To choose.'

'Yes.' Mr Butler was looking narrowly at him. 'To choose.'

'I've chosen the priest, sir,' Nicholas stammered.

'A boy of your sense,' fussed Mr Butler. 'It's ... you truly amaze me.' Then, after a pause, 'It's not as if you believe their nonsense. Do you?'

'No, sir. No, I don't believe.'

'I've tried to get you out of there, you know. You may still have an appointment if you wish ...'

Nicholas said nothing. He had his appointment! His lip curled. The priest's lackey. His nursemaid. Running his errands, sweeping his floors, washing his linen and hanging it out to dry behind the Presbytery orchard like a washerwoman!

They passed some sunken hovels at the side of the road. The people stared and at one point a whole family of them, filthy and ragged, a mother and a whole litter of them, came and walked some distance alongside the carriage peering in with that special naked intentness of the very poor. The driver yelled at them and eventually put the horses to a trot but Mr Butler didn't seem to mind, rather leaning forward the better to study them and when they were gone he leaned back with a sigh like regret.

'What,' he asked suddenly, 'have you learned from him?'

'Is it Father Lannigan?'

'Yes.' Mr Butler waited and then snapped his fingers. 'I insist on an answer!'

Nicholas disliked his tone and looked out the window.

'Well?'

'I can't answer, sir.'

'Of course you can't.'

'What I mean ... there's no dogma, if that's what you ... I haven't learned ...'

'Precisely,' stabbed Mr Butler, satisfied. 'No dogma.'

'It doesn't matter if he's wrong!' Nicholas turned back to him heatedly. 'I don't care! That's not what's important ...' And he began to shake all over trying to hold himself still with his hands on the cushions but he couldn't stop and the whole world thundered about his head. Oh God yes! If ever a man was wrong it was Father Lannigan, a blunderer, a great floundering innocent like when he claimed in the night after all that had happened that he still believed, was still sure, Nicholas, that the people were with him, the good people, his people, oh God! As if it wasn't his good people, as he called them, his respectable, pious people who were the real villains and not the louts because you measure evil by its claims to virtue and measure violence by the claims to peace of the men who provoke it ...

'I should have thought you had more possession, young man,' came Mr Butler's cool voice.

'I'm sorry, sir,' Nicholas replied grimly, 'to disappoint you.'

'Hm ...'

Nothing more happened for several minutes and then Mr Butler rapped on the floor with his cane and the carriage was turned about, with a great heaving from the horses, in the opening of the next laneway.

'We had better not exhaust all our pleasures,' Mr Butler gave one of his high laughs, 'on the first day.'

'No, sir.'

Mr Butler began to struggle with his pockets and produced a piece of newspaper. 'Have you seen this?' He thrust it at Nicholas. 'That's something to show him! Take it with you! *The Freeman*. Only the day before yesterday ...'

We are pleased to report that the recent unhappy history of the town of Kyle has now suffered a change for the better. In the last Petty Sessions scarcely any outrages were reported in the area. The recalcitrant clergyman, Mr. Lannigan, continues to hold his benefice without consent of his superiors. It is reported, however, that all his followers have been drawn away

*by peaceful means and that it is but a matter of time until
normal Christian habit is restored in the town.*

'... normal Christian habit ...' repeated Nicholas.

'Yes,' Mr Butler's eyes flashed. 'I must say I like that, don't
you?' And then, 'All his followers. Hum! I may send them a
letter of correction. I may do that! Eh-hee. And inform them
that he still has one follower left, at least.'

'I'm not much of a follower, sir.'

'Never denigrate yourself, young man! Never set yourself on
a low shelf. Always keep your worse perceptions of yourself to
yourself ...'

'What I meant, sir, is that Father Lannigan deserves ...' He
shrugged, red-faced, deeply unhappy. 'He can look into himself, Father Lannigan. I can follow a man like that, sir.' He
might as easily have said, I have to, I have to ... He felt if he
had to think of himself for one minute long he'd go and throw
himself in front of the horses.

'Never mind that, now. What will he do next?' Mr Butler
had a strange, remorseful look on his face.

'Nothing. There's nothing for him to do. What can he do? I
suppose they'll come and take him one day ...'

'He's give up the fight, then? He's lost!' There was anxiety
in the way he said it.

'He believes posterity, sir, will reclaim him.'

'Oh, posterity, fiddlesticks!' cried Mr Butler.

Nicholas closed his eyes. He could smell the clean leather
and the brass polish, all the wonderful aroma of harness and
horses that he associated with the stables of Whytescourt with
their huge oaken beams and stone floors where he loved to
stand whenever he approached the house from the river-path.
Shouldn't he confess that when all was said and done, all the
arguments and controversies over, that what really mattered
was that sometimes there in the Presbytery, just doing things
for him, tidying up or sorting papers, he loved the man more
than he had ever or could ever love his own father?

'The result of the trial determined his fate, didn't it?' he
heard Mr Butler say. 'I mean it was scarcely the victory he
looked for.'

'No. No, it wasn't.'

'You must understand I was unable to assist him with money at the time . . .'

'I understand, sir.'

'It was not an auspicious time for him to appeal to me. My mind was much preoccupied. With burglaries . . . and death . . .'

'Yes, sir.' Nicholas was very embarrassed. Old Mrs Butler had died that previous May and strange stories had come out from Whytescourt at the time.

'I rather thought it was all over last May,' exclaimed Mr Butler. 'I realized he could scarcely recover himself after that.'

Outside the courts, as they stood on the steps, Mr McAllindon had come up and clapped the priest on the shoulder. 'You won, sir!' His winterish smile. 'A victory of principle! I said so, didn't I-ah Mr Houston? I said the Chief Justice wouldn't tolerate Romanist dictation. Never ye mind, Mr Lannigan about the wee award. It's not much, I grant ye. But juries are like that. Aren't they, Mr-ah Houston? Juries are like the women! Direct them as to what to do and they'll do it but they'll make ye pay for the honour. Leave them alone and no man alive may say what they'll come up with.'

The jury, in bringing in a verdict in favour of Father Lannigan and against the Cardinal, had made an award of one farthing.

'Yes, yes.' Nicholas hardly moved his lips. Yes, May was the month.

Mrs Butler died at Whytescourt House in the last weeks of the Lannigan trial, that May. Miss Pabst the German nurse went away, as mysterious in her going as in her coming and people suddenly realized that she had been living in the place for over twenty years. The story that came out of Whytescourt at the time of the old woman's death was that Mr Butler had had his dog Lincoln shot that very same afternoon, telling the frightened yardsmen who buried the dog, that it would save the necessity of another occasion . . .

But the death which seems to have taken hold of Butler's imagination was that of John Stuart Mill who also died that May, of erysipelas. In his Journal Mr Butler began assembling notes for what appeared to be an obituary tribute (*He could not*

speak but his Mind was Open to the End). At one point there is
a projected title, *Prophet of a New Age* and the words, *to be
submitted to the* Kilkenny Journal, but a careful search of the
files of that newspaper has failed to turn up such a contribution. The tribute must never have matured beyond the scattered notes.

This was also the time in which Butler was quite convinced
that his house was being burgled or about to be burgled. He
had persuaded the District Inspector to allow him one of the
reinforcement of constables still quartered on the town and
this was granted because Kyle had now been quiet for months.
He had the man posted at the Gate Lodge where he could see
him, if he wished, from an upper window of Whytescourt.

The notes on Mill begin with a remarkable account of Mill's
interest in Botany and of his life at Avignon. But all pretence at
biography is soon abandoned and the rest is a mixture of
quotations from the philosopher (*No one can be a great thinker
who does not recognize that as a thinker it is his first duty to
follow his intellect to whatever conclusions it may lead*) or
antithetical summations of the man's achievement (*He has
been a bulwark against the Modern Idolatory of the Machine,
against squalid Mercantilism and the Dynamo. He has been the
Apostle of the Word over the Deed, of Reason over Might, of
Thought over Action, of the Open Mind over the tyranny of a
Particular Opinion, of the Religion of Man over the Religion
of God*). There is a long rambling critique of Carlyle which
is hardly relevant in the present context and what seems to be
the beginnings of an essay on the Anglo-Saxon character.
(... *Janus-headed, we hunt the Fox in the afternoon and the
Truth in the evening, we applaud Liberty and practise
Tyranny* ...) but all of this is of less account than that in the
middle of his obituary notes on Mill, Butler begins to write,
without even bothering to indicate the shift, about the Reverend William Edward Lannigan.

He came yesterday to Whytescourt with the Scully youth
looking for money. He has been to all the houses. The boy
carries the bag for him. When they are seen coming it is
the occasion to retreat to the bedrooms. Proctor had the

dogs on them. I saw them on the high road and indicated to the Constable with my signalling napkin that they be let through. He has humour. I hadn't thought, sir, he said, to be prevented by a constable. I am being burgled, sir, I said. They have already ransacked several rooms, valuable papers ETCETERA. He talked much of his trial. Of what he called Civil and Religious Liberty. I said the first I acknowledge, the second is a contradiction. I said Christianity defined Man by his capacity to Sin. As men, I said, our very condition is slavery. We must spend our lives devising freedoms, not forms of slavery. I said they could return some other day. I did not contribute money since it might engage the attention of miscreants on the public road. They were AMAZED when I showed them the broken window, the footprints on the lawn and other evidence of INTRUSION.

'Marcus isn't here,' she said trying to close the door on him.

Since he had chosen a time when his brother would be at work he knew this.

'What about my mother?'

'She isn't here either.'

'Well, d'you mind if I enter my own home?' She sniffed and turned on her heel leaving him at the open door to go away or go in. He watched her retreat into the kitchen, anger in the stiffness of her slim back, in the swish of her long skirts. She had nearly finished painting the whole place for the wedding. 'It's nice,' he said lamely, standing in the middle of the kitchen floor.

'What do you want?' She stood with a brush in her hand and a smudge of black on her cheek.

'I thought ... I just thought I could do something for ye before the wedding.'

'You thought no such thing.' She turned, ignoring him and continued to paint around the fireplace.

'Oh Nina ...'

'Oh Nina!' she imitated as if they were still children.

And they remained like that for a while, he standing awkwardly in the middle of the floor and she studiously painting over the same corner of the fireplace, again and again. It was this impotence that he raged against and raged against in all the hours of loneliness as he planned his mad schemes of revenge against her but when he was faced with the germ of it all as now, the thing itself, he was tied, paralysed by it . . .

'I only wanted . . . all I wanted was . . .'

'Look Nicholas,' she tossed her hair up off her dark decided face, 'I don't want to see you in . . .'

Suddenly Marcus was in the kitchen with them although neither had heard him come in. He said nothing but brushed past Nicholas and began to take off his coat which was filthy with some kind of oil. There was a fire going under the dinner and Nicholas wanted them to invite him to eat with them. He wanted it desperately. To have to walk back up to the desolate Presbytery, to the scraps on a plate, to the priest like a corpse in the chair was a sudden ordeal.

'Well?' said Marcus unexpectedly turning on him. 'What is it, so?'

'He doesn't want to marry you,' Nicholas announced although he had no intention of saying any such thing.

She said nothing but she took in everything with her dark eyes and his hate for her was almost unendurable.

'Why doesn't he? Why?'

'I don't know why.'

'You must know why.'

'Maybe,' said Nicholas, pale, trying to meet his brother's eyes without flickering, 'maybe he doesn't think it's right.'

She was somewhere behind them, listening.

'Maybe *you* don't think it's right! Hah? Isn't that it? It's not Father Lannigan at all. It's you . . .'

Nicholas tried to scoff at this, a hollow croak in his throat.

'You're a shit!' roared his brother, the veins pumping out on his forehead, 'you're a . . .'

He heard her, out of sight, the gasp of the name, the punctured dismay of it . . . 'Marcus!'

Listening to him in those long Wednesday afternoons of that year as the carriage rolled along the country roads or in the high, cramped Observatory as he pored over his specimens Nicholas came to realize how alike they were in a way, Mr

Butler and Father Lannigan, for all the gap of blood and place and belief that separated them. He thought he saw, too, how in crossing the town and the bridge from the Presbytery to Whytescourt, he hadn't come that far. He enjoyed hearing each man warn him direfully against the evil influence of the other. They are both victims, he thought. Men with visions but hanging between the world and their vision of the world without being able to bridge the two or at least make a bridge substantial enough to invite across any but the most foolhardy. People like himself, maybe. That was it; each of them believed he was the only possible convert either of them was ever likely to make...

It was because he said something like this aloud to Mr Butler that they finally quarrelled.

Mr Butler had embarked on a series of experiments with lichen and fungi in his Observatory and Nicholas liked the curious earthen smells of yeast and peat-moss that filled the room. Mr Butler told him there was little time left, that he had abandoned his wild flowers, that he was convinced a clue to it all could be found in the study of lower forms of life, that the lower levels of life were constant, it was only the upper reaches of human development that stretched away beyond our present sight. Deliberately Nicholas annoyed him by saying that this was an image of religion. 'Religion, fiddlesticks!' Mr Butler shouted.

Together, with minute particles of meat and white of egg they observed the insectivorous habits of the parasitic sundew. In the pale sunlight from the window the leaves lay open to the bait, the whole plant like some attentive creature as it floated on in its moss bed in a soup plate. Mr Butler dropped the bait on the sticky surface and they watched it secrete and finally curl over in the swallowing. When the leaves re-opened nothing remained but a smear of black.

'The purpose of this exercise,' Mr Butler lectured in a high voice, 'is that I may observe the ravages of life, a daily reminder, but I may do so while I control the matter here under a bell-jar.'

His eyes flashed behind the eye-glasses and Nicholas suddenly realized that he might be losing his sanity.

'Yes, sir,' he gulped.

But Mr Butler was drying his hands on an old towel and had begun again to expound his doctrines of the New Order of Socialism. He went on and on about Saint-Simon and Robert Owen. About Cooperation and the Community. He urged Nicholas to set himself up as some kind of teacher among the people in the town. He would help him with books and money, he said. Nicholas inquired why he wouldn't go and do it himself.

'Eh? What's that?'

'I said it's not my concern.'

'Don't be impertinent, young man.'

'No, sir.'

'I believe in the day when man may be able to accomplish his intentions.'

'Yes, sir.'

He wouldn't leave the matter alone but pressed on and on about his social theories so that Nicholas' head began to throb. There was a defensiveness about the way he spoke and Nicholas knew he had provoked him.

'You'd prefer, sir, to choose your religious humbug! You'd prefer superstition. You'd prefer ...'

'I wouldn't want to prefer either,' said Nicholas in a low voice.

'You said you chose the priest!' accused Mr Butler as if it were a crime.

'Father Lannigan is a man,' said Nicholas hardly knowing what he said. 'Not a religion.'

'You said you'd choose all that ...'

'If I had to ...' said Nicholas angrily, 'if I had to, sir, choose I'd take a cause any day – even if it was doomed – that recognized men as they are to one that looked to the day when ... when the nature of man would be, in some miraculous way, changed ...

'You're impertinent, sir,' huffed Mr Butler and Nicholas left.

There is nothing of all of this in the Butler Journals of the period, filled with their descriptions of sepals and pistils and lower vertebrates. In fact the Butler Journals from this time on cease to be of any relevance to the case of the Big Chapel. Nothing, then, except this, from an entry on the NEW YEAR, 1874.

> The Old has passed away but, alas, the NEW appears not in its stead; the Time is still in pangs of Travail with the NEW. Situated in a time, as we are, of wholesale MORAL FAILURE such as has never before been known to history it behoves us to beware of all IDEAL constructions and solutions.

Each morning Nicholas used to tidy up the two bedrooms, wash a few things and put them out to dry if it wasn't raining and then he'd walk down to the laurel bushes just inside the Chapel gates and there he'd find a saucepan of potatoes and vegetables and a half of can of fresh milk. Without this they might have starved. Or begged. He put back the empty pot, clean and scoured, each evening.

The priest never questioned where the food came from but ate everything that was put before him with a trembling, ravenous appetite. If there was no food he never asked for it. After several weeks of this Nicholas asked him if he knew who was leaving the food.

'What food? What...?'

'The food we eat every day.'

'I thought you were getting it up from your sister below.'

'No-o ... I find it. Out ... out beyond.'

The priest looked at him with a perfect, unquestioning comprehension of it all and Nicholas never mentioned the matter again.

Their sessions together were of two kinds. One was what the priest called 'working at the desk' except it wasn't a desk but the big mahogany table in the parlour where they would sit before the mountain of newspapers, scraps, cuttings, files, letters, calculations, drafts. They attacked the great heap almost daily, the sludge of print, the refuse of words from years of controversy; they ransacked and scavenged about it, Nicholas didn't know for what. He supposed it was in the hope that the mystery of it all was imprisoned there somewhere in a net of ink waiting to be found and flourished before the world. Wasn't there an ancient philosopher who gorged himself upon his own writings and died choking trying to ingest pansophia? Or was he only imagining it?

'I sometimes think,' Father Lannigan said to him, helplessly, gesturing at all the paper before them, 'that I'm laid out here, boy, in bits and pieces.'

Dear Sir: Strange as it may appear to you, I believe that few people love seclusion and privacy more than your present correspondent . . .

Sir: Unhappily for my peace of mind I am become one of the most remarkable men in the community . . .

Nicholas wondered if all the opening sentences were so revealing. He picked up another batch of letters.

'That one there,' the priest pointed, gloomily, 'was one of the ones I wrote to Mr Gladstone.'

Your Excellency: Poverty, it is said, makes us acquainted with strange bedfellows, but my poverty has made me acquainted with the greatest men in England . . .

'I see that.'

'I'm an arrogant man, Nicholas.'

Nicholas began to tidy the papers with unnecessary attentiveness.

'Will you look at the spectacle I made of myself in those letters. I must be the right. . . !'

Nicholas still didn't say anything. It was an innocence in the man that had first set him off those years ago and it was an innocence that left him now, crumbling, without much left to console him. Only the day before Father Lannigan had cried out that he'd have ended up long ago in the madhouse in Kilkenny, chained and raving, but that he knew his God to be so above the small passions of this world that he was able to . . .

'I sometimes think,' Father Lannigan said, absently, 'that I only exist in the words that come out of my mouth. If a light was put to that paper there there'd be little left of me but the black ash.'

'That's not true,' Nicholas said, hotly. 'I mean you're true to yourself and that's important. You haven't betrayed yourself!' He stopped, trying to think of something more lasting to offer.

226

'Yes,' said the priest, looking through him.

'You've fought a fight that ... some people ... I'm sure someone, anyway, will get courage from ...'

'I sometimes think,' Father Lannigan turned away, 'my fight is only about to begin, I do.' And he was silent.

And it was out of this or a similar silence that the second kind of session between them developed. Sessions of silence, a hollow silence while the priest sat, sealed into some private chamber of anguish and Nicholas sat miserably opposite or moved in and out of the room quietly because he learned early that there was nothing to be said when the priest was like this.

In the final years when he sank into his torpor Father Lannigan simply took to his bed altogether and Nicholas would take him up warm milk in a soup bowl. Then he'd come back down alone into the parlour where he'd sit, sometimes for hours, before the remains of verbiage there on the table. As if he were waiting for a visitor. It was only on very exceptional occasions that he felt the urge actually to go out, into the town.

Amazing balloon ascent from the grounds of Whytescourt House... Kyle witness to daring feat of Frenchman... Gallic Icarus defies physical laws... Aviationist chaired by populace through streets of town... Major Wymnes travels with party to see flying machine... 'On threshold of new travel,' says M.P...
On that celebrated day in the autumn of 1874, a day which was to pass into the balladry of South Leinster and even of the adjacent counties of East Munster, Nicholas Scully stood with the hundred odd locals on the Dairy Lane beside Whytescourt House watching the scene down near the river. When Mr Butler had first given over the grounds of Whytescourt to the airman, Monsieur Achard, he had invited Nicholas to join in the Great Adventure. Nicholas had declined. He had enough to do now attending the priest and besides he was no longer able to talk to Mr Butler.

The huge black balloon strained to free itself and it was barely held by the grappling irons that ran into the trees all around on long cables. Monsieur Achard, moustachioed, his fat bulk encased in a tight-fitting, head-covering costume, had

227

been in place in the basket for over an hour now. He watched with aplomb as his minions ran hither and thither or up and down ladders to stoke the furnace under the balloon up over his head. Sometimes he gestured directions but no one seemed to bother with him.

'It's a wonder,' said someone near Nicholas, 'the whole fukin' thing doesn't g'up in fukin' smoke.'

'Not at all,' said another, 'isn't the fire stopped off by dampers . . .'

'Dampers! What d'ya mean, dampers!' sneered the first. And there followed a big argument about flues and colanders and the properties of rye straw, whether it would smoke or not.

'Well, I ask you!' An old man to the side shook his head, unbelieving. 'What'll they do next! Wouldn't you think they'd be content with their feet on the ground like the rest of us!'

But everyone was really very proud that this was happening here on their own doorstep with half the county watching. When Mr Butler came by at a trot a wild cheer went up. Nicholas hadn't seen him for months and he was shocked by the appearance of him. He was carrying a piece of mangled machinery and his hands and his clothes were black with some kind of grime, a blotch of soot ringing his eyes. He spotted Nicholas at the hedge and came running over.

'Come down!' he called. 'Come down into the field . . .'

'I'd prefer to stay here, sir,' Nicholas replied, feeling the people draw back in deference to the Master of Whytescourt.

'I shall expect you!' Mr Butler hadn't heard him. He turned away again but hadn't gone far before he was back once more. He looked frantic under the black grease and powder and he thrust his face right into Nicholas'.

'I have little patience,' he shouted, 'with mobility,' and Nicholas could smell the sharp, acrid odour of the machine from him, 'when it's parallel to the ground . . .'

'Yes, sir,' breathed Nicholas not knowing what more to say. There was a dark, sulphorous, infernal aura about the man and his clothes.

'I like the balloon!' Mr Butler became very belligerent and without his Conversation Tube had clearly no interest at all in any response. 'It has aspirations in the other direction,' and he

228

shot his hand up towards the heavens, 'which is the only direction that counts. I'll assist anyone, sir, who wishes to flaunt Newton! I'm with the man who wants to get off the ground!'

This time he was really gone, in a loping trot down among the helpers about the balloon which was now leaping like a fat monster on the ropes, trying to be off. Nicholas, sad at this encounter with Mr Butler, turned his back and pushed his way through the people in the laneway.

As he passed the Big House he heard a loud bellowing and guffawing from the terraces and looked over a wall. A large crowd of young gentry had arrived from the hunt, still in their riding kit, about thirty young men and women, young boys and girls. They had dragged out furniture from the drawing-room and there they sprawled, watching the action down below them. There was an immense animal joviality about the whole group so that they looked like drunken whippets or foxhounds or fat retriever bitches, stuffed into tight riding breeches and coats and muddy leathers and skirts, their jaws loose, their movements towards the drink before them and the spectacle beyond them the movements of a consuming, baying pack. As he watched, several of the priceless chairs fell over with a crash amid laughter and shouts. He had heard it said that the house had become the target of all the idlers in the county and that at this rate there soon wouldn't be much left to the place.

Out on the road he had to make his way past carriages, tethered horses and tired grooms, hawkers with their penny stalls and more people were arriving every minute from all points of the compass. Still farther on towards the town with the Commons cottages away to his left he met a long line of townspeople walking out, gesticulating excitedly at the sky and it was then that the balloon went up.

First a rapid, farting sound came from down near the river and then the balloon itself and then Monsieur Achard in his puny, dangling basket rode into sight. A thick trail of evil black smoke followed them slowly as they rose into the air while the machine seemed to labour and to belch with the effort. It slowly moved past the roof of the Mill opposite Whytescourt, Monsieur Achard narrowly skirting the masonry. And then it happened! No one watching had been quite prepared for it.

At one moment Monsieur Achard dangled, an object of humour, derision even but certainly not admiration, just above the rooftops. The next moment some unseen and terrifying force took hold of his invention and propelled it upwards in a great suck, up into the clouds. Nicholas held his breath with the rest of the world below. The trail of black smoke became a frail, lingering connexion in the sky between them and this Man in the Heavens and every mortal watching was stirred by the sight. The mystery lasted only a moment. Then Monsieur Achard descended in a slack deflation towards normality once more and Jenningstown Wood some five miles from the town where he was later rescued, as subsequent reports have it, more dead than alive, from the branches of a high tree.

Nicholas began to walk home. He tried to put the demented face of Mr Butler out of his mind. As he came out on the Kilkenny road and began to enter the town through Bridge Lane and River Street. But he couldn't. Past Jude Hennessy's pub which was going down rapidly, they said, since the old man died. Past where Martin Donovan used to have his stables before he left the town. Past Bun Hipps' Bakery with, as Nicholas noted with bitter amusement, its prosperous, new paintwork.

He walked more quickly when he reached the Cross, Mr Fincheon at his doorway called out something to him but he didn't hear. He dreaded to look up and see her standing at a window as she often stood with that puffed, impervious stare which she had continually now since she had become swollen with child. But even without looking up he felt her eyes bore down upon him as he passed, in hatred and triumph.

Up the hill he almost ran in a senseless haste, his long black coat flapping about his ankles. Mr Bergin's Tea Hall. Mr Dubby's Depository for Medicated Produce. Nugent's Stores and, under the brow of the hill, Grace's Shoe Shop. And then the Big Chapel. He stopped, breathless, at the gates and as always had to make a definite act of will to walk in. But having passed the pillars and the shadow of the great spire his step quickened and he almost ran down the avenue and into the Presbytery to where he knew the priest would be dozing, labouring each breath, in a parlour chair.

A Chronology

1877   The body of Nicholas Scully is found in the fields below the Fair Green of Kyle and his brother Marcus
Antony is arrested and tried on a charge of murder.
There are conflicting accounts as to what happened.
Marcus pleaded guilty at the trial but claimed in evidence (as is recounted in A. T. Ball's chapter on the
case in his *Memories of an Irish Barrister*) that his dead
brother waylaid him and threatened him with a pitch-
fork. There has always been a curious tradition in the
town that Nicholas Scully killed himself before the eyes
of his brother and that Marcus Scully deliberately
chose responsibility. The field there is still known as
Cain's Plot.
Emerine Scully leaves the town after the trial of her
husband to work in England. She leaves a child,
Michael Davitt Scully, with a Mrs O'Shea in the town.
It would appear that Henrietta Scully and the other
son, James Florence, were still in the house on the
Cross at this time.

1878 or 1879   Marcus Antony Scully dies of pneumonia on
the Farm Prison at Lusk, County Dublin.

1879   Mrs O'Shea is brought to Manchester to identify the
body of Emerine Scully, a suicide. Henrietta Scully
still seems to have been living in the town.

1880   Father Lannigan's letter of submission to his bishop
is published and he leaves Kyle. The letter is witnessed by M. O'Brien, Apothecary and J. J. Cullen,
RIC.

1883   Father Lannigan dies in the County Home and is

231

buried in Newtown churchyard. The following is the inscription on the tombstone:

> This tomb has been ordered by Mrs. Elinor Lannigan as a small but sincere tribute to the memory of her husband, Mr. John Lannigan who died the 10th Oct. 1815. His various virtues as a husband and father, his affability of manners, benevolence of heart and correctness of conduct will make him to be remembered and his loss to be deplored. Also Mr. John Lannigan, eldest son of the above, died the 9th Novr. 1833. He was a young man of much virtue. Peace be to his soul. Also Mrs. Elinor Lannigan died Sepr. 1841. Also her other son, the Very Reverend William Edward Lannigan, died July 20th 1883. Also her daughter Eileen Rowen nee Lannigan, died Janr. 8th, 1888.

Late 1880s Mrs Henrietta Scully dies in Dublin in the Sir Ambrose Hammond Home for Indigent Christians. It is said that she died of cholera. There is no further trace of the other son, James Florence Scully.

1901 Within weeks of the Queen's death Horace Percy Butler dies at Whytescourt and the timing, which he anticipated towards the end, caused him some considerable annoyance. He was renowned throughout the Provinces for his eccentricities and ill-judged forays into public controversies. Whytescourt House was burned down during the War of Independence in 1922.

1920s (Michael) Davitt Scully was still to be seen in the town. A butcher's help with a hare lip he was frequently pointed out as an example of the priest-curse that was said to affect with deformity all those families who had sided with the Red Priest, years before.